What the critics are saying...

"*Bound Hearts: Sacrifice* by **Lora Leigh** is absolutely wonderful. The intense sexual chemistry between Kimberly and Jared will hook you from the beginning. The choices that Kimberly must make for her life are monumental. This story is not for the faint of heart. There are several menage a trois scenes. But overall this book is definitely a keeper." ~ *Fallen Angels Reviews*

"SACRIFICE is a sizzling story about love, lust, and the SACRIFICES that fall between. Jared's infatuated with Kimberly and the idea that he would go to such lengths to pursue and then have her, is admirable and honorable. The passion that they share rages throughout the pages while the fact that they can't act on their desires in the usual way makes for a more unique and tantalizing read. Ms. Leigh delivers a red-hot read…" ~ *The Road to Romance*

"Lora Leigh has done it again with this interesting ménage of colorful characters. Definitely a keeper on my shelf, this book is sure to please lovers of the erotic genre." ~ *Just Erotic Romance Reviews*

An Ellora's Cave Romantica Publication

www.ellorascave.com

Wicked Sacrifice

ISBN 1419953966, 9781419953965

Cover art by Syneca

This Book Printed in the U.S.A. by Jasmine-Jade Enterprises, LLC.

Trade paperback Publication November 2006

This book printed in the U.S.A. by Jasmine - Jade Ent., LLC

Content Advisory:

S - ENSUOUS
E - ROTIC
X - TREME

Ellora's Cave Publishing offers three levels of Romantica™ reading entertainment: S (S-ensuous), E (E-rotic), and X (X-treme).

The following material contains graphic sexual content meant for mature readers. This story has been rated E–rotic.

S-*ensuous* love scenes are explicit and leave nothing to the imagination.

E-*rotic* love scenes are explicit, leave nothing to the imagination, and are high in volume per the overall word count. E-rated titles might contain material that some readers find objectionable—in other words, almost anything goes, sexually. E-rated titles are the most graphic titles we carry in terms of both sexual language and descriptiveness in these works of literature.

X-*treme* titles differ from E-rated titles only in plot premise and storyline execution. Stories designated with the letter X tend to contain difficult or controversial subject matter not for the faint of heart.

Also by Lora Leigh

A Wish, A Kiss, A Dream *(anthology)*
B.O.B.'s Fall (*with Veronica Chadwick*)
Bound Hearts 1: Surrender
Bound Hearts 2: Submission
Bound Hearts 3: Seduction
Bound Hearts 6: Embraced
Bound Hearts 7: Shameless
Broken Wings (*Cerridwen Press)*
Cowboy & the Captive
Coyote Breeds 1: Soul Deep
Elemental Desires *(anthology)*
Feline Breeds 1: Tempting The Beast
Feline Breeds 2: The Man Within
Feline Breeds 3: Kiss of Heat
Law and Disorder : Moving Violations (*with Veronica Chadwick)*
Manaconda *(anthology)*
Men of August 1: Marly's Choice
Men of August 2: Sarah's Seduction
Men of August 3: Heather's Gift
Men of August 4: August Heat (*12 Quickies of Christmas*)
Wizard Twins 1: Ménage a Magick
Wizard Twins 2: When Wizards Rule
Wolf Breeds 1: Wolfe's Hope
Wolf Breeds 2: Jacob's Faith
Wolf Breeds 3: Aiden's Charity
Wolf Breeds 4: Elizabeth's Wolf

About the Author

Lora Leigh is a wife and mother living in Kentucky. She dreams in bright, vivid images of the characters intent on taking over her writing life, and fights a constant battle to put them on the hard drive of her computer before they can disappear as fast as they appeared.

Lora's family, and her writing life co-exist, if not in harmony, in relative peace with each other. An understanding husband is the key to late nights with difficult scenes and stubborn characters. His insights into human nature and the workings of the male psyche provide her hours of laughter, and innumerable romantic ideas that she works tirelessly to put into effect.

Lora welcomes comments from readers. You can find her website and email address on her author bio page at www.ellorascave.com

Tell Us What You Think

We appreciate hearing reader opinions about our books. You can email us at Comments@EllorasCave.com.

Wicked Sacrifice

WICKED INTENT

Dedication

Hey, Tally, this one is yours!
And it wasn't easy either! ☺

Prologue

"Hi, Jaded, how's tricks?" The words popped up on the computer screen, drawing an amused smile to Tally's lips.

"Slow, Wicked. Very slow," she typed back, snorting at the understatement.

The online life she led was the complete opposite of the real life she escaped each evening. The same men, the same parties, the same crap. She had grown bored with the endless round months ago. Why she had grown bored she had yet to figure out.

"Your boss still doing his own files?" It was a running joke in the online chat rooms she inhabited. She had told the story the first day it had occurred. Everyone had seemed awed by her accomplishment. She had personally hoped for at least a good argument out of Jesse Wyman at the time. She hadn't expected him to actually do his own fucking files.

"Hell if I know," she finally typed in. "I think he fired me today."

Repositioning, firing, it was the same thing. She liked working with Wyman. It wasn't exactly challenging but it left her plenty of time for shopping.

"Fired?" The words popped back. "He wouldn't dare fire you."

She laughed to herself. There were days Wyman had wanted to kill her, but he had resisted the urge with more self-control than she had given him credit for. Of course, the wedding Terrie was planning was keeping him pretty tired. That or her afternoon visits to his office.

"He says it's repositioning. He sent me to hell, Wicked." She sighed at the thought.

The merger between Conover's and Delacourte's had been more than a surprise last month. Even bigger was the surprise that she would now be the personal assistant for Lucian Conover.

"Repositioning?" The short question was so typical of Wicked. She could almost feel his impatience. *"In Hell?"*

"In Hell." She sighed. "My new boss is Lucifer. This is not going to be fun. There goes all my playtime. (pout)" She typed in the expression huffily. Lucian Conover was not her idea of the perfect boss. "Let's hope he's at least hiding a sense of humor under that scowl he wears. I bet he doesn't even know the difference between a ménage and a margarita. Who will I tell all my dirty jokes to?"

* * * * *

Lucian scowled. Son of a bitch. Lucifer, was he? Didn't know a ménage from a margarita? He bit off a series of volatile curses as he jumped up from the computer and paced the den furiously. Smart-mouthed, viperous little termagant. He would show her a fucking ménage she'd still remember into her next life if she kept this shit up. She had no sense of decorum and had shown him zero respect each time he showed up at Jesse's office.

She stung him with that waspish tongue of hers, smirked every chance she had and showed in a hundred different ways that she expected him to grovel at the perfection of her tiny feet. Son of a bitch. For a taste of that sweet little body he just might do it, too, and that was what really rankled.

"You still breathing?" Her tart question came over the instant message with a soft ring.

"Yeah, just wondering what the connection was between the ménage and the margarita," he typed in, damning himself a

thousand different ways. He was insane to have demanded her as his personal assistant. He had lost his ever lovin' mind.

"No connection." He paused at her answer, frowning. Jaded always had a reason for damned near everything she said. Unless she was unhappy. Unless she was lonely. He had learned that over the past year. Had made it his business to learn everything he could about her.

"You okay, Jaded?" He really shouldn't care, but he did.

"Oh yes, I'm fine." Her words rang hollow, even through the impersonal communication box. "Maybe I'll go shopping tomorrow. I hear there's a sale on shoes..."

"Uh oh. Poor cows, sacrificing their lives to support your addiction." He shook his head, yet still he worried. She wasn't acting normal.

"Cows, alligators, whatever." Nope, that wasn't his Jaded.

"Hey, babe, you can talk to me, you know." He needed her to.

There was a long silence.

"She's my friend." The words finally came through with a sense of sadness. "I can't believe she has such horrid taste in men."

"Yeah?" He didn't even pretend to understand that one.

"I love her like a sister." She had to be talking about Terrie.

He waited to see what else she said.

"I can't believe she actually fucked Lucifer! Was she insane? Has she lost her mind? The man is an outcast. He has no style, no class, and I doubt he has a cock over five inches long. He probably only needs a finger or two to jack off with."

He sat back slowly in his chair. His cock, all five inches and several more, pulsed in outrage. His eyes narrowed.

"The man scowls. He sneers. Stomps around like a bull in a china shop. He is such a bore. Geez. I need a new job."

His fists clenched, his teeth ground together as he saw red. The viperous little witch. A bull in a china shop? Five-inch cock? *Five-inch cock??* Ohh, he would show her a hell of a lot fucking more than five inches. Damn her. The woman had a bite that would do a rabid dog proud.

"If you quit, just think of all the shoes that would cry." It was lame. Real lame, but he'd be damned if he could type his outrage to her over the Internet. She would probably save the fucking message to show all her chat room buddies. He sneered. Oh, was she in for a surprise.

"Well, this is true. But I'm definitely looking."

He stilled. Looking, was she? He'd see about that one.

"Well, good luck, darlin'. Now I'm off. Hot date tonight."

Nothing came back for long moments.

"All right. Goodnight."

"Night, darlin'. Cheer up, maybe you'll get lucky and he'll at least have more than five inches." He growled.

"As though that can help him." He could almost hear the haughty vibration of the words. "Where, oh, where have all the alphas gone? Your mothers must have breastfed you overly long."

"Or yours fed you venom and spice rather than sweet milk," he typed back furiously. And he meant it.

"LOL. Good one, Wicked. Have fun for me while you're out. Talk to you later."

He clicked the box away. He shut down the program, damn near shaking with rage and arousal. He came to his feet, pushing his fingers ruthlessly through his hair as he clenched his teeth against his anger. Damn her. Lucifer, was he? Five inches, was he? He snarled as he stomped through the house, jerking his leather jacket from the staircase post as he headed for the door.

Miss Jaded Tally was in for one hell of a surprise.

Dev had warned him she wouldn't be as easy as he thought she would be. Of course, Dev was often warning him about Tally. He snorted derisively at that. His twin had stayed in the background during this phase, though under protest. From the first moment Lucian had met Tally, he and Devril had both been lost.

His brother had commented often that only Lucian would have chosen to make them fall in love with such a sharp-tongued little vixen, but Lucian knew his brother would have been just as helpless in the face of her haunted eyes, her unique features and sheer bravado.

Now, they were both in a hell of a predicament. And neither of them was happy about it. Tally wasn't coming around as they had expected. She was no closer to admitting to the lust that heated between them than she had been six months before. It was time to fix that. It was time to master Tally Raines.

Chapter One

It was just called The Club. It was a large southern plantation house set on the outskirts of town in a small wooded area, perhaps a mile from the main road. Not easily accessible, but neither was it hard to find.

A stone wall enclosed the four square acres of property; a guard sat in a small booth at the iron gated entrance. The house itself was surrounded by majestic oaks, giving the estate an air of graceful wealth.

Lucian pulled into the hidden parking lot, surveying the vehicles already parked there. The Club served a large clientele from around the world, but still maintained an atmosphere of personal friendliness. Not just anyone was invited through its doors, only a select few. It took more than money, breeding or influence to receive an invitation from The Club's members. It took a lifestyle.

"Good evening, Mr. Conover." The butler and peacekeeper, Matthew Harding, opened the door and stood aside as he entered. "May I take your jacket, sir?"

He wasn't your typical butler. Lucian couldn't see Matthew attending to any of the influential families he knew. The six-foot plus ex-Special Forces soldier could have had his pick of any security agency he could have worked for. Instead, he had accepted a position as butler and head of security at The Club's house. The benefits, Matthew often said, were better than the pay, which was damned good.

"Thanks, Matthew. Looks like a full house tonight." He could hear the voices raised in laughter from within the main room.

"We have several out-of-towners in for the week, as well as many of the regulars." Matthew hung the leather jacket in the wide closet to the side. "The house is definitely full for a while."

The Club maintained the plantation for the convenience of its out-of-town members. There was no need for hotel accommodations when doing business near or around the area. The three-story house counted a dozen fully equipped bedrooms, a kitchen staff, and maid service. A trust set up nearly twenty years ago by the founder of the private club took care of most of the day-to-day running of the house. The membership fees, which were not cheap, went into an account to offset general expenses.

"Has Devril arrived yet?" Lucian asked as they headed to the main room.

"Mr. Devril should arrive shortly." Matthew grinned, his pale blue eyes lighting in amusement. "I believe he was picking up Miss Hampstead from the airport before coming here."

Alyssa Hampstead was one of the few subs whose membership had been approved. She was a delicate, haughty heiress with cool hazel eyes and a cold exterior. Heating her up was a challenge that many of The Club members embraced enthusiastically.

Lucian walked into the main room, a cavernous ballroom that had been remodeled to fit The Club's needs and was outfitted for the enjoyment of the members. A bar stood at one end; the rest of the room was filled with comfortable leather couches, chairs and small nooks for the enjoyment of its patrons. His welcome was a high-pitched female scream of pleasure and pain.

He paused, his gaze moving to a nearby couple. Sax Brogan had his shaved head thrown back in ecstasy as he held a petite redhead down on the thick cock spearing her ass. The woman's creamy white skin contrasted sharply with the chocolate tones of the big man's. Her legs were spread wide as

Sax gripped her small waist and lifted her, only to lower her slowly on the rigid shaft parting her buttocks.

Dazed blue-green eyes stared back at Lucian as he watched her lips part in excitement. Her face was flushed, and below, her full breasts were swollen, the pierced nipples standing hard and proud in excitement.

Her pussy was shaved smooth, or waxed. Some of the female patrons enjoyed the painful stimulation of the waxing that the house provided. Her cream stood thick and glistening on the small pussy mound. Her clit was engorged, a shining little pearl standing out from its protective hood as her fingers worked over it desperately.

The woman was younger than most of the female members. Barely twenty-four, she was the daughter of a staid, stuffy Senator who would have a heart seizure if he ever imagined his perfect little girl was a member of an establishment that catered to sexually dominant males.

"Fuck me, Sax." She was riding the thick pole with halting movements, weak with lust as her head fell back against Sax's shoulder. "Fuck me harder. Now. Please, now."

Sax groaned behind her. Despite her words, everyone knew that hard and fast wasn't what she liked. She loved being sexually delayed, being pushed to the boundaries of control and stripped of the natural reserves she had forced on herself for so long.

Sax would have her begging before he was finished with her. Her screams would echo through the window-lined room, her pleas becoming desperate before he would allow her any release.

The sight of it wasn't doing Lucian's cock any good, either. Her tender pussy had flowered open, dripping in excitement, flushed and swollen. Unfuckable. It was one of the few restrictions she had stated upon entering the membership. The woman's pussy had never been breached and for the time being, wouldn't be.

A fucking virgin with a dick up her ass. It never ceased to amaze Lucian.

Shaking his head at the sight, he turned and headed for the long bar and hopefully a strong drink. Tally had him too angry to even consider fucking the tension out of his system tonight; besides, it wasn't one of the lovely lustful women there that he was in need of. Tally had created the monster throbbing in his pants and he had just about set his mind that she would be the one to take care of it.

"Hey, Lucian." Thom Briner, the bartender, greeted him jovially.

Thom wasn't a handsome man in any sense. He was nearly six feet tall, with long dark brown hair pulled back in a ponytail. His tobacco brown eyes were cynical, his scarred face sinister. He was dependable and loyal, though, and for the job, that was what counted.

"Give me a whisky, Thom." Lucian sighed as he tried to ignore the little redhead's gasps from across the room. He wondered if Tally would let go so easily. Then he grunted. There wasn't a chance in hell anything with Tally would be easy.

"Sax is going to have a hell of a time pushing her over," Thom commented as another female cry reached them. "He's been fucking her nearly half an hour already and she still hasn't peaked."

There was an edge of sympathy in Thom's voice. Lucian shook his head wearily. Red was a virgin, tested regularly on the orders of her morally upright father. It was rumored that the day she turned up without her virginity, or the benefit of a marriage license that her father had approved, then the vast estate her mother had left her on her death would revert to her father in full. Privately, Lucian suspected there was much more to it.

He glanced back at the couple.

"No. No. Not yet..." she cried out brokenly as Sax thrust hard inside the tight depths of her bottom and began to shudder in release. Thankfully, for her, he kept thrusting, though.

Lucian downed the whisky and slapped the glass to the bar for another. Every time he glanced at the other woman he saw Tally instead. Her long black hair sweat-dampened, her face flushed, her thighs spread as his cock tunneled up her pussy or the tight confines of her ass. He wanted to hear her screaming brokenly in lust, her voice husky, pleading, begging.

It was his own fault. Devril had been after him for months to make his move on her. His twin, Devril had slightly less patience than Lucian did. He was extremely put out over the fact that Lucian was taking so much time in testing Tally's limits. They had, as brothers, set their sights on her when she first went to work for Jesse Wyman. Unfortunately for Tally, it wouldn't be a matter of sharing a night or two with the brothers simultaneously. It was a matter of sharing her life. The bond Lucian and Devril shared wouldn't permit otherwise. What Lucian lusted after, Devril naturally knew a hunger for as well.

What Lucian loved, Devril loved. And they were both becoming much too attached to the smart-assed, viperous Tally Raines.

Lucian could feel Devril's anticipation beating at him. They were each one half of a whole it seemed. What had begun with their separation as children had only solidified as they reached puberty and then adulthood. The natural bond that twins share had been intensified, strengthened somehow, until they could sense each other's pain, their pleasure, and sometimes their very thoughts.

They had battled it through their teenage years, denied it as they each fought to develop their individual personalities. But as they reached adulthood, they had learned to accept it.

"Hey, Lucian." Devril took a seat beside him, his dark face reflecting his own tension, deep green eyes concerned.

Lucian turned his head. Night and day, that was what they were. Devril was black-haired and looked like a poster child for lust and sin. His features weren't classically handsome; rather, they were hard-edged, almost savage. The same features Lucian possessed, except his coloring was almost a pure, vivid blond.

"She's pushing too far." Lucian sighed, aware that Devril would know he was talking about Tally. "I'll start tomorrow."

Devril tensed in expectation. "What do you want me to do?"

Lucian swallowed the drink, wincing at the burn that tore through his throat. "Just be ready. My control is damned weak right now, bro. I'm ready to paddle her ass, and I don't mean in a good way."

Devril's dark brows lifted in surprise before his lips tilted upward in a wicked grin. "Long as I get to help," he chuckled. "Remember, keep her off balance. I'll provide a distraction. We'll bring her down yet."

Lucian grunted. "Or she'll bring us down. Stubbornness should be her middle name. But we'll see what happens."

Behind them, Red screamed out in release. Turning, Lucian saw that Sax had bent her over a convenient table, plowing hard and deep up her ass as his fingers tucked between her thighs, milking her swollen clit as she exploded. There was a grimace of pleasure on his face as he filled her ass with his release again, but this time, he had driven her over as well.

Turning back, Lucian sighed heavily. If only Tally were as manageable.

Chapter Two

Lucian Conover was going to be the death of her. Tally Raines inputted the last of the figures he had requested into the data file and sighed in boredom. The afternoon stretched out ahead of her and there was a sale at Brighton's, the exclusive shoe store in the city.

Sneaking out of the office was becoming harder to do daily. She swore Lucian had hidden cameras in the office to record the time she spent away from her desk. She had one hour for lunch and one hour only. That was barely enough time to get to her favorite café and order a cappuccino, let alone eat or check out the sales. Working for Jesse had been much easier. Whatever had made her think she could tolerate working for Conover?

Of course, she had tried to object to the move, but to no avail. Jesse had been gleefully satisfied at having her out of his office. She snorted. That new battle-axe he had hired probably did his filing for him too. The man was much too spoiled, especially after his marriage to Terrie.

Thinking of Terrie had a bittersweet sadness running through her. Jesse had ordered no more piercings, no more tattoos, and he seemed determined to tag along on every outing she had with the other woman. No more adventures. There were so few of her friends who could appreciate some of her more daring escapades.

Not that there had been any in the past weeks. Trolling her favorite spots had dimmed a bit, though she wasn't certain why. The fact that it had begun the night she walked in on the little ménage with Jesse, Terrie and Lucian had nothing to do with it, she assured herself. But she couldn't get the vision of it out of her mind.

Terrie had been sandwiched between the two men, Jesse's cock spearing up her ass as Lucian fucked her pussy with wild lust. Tally had left quickly, but she couldn't forget what she had seen. She couldn't get the arousal it had sparked out of her body and it was driving her insane.

Not that she *really* wanted Conover, she assured herself firmly, ignoring the pulsing heat between her thighs. Arrogant, snide, self-important ass that he was, she could definitely do much better. Couldn't she?

"Tally, I need the Charter file." Lucian stepped from his office, a scowl on his face as he stared over at her.

She lifted a brow with cool inquiry. "The Charter contract was dropped last week."

She turned back to the computer and saved the data information before picking up the file she had been working on and placing it on the side of her desk with a dozen others. She could practically hear Lucian grinding his teeth.

"Did I ask you when it was dropped?" he questioned her softly. "I don't believe I did."

Now that voice… Tally tensed to control the shiver that wanted to work up her spine. It took all her control, but she kept her movements smooth, languid, as she exited the program then sat back in her chair before swiveling around to meet his gaze once again.

She crossed her legs lazily, ignoring the thrill of excitement as his gaze flickered to the silk-covered flesh and heated up with a flare of lust. And if she wasn't mistaken, he was definitely aroused.

Keeping her expression calm in the face of the sudden fire flickering in his green eyes wasn't easy. His hard features were almost savagely outlined, the full curve of his lower lip tightening as his gaze rose to hers once again.

She lifted a brow slowly, more than aware that the perfect arch of the wing-tipped brow would make him furious. If he was angry, he was off balance. An out-of-control Lucian she could handle. The calm, determined Lucian had sent trepidation skittering through her system.

His brows snapped into a frown as his green eyes darkened for long seconds. Then, like the calm before a storm, his expression cleared. This could be interesting. She forced herself to remain relaxed as his face hardened.

"The Charter file," he said carefully. "Now."

She sighed with exaggerated forbearance. "Very well. Though I don't understand why you need to go over a contract that was obviously dropped a week ago. Besides, the owner is a maggot. You wouldn't like him."

She rose to her feet and walked slowly over to the file cabinet as she restrained her own anger. Whereas Jesse had most likely understood her reluctance to deal with the tall, imposing metal cabinets, Lucian merely stood negligently against the doorframe and watched her with narrowed eyes.

He *would* want a file that was stored in the upper drawer. The cabinet was over five and a half feet tall; Tally was barely five two. Pulling the drawer out, she stood on her tiptoes and began riffling through the files until she found the one he wanted. Lifting it out, she pushed the drawer in and walked sedately over to him.

His gaze was hot, but not from anger now.

"Your file, Mr. Conover." She handed it to him, fighting the flush she could feel gathering on her cheeks as his gaze dropped to her breasts. She couldn't keep her breasts from tingling, though, or her nipples from heating beneath his gaze. She breathed slow and evenly, but her heart was racing out of control.

"Your shirt..." He ignored the file, his hand reaching out as his finger slid beneath the parted fabric.

Tally dropped her gaze, almost flinching as his finger slid beneath the edge of her lacy, low-cut bra. The two buttons had somehow slid free on the white silk shirt, leaving her all but bare to his gaze. The sight of his flesh, dark, yet not as dark as her own, sent vibrant trails of awareness blazing through her body.

Suddenly, the memory of him naked, his cock working between Terrie's thighs, sent anger pouring through her system. Unaccountable, uncharacteristic anger. She shouldn't care who he fucked or how often he did it. It shouldn't matter.

She lifted her hand, casting him a look from beneath her lashes as she ran her finger up one side of the parted fabric.

"Do you want this file?" she asked him, her voice low, seductive at first. A second later she raised her gaze, and allowed the ice beneath the surface free rein. "Or the one I'll present later for sexual harassment if you don't move your hand?"

His gaze rose slowly back to hers and the heat in his eyes nearly seared her. She could feel her pussy swelling, her clit aching in response to that look. She lifted her brow in haughty inquiry.

"Would you?" he asked her. "I never figured you for a hypocrite, Tally. But if that's the way you want to play…"

He pulled his hand back reluctantly as he took the file from her hand. A small smile edged the corner of his sensual lips.

No, she wasn't a hypocrite, but she would use whatever edge she could get.

"If that's all you need then, I'll be going to lunch." Without looking she casually re-buttoned her shirt before turning away from him.

"It's a half hour before lunch, Tally," he reminded her smoothly. "I'll have to dock your pay."

Tally shrugged in unconcern. It would be worth it.

"I'll survive." She collected her purse and headed for the door.

"I didn't take you for a coward. Maybe I was wrong." His voice had her stopping, anger seething through her body as she turned back to him.

"A coward?" She lifted her brow as she assumed an expression of haughty disdain. "And you came to this conclusion how?"

She crossed her arms beneath her breasts as she stared back at him. Damn him for the arrogant ass he was.

"Because you want me. You know it and I know it, yet you fight it." His voice was low, dark and husky. She hated it when he used that voice. Hated the way it made her pussy pulse and tingle, made her yearn for his touch. Unfortunately, she was also well aware of the fact that there wasn't a chance in hell it could work.

"My dear Mr. Conover." She sighed mockingly. "I'm old enough that I understand I can't have everything I want in this life. Perhaps this is a lesson you should learn as well."

It was one she took to heart. Some things, men like Lucian topping the list, just weren't good for the emotions or the general stability of life. Tally prided herself on her stability. If she had thought for one moment that she could go to bed with him, enjoy a few hours of wild sex and have it done with, then it would be a different matter. Something warned her that this would not be the case, though.

She stood still, in control, as he paced over to her slowly. He was tall, broad, and if the bulge in those slacks was any indication, he was fully aroused and just as large as he had looked while fucking Terrie.

He stopped directly in front of her, staring down at her, forcing her to raise her head to stare back at him in unconcern.

"Funny," he said with apparent gentleness. She wasn't fooled in the least. "This suddenly antagonistic attitude didn't show up until you walked into that office while I was fucking Terrie. Jealous, Tally?"

Her breath caught in her throat and she knew he caught the tightening of her eyes at his shocking question.

"Oh yeah, I saw you come in." He dropped the file on a nearby shelf as she backed away from him.

He was too close; she felt too overwhelmed, too weak when he towered over her like that. Unfortunately, there was no place to retreat. Her back came against the door as his arms bracketed her, holding her firmly in place.

"Your nipples are hard, Tally," he growled. "And that cold little expression can't hide the fact that you're fucking hot as hell right now. You want me, and you're damned scared to take it."

"Scared? Of you?" She only barely managed the disdain she was trying for. "Not hardly, Lucian. You're letting your imagination run away with you. You're not the first man to make me respond sexually and you won't be the last. Never doubt that. But I decide who I fuck and who I don't. And I won't fuck you."

"Because you're scared." She watched as his gaze softened, the brilliant green color warming drastically. "You're small, baby, but you can take me."

His outrageous words had flames of anger—or was that violent lust—shooting through her.

"Oh, get away." Sarcastic amusement filled her voice; her hands flattened on his chest as she pushed him back forcefully. "You think your dick's so big I'm afraid of it?" She straightened the shoulders of her silk shirt, smoothed the crease at the top of her skirt before staring back up at him, allowing her lips to curve with seductive knowledge.

"Dream on, Conover. It's not your cock I reject, or even your hedonistic lifestyle, such as it is. Quite frankly, you couldn't handle me, and I'll be damned if I'll deal with the complications of your bruised pride when you realize that. It's not fear; it's fact. Now touch me again and I'll resign. I don't have to deal with your advances as well as your snappish attitude. I'll quit first."

She gripped the doorknob and jerked the door open as she rushed to leave, only to be stopped abruptly as she ran into the dark, devil's version of the wicked apparition behind her.

"Easy, sweetheart." Devril Conover's voice was rough sex, whisky at midnight and depraved desires all rolled into one. The same as Lucian's. She was trapped between the two men now as Devril gripped her hips and eased her backward as he came fully into the room, pushing her flush against Lucian.

"Everything okay?" Dev asked her when she didn't speak. She couldn't speak. Lucian enclosed her from behind as Devril pressed against her breasts. Heat enveloped her. Like bands of invisible steel it held her motionless, curiously shocked by the sudden impression of protectiveness and strength that emanated from the two men. She was surrounded by their warmth. Wrapped in it.

She stared up at him in surprise. He was the devil's image of the man behind her, watching her heatedly, reminding her of exactly what she was passing up by walking out that door. It was bad enough to have Lucian tempting her, but to have Dev, the dark-haired vision of the sin twin helping him? That was completely unfair as far as she was concerned. Fate had it in for her, that's all she could say.

"Just what I need." She sighed with mockingly false patience as she stared up at Devril and batted her eyes seductively. "Tweedle Dee to join Tweedle Dum. Do you boys ever do anything solo?"

"Where would the fun be in that?" Lucian asked her as his lips settled against her ear, his hands on her shoulders as she felt the hard length of his cock against the small of her back, Devril's against her lower stomach. "Or the challenge? I'll make you beg me to touch you again, Tally."

The sexual tension thickened as she realized the implication behind his words. The breath locked in her chest and lust sizzled through her veins. Both of them? Brothers? The temptation was damned near impossible to deny. She couldn't have thought of any sexual experience that would have possibly been better. Or one that came closer to her fantasies.

Except.

Lucian was her boss. Her position as assistant to the vice president of Delacourte-Conover could become extremely precarious and even if she did quit, resign or walk out, the gossip that would abound could destroy her career. They could destroy her heart.

"Ohhh, so confident," she mocked him waspishly, well aware that she had lost her appearance of calm disinterest as she pushed her way past Devril and made it to the door again. "I could make you beg." She rolled her eyes with forced patience. "Not hardly."

She turned back to them. They were like night and day. Devril watched her with blatant lust while Lucian watched her with a mix of predatory interest and a flare of anger.

"We'll forget this episode ever happened," she drawled coolly as they watched her with their ever-present amusement. Fighting back the knowledge that she was walking away from the ultimate sexual fantasy, she bit back her sigh of regret and informed them instead, "I'm going shopping. I'll be back when I get back." Her gaze hardened on Lucian. "And if you dock my pay then you better make certain you bring your own coffee to work. Because anything you get here won't be safe to drink."

She turned and walked sedately from the room, though she closed the door a bit harder than she intended. The blood was rushing through her body, heat and lust curling through her womb as her cunt trickled with her juices. Had anything ever been so intensely carnal? Not that she knew of. Which was terrifying. They were a weakness she could ill afford.

She had turned them down. She drew in a hard breath and gave herself a mental pat on the back even as the darker part of her desires mentally kicked her. Could there be anything more seductive than the thought of being mastered by the two fallen angels of Delacourte-Conover? Not to her mind there wasn't. But, she reminded herself, was there anything more dangerous?

Chapter Three

Okay, so she had choices to make. Tally sat alone in the small gazebo in the center of the park, staring out at the placid blue of the pond, on whose banks it had been built. The wooden bench was hard but not uncomfortable. The slight breeze that flowed through the branches of the trees above her was soothing, even if it did little to cool the fires raging in her body.

She was out of control. Or at least as out of control as she felt it was possible for her to get. She was nothing if not well aware of the fact that she had run from that office and from Lucian and Dev like a scared little virgin. She was anything but a virgin. And just because they may not be aware of it, she was honest enough with herself to admit the truth.

She was scared.

She hadn't anticipated that when she had first been moved to Conover's. She knew she lusted after Lucian, knew she wanted a chance to experience his touch, to fuck him until she knew at least some small relief from the desires tormenting her. When Dev had been added to the equation, she had been positively gleeful. Two men at her beck and call, she had thought. Amazingly virile, able to provide her with her every carnal desire. She hadn't expected the dominance as well. Nor had she expected the growth of her desires. Her needs were almost consuming her now. Needs she had no business seeking.

She watched a small flock of ducks waddle across the grassy bank and slip into the cool water. Their lazy quacks and playful antics in the water brought a smile to her face. Once, a long time ago, she would have followed them. She would have splashed in the water and dared anyone to deny her the pleasure of it.

Now, she hid her pleasures, kept them in the dark and allowed them out only under the strictest circumstances. She could tell Lucian and Dev were not going to allow her to decide where and when those desires came out. Or how they would be played.

"Still pouting?" Dev's dark voice had her jerking in response, her head swinging around as he stepped into the sheltered gazebo and took a seat across from her. His legs took up most of the space; his big body seemed to fill the small open building to capacity.

"I never pout," she informed him with a patient little smile. She wished she felt as patient as she forced herself to appear. "I was merely enjoying the peace."

A peace she was certain was gone for good now. Dev Conover looked like your typical bad boy. From his overly long jet-black hair to his intense green eyes and hard body, he was every woman's ideal of carnal pleasure. He was the dark to Lucian's light, as different physically from his brother as you could get. But she had a feeling that inside, where it counted, they were too damned much alike.

He watched her intently, leaning back against the bench, his arms stretched out along the back of it as amusement tilted the corners of his lips.

"I had you pegged as the Dragon Lady," he finally mused quietly. "I expected you to come out with claws drawn, not to see you run away as though afraid of the two of us."

She lifted her brow mockingly, despite the fact he had described exactly what she had done.

"Devril, really," she said, shaking her head. "Some things are worth drawing claws over. Others aren't really worth the time. Perhaps you and Lucian fall into that latter category."

"Perhaps?" That demonically sexy quirk of his lips made her mouth water.

She breathed in deeply, refraining from rolling her eyes, though resisting the urge was a test of her patience. No matter how sexy he was, he was infuriating as hell.

"Fishing for compliments, Dev?" She fought to keep her voice calm, modulated. It wouldn't do to let him sense any weakness. Like Lucian, he would pounce on it immediately. "You'll need to bring better bait next time." She lifted her brow in mocking amusement as she glanced at his lap insultingly before looking away. No way in hell would she admit that bulge was more than outstanding.

He was silent for long moments. Just long enough for her to grow comfortable with the sounds of summer that filled the hidden spot. Soothing, relaxing, she found comfort here more than any other place she knew of.

"Have you ever had sex in public?" he finally asked her with devilish amusement.

She glanced at him mockingly. "Of course I have. I've grown out of the urge to tempt a charge of public indecency, though. As you should have."

His eyes were assessing and filled with an outright challenge.

"Hmm. Maybe." His lips tilted into a sexually knowing grin. "But isn't that all a part of the fun?" He lowered his arms from the bench and braced his elbows on his knees. Leaning forward as he was now, he was much too close to her; the small gazebo seemed filled with him, the sexual tension heightening unbearably.

Hard, calloused hands settled on the sides of her knees, his thumbs smoothing over the sensitive, silk-covered flesh. Tally's gaze fell to those large, competent hands. It was much too easy to imagine them on her skin.

"I want to fuck you, Tally. So bad it's like a hunger. You've flitted around and teased us for a year, determined to control every step of this little dance we've been involved in. Haven't you learned yet? There's no control here."

Tally narrowed her eyes at the challenge. Drawing in a slow, deep breath, she leaned forward, noticing rather smugly the small flare of surprise in his gaze as her hands ran up his arms, her nails dragging over the hard, muscular flesh of his biceps. She felt him tighten, his knees shifting as he moved forward, enclosing her legs within his as she stared back at him.

"There's always control." She blew a soft breath over his lips as they parted, only slightly. "It all depends on the control you're seeking."

Her hands moved from his shoulders to the buttons of his shirt. She undid the first, then the second, spreading the material enough to allow her hands to lay flush against the heat of his chest.

The glitter of battle entered his eyes then. "You could be biting off more than you can chew, kitten," he whispered as her nails flexed against the hard muscle beneath them. "I'm not the least bit afraid of an indecency charge."

He wouldn't be, she thought silently. But as she had told him, it was all in who controlled it and how.

She leaned closer, her tongue peeking out to lick her lips, but glancing his lower one instead as his gaze sharpened with sexual heat.

"Would you give up control, Devril?" she asked him as his hands moved to her waist, his fingers gripping her lightly. "Would you allow me to do whatever I wished, whenever I wished?"

All she needed was the promise. She leaned forward a bit more, her teeth catching the temptation of his lip and nipping at it gently.

His hands tightened further.

"How much pleasure can you take, Dev, before *your* control breaks?"

Her hands slid down his chest, nails rasping as his eyes suddenly narrowed. There was no warning. There was no teasing, no asking permission. Before she could evade him he had her across his lap, one hand tangled in the long strands of her hair, tilting her head back as his lips claimed hers.

He devoured her. His tongue pressed past her lips as the sharp flare of heat at her scalp had her gasping in pleasure. It was so decadent, the thrill she received from hard fingers gripping and pulling at her hair as his lips moved expertly, heatedly over hers.

There were kisses and then there was a conquering. This kiss conquered. His tongue opened her lips, pressed forward and claimed her mouth as though it were created for him alone. And her mouth was in ready agreement.

A moan tore from her throat as fierce, alternating sensations swept through her body; the dominance of his lips and tongue taking what he wanted, his hands, one tangled in her long hair, the other splayed against her lower back as he held her close in his grip, the heat of his chest, his cock, hard and insistent beneath her ass. She wiggled against the heavy erection, thrilling to the hard male groan that vibrated against her lips.

Had she thought he had control? Of her, perhaps, but not of his desires. His lips ravaged hers, but they didn't mind. His tongue tangled with hers in a masterful stroke, but it had no objections. Her arms wrapped around his shoulders, hands holding tight, her nails digging into his back as she fought to maintain her own control, but she could feel her senses scattering beneath his kiss.

The hand at her back moved, swept over the curve of her ass, down her thigh to the hem of her skirt.

"Son, you go much further and we might have a problem here."

Tally froze at the amused voice. Her eyes flew open in horror as Dev's head raised slowly. Lust and heated demand filled his eyes, but the smug curve of his lips spoke for itself.

"Oh. You..." She jumped from his lap, slapping at his hands as they reached out to steady her when she stumbled.

Shame coursed through her as she stared at the park official standing several feet from the gazebo. He had that look of indulgence that other men gave each other. A smirk that made her want to rip their faces from their heads and feed their dicks to the dogs. Infuriating.

"Now, Tally." The amusement in Devril's voice was like gas to a fire.

Narrowing her eyes furiously, she ignored the guard. Leaning forward, her hand fisted in Devril's hair, her lips lowered to his as though in a surge of lust as her knee came down between his thighs.

Her lips were a breath from his when she exerted just the right amount of pressure on the tender, sensitive scrotum just below her kneecap. His eyes widened, his face paling ever so slightly as the guard chuckled behind them.

"Uhh, Tally," he said hesitantly. "Do you know where your knee is?"

"Ohh baby," she drawled with seductively heat. "Of course I know where my knee is. Remember, darling, no pain, no gain. Are you sure you want to continue to tempt me in such a way?" She increased the pressure by the slightest degree, watching him swallow tightly.

He cleared his throat, his green eyes watching her cautiously. "Think of all the fun you could miss out on later."

She watched him wince as she leaned in more, knowing the pinching pressure he would be feeling now.

"There's such a fine line between pleasure and pain," she told him, keeping her smile intentionally innocent. "Shall we see where your line is drawn, Dev?"

Small beads of sweat stood out on his brow, but his eyes glittered with an amused knowledge of his defeat.

"I surrender." He held his hands out from her, his thighs tight, his body drawn in anticipation of the pain to come.

She leaned down, gave that tempting, full lower lip a quick little bite before moving back from him calmly.

"You're so easy." She sighed regretfully. "Too bad. I had hoped for more of a challenge."

Still ignoring the park official, she pulled the tattered remains of her pride around her. She shrugged her shoulders, adjusted her shirt and smoothed the slight creases from the silk covering her hips before she gave both men a disdainful look and marched from the gazebo.

"Tally, Lucian asked me to find out where the Gallagher file was. He was searching for it when I left." Dev's amused voice brought her to a halt.

She turned carefully, keeping her expression blank as she stared back at him, fighting to control the fury rising inside her.

"In hell. Where he can go," she suggested sweetly before turning on her heel and heading back to the office.

Chapter Four

“Stay the hell out of my files!” Tally slapped the Gallagher file on Lucian’s desk, right in front of his face.

He swiveled the chair around to face her, looking up at her broodingly. His thick, almost white, blond hair fell over his brow, lust glittering in his eyes.

“Don’t you even think about it,” she warned him, unable to still the harsh anger that pulsed in her voice. “If you touch me, I promise you’ll regret it.”

He leaned back in his chair, watching her with narrowed eyes.

“This is an office,” she told him with cold disdain. “A place of business. This is not an orgy palace, nor is it your own personal fuck central. I will not be molested here on a daily basis.”

“I own the damned place,” he snarled back at her. “If I want to fuck in it, then I’ll do it *on a daily basis*, Tally.”

“Not with me.” She bared her teeth at him, her fists clenching with the need for the action. “I am not some weak-kneed office bimbo who’s going to spread out on your desk for your pleasure. I am a professional, Lucian, and I expect to be treated as such.”

He rose slowly to his feet. She should have felt intimidated, instead she felt enraged.

“I never act in any other manner while conducting business,” he reminded her, his soft voice in no way disguising his anger.

“While we’re in this office…”

"Tally." He never raised his voice, but the sharp edge had her brows lowering in growing anger. "This is my office. You're my woman. While no longer conducting business, if I want to fuck the hell out of you, then it's my choice and my prerogative."

"Oh, is it now?" She crossed her arms carefully beneath her breasts. "And exactly who decided I was *your* woman?"

He smiled slowly. "Our woman," he said, his voice dark and confident as he leaned closer. "Don't doubt it, Tally. I know who you just came from. I know how hot you burned in his arms and I know damned good and well you would burn the same in mine. The pain in my balls was well worth the experience. So never doubt you haven't been claimed."

The hard throb of ownership in his voice sent tremors of excitement racing up her spine even as a firestorm of fury raced through her blood veins. But it was his words that shocked her. He had felt that? They could sense what the other felt? That information she would use later; for now, she had Lucian's attitude to deal with.

He was taller than her by quite a bit. Her head barely reached his upper chest, so she was forced to tilt her head back as she allowed smug disdain to fill her expression.

"Do you really think you can control me with sex, Lucian?" she asked him, her voice cold, filled with loathing. "Do I really appear to be such a twit that all you have to do is fuck me to handle me? You have another think coming." She punctuated her words with a forceful jab of her finger into his hard, muscular chest. "No one handles me. No man controls me. Not now. Not ever."

He glanced down at her finger. Slowly. A second later his gaze speared into hers once again.

"I'll control you, Tally," he told her, the tone of his voice whispering of a sexual dominance, an excitement she had only imagined before. "We'll control you, and I promise you, when we do, you'll beg for it."

Her lip curled as a snarl begged to be free. In her life, she could never remember being so furious, so intent on slapping a man to his knees as she was now. And she would have. She could have. If only she could force the required words past her lips. Her repertoire of cutting phrases refused to come to mind now.

"And you'll learn just how quickly your own arrogance will kick your ass," she informed him coldly before spinning away and stalking to the door. "Stay the hell out of my file cabinet or do the damned filing yourself. Your choice. I won't warn you again."

"Tally."

She stopped at the door, turning back to him slowly, fighting the compulsion to go to him, to give him what he needed, what they both wanted.

"You're not fighting me, baby, or Dev. You're fighting yourself. And I think you're smart enough to see that."

"You're wrong," she told him softly. "Now, I just left Tweedle Dee in the park with my kneecap imprinted on his balls. Keep fucking with me, and I'll slam yours up your throat. I'm going back to work now." She gave the information, pretending she had missed his earlier admission. Revenge was best dealt in surprise, she chuckled to herself.

She swept from the room before he could respond, before she could glimpse any knowledge or emotion in his expression. She had a job to do. A job she enjoyed, and she needed to remember that. Even if Lucian and Dev refused to. And she had revenge to plan. An exacting, satisfying revenge before her fury ended in bloodshed.

Chapter Five

Planning her revenge took a day or two. Tally knew it wouldn't be easy to separate them, nor would it be easy to convince the other to go along with her. Especially as furious as they had known she was. But she managed it.

Two days later, as Lucian was settling down to a meeting with several military liaisons, Tally picked up a file she had held back the day before and walked into Dev's office, careful to keep her hand behind her back as she turned the small locking mechanism on the door knob that would automatically secure the door.

"I need you to sign these, Dev," she told him briskly as she walked over to his desk and moved behind it as though she had no qualms at all in being so near him.

She laid the file on the desk in front of him, opened it and straightened as she turned to look at him.

He didn't appear interested at all in the papers laid out before him. He was more interested in the fact that several buttons had slid free on her royal blue linen shirt.

"You've been in the files again," he said softly as she glanced down. She knew that was what he would believe. Both brothers, it seemed, immensely enjoyed the fact that the file cabinets managed to strain her blouses until the top buttons slipped their moorings.

She sighed with false impatience. "Of course. Isn't that the purpose of making me do your filing now? Perhaps you should be the one to button my blouses when it happens."

A grin tugged at his lips. He shouldn't be so damned sexy and rakish looking when he smiled like that, she thought, deeply perturbed by it.

"I would be more than willing," he promised her silkily as he swiveled the chair around to face her and patted his lap. "Sit down here, baby, and let me see what I can do about that pretty blouse."

She knew he expected her to kick his teeth in for the offer, but rather she sat down sedately on his thigh, staring into his surprised expression with an innocent smile.

"Like this?" she whispered seductively, her body turning into his as one arm came around her back.

"What are you up to?" There was a flicker of suspicion in the jade depths of his gaze as he watched her.

"Me?" she asked him, her eyes narrowing in false anger as she watched him carefully. "Really, Dev. You offered. But if you would prefer not to." She shrugged her shoulders as she moved to rise, aware that he would catch a glimpse of seductive sheer lace beneath the edges of her bra.

"Now, I didn't say no." His arm curved around her back, holding her in place. "I was just questioning your motives, baby. You haven't exactly been eager to play here lately."

She would have laughed if she weren't so determined now.

"Well really, Dev," she snapped. "The two of you together can be rather intimidating. It's enough to make even the most jaded of us wary."

She injected just the right amount of irritation and watched with silent glee as his gaze darkened reflectively.

He sighed, shaking his head slowly. "Why don't I trust you, Tally?"

She smiled innocently, blinking up at him with a rare display of charm. She could be charming when she wanted to be. She had done so often in the past.

"Because your balls still carry the imprint of my knee cap?" she asked wickedly.

He chuckled, relaxing marginally. "That could be it." His hands gripped her waist. "If you're serious about the blouse, come here where I can get to you."

Now how did he manage that? Tally was staring down at him in shock seconds later as she sat on the edge of the desk, her bare buttocks meeting the cool wood as her skirt pooled along the desk around her.

"Sneaky." There was a vein of grudging respect in her tone. It had been done so smoothly she was unaware of his hands sliding her skirt up her legs as he lifted her.

"Thank you. I thought you would appreciate the move." He chuckled wickedly as he moved closer. "Let's see about these buttons now."

Another came undone.

Tally frowned down at him darkly, though silently she crowed in triumph.

"Wrong way, Conover." She allowed her voice to become breathless, the arousal that was ever-present around them to glitter in her gaze.

"Really?" Another came undone. "Are you sure?"

He watched her, gauging her, testing her. She allowed a cool smile of confidence to shape her lips.

"You wouldn't dare. Lucian would be very put out," she warned him softly.

"Would he?" he asked her. "Is he busy right now?"

She frowned as though not certain. "He was going over contracts before I came in here. Why?"

She pretended ignorance. She was good at that when she needed to be. But if what Lucian had said after her little escapade in the park with Dev was true, then he would feel every touch his brother knew. Tally was going to make certain he felt quite a few touches in the next few minutes.

"Just curious." He cleared his throat, another button falling victim to his fingers as he pulled the material from the waistband of her skirt. "So, Tally, how much are you wanting to play this afternoon?" he asked her curiously.

"I don't know, Devril." She smiled slowly, seductively. "How much control do you think you have?"

He lifted one dark eyebrow mockingly. "Do your worst, baby."

Ohh, a dare. She smiled slowly, her tongue peeking out to lick her lips as she shrugged her shirt from her shoulders, slid from the desktop and straddled one hard, male thigh.

"My worst, huh?" she asked him curiously as she leaned close, her knee pressing, but exerting no pressure to the sensitive area she had nearly abused before.

He cleared his throat. "Pleasure-wise."

"Of course." Her fingers went to his shirt, buttons loosening with each breath he took as she leaned forward and allowed her tongue to rim his lips. "Only pleasure, Devril. For now…"

* * * * *

Lucian tensed. Son of a bitch. It was all he could do not to curse aloud as he tried to follow the conversation between Jesse and the General regarding the new military contract they were being offered.

He could feel her. What the hell was Dev doing? He knew better than this. He knew not to allow that little vixen around him alone during business hours. But somehow the conniving little witch had managed to convince him otherwise. And Lucian was stuck. There wasn't a chance in hell of escaping the meeting, and no way to stop what he knew was coming.

He felt her kiss, that tempting tongue first rimming the lips then sliding softly, easily, into Dev's mouth. Heat surged through his body as his cock responded immediately. Hard, demanding, it strained against his slacks as he suffered through the impression of a feast of lips, tongues and breathless moans. Damn them, he was going to kill them both.

He fought to control his breathing. It wouldn't do to be panting in front of a General, a Senator, a military contractor and, worst of all, Jesse. But he could feel the perspiration gathering on his forehead, the heat whipping through his system.

Where was telepathy when a twin needed it? Unfortunately, that wasn't a bond he and Dev had ever developed.

Jesse had warned him about Tally. Warned him to never, ever let her suspect the weakness the two men shared. When she had stomped into his office from the park, he had a feeling he had done just that with his hastily spoken words. Now, he was paying for it.

The sensation of hot lips moved down his neck, his chest. Teasing fingers ran along the length of his cock, then farther down, rasping the tightening scrotum before caressing the sensitive flesh just behind it. He was going crazy.

Even worse though, he sensed the feel of her soft flesh against his fingertips. Hard nipples surrounded by little gold bands. Slick, fiery heat as two fingers pushed slowly inside her tight pussy. His fist clenched as he fought for control and prayed he could hold out against the exquisite pleasure. Coming in the middle of a business meeting wasn't acceptable. But he had a feeling Tally was pushing just for that.

"You okay, Luc?" General Mornay watched him closely for long seconds as Lucian fought to clear the dazed pleasure from his mind.

"Fine, General." He cleared his throat, glancing at Jesse for help. Was he supposed to be contributing here?

Jesse gave him an odd look before turning to the General, thankfully with an explanation to whatever question he had asked.

Lucian's thighs tightened; his whole body screamed with the need for release as the impression of a hot, moist mouth surrounded the head of his blazing erection. Sweet Heaven, he prayed, he was not going to survive this. It wasn't possible.

He could feel sweat gathering at his temples now, a rivulet running down the side of his face and didn't dare move to wipe it away. His hands were shaking as his palms heated with the feel of her silky hair gliding over them, his fingers clenching as Dev's tightened, holding her mouth on his cock, torturing Lucian with the feel of it.

He stared around the room wildly, his gaze finally connecting once again with Jesse's and he knew then he would kill Tally. Jesse stared at him for a second, confused, then with slowly dawning awareness of what must be going on. There were few people who knew of the bond Lucian and Devril shared. Jesse was one of them. And if the gleam of evil amusement was anything to go by, Lucian was getting ready to pay for baiting the other man months before while Terrie had obviously been getting right friendly beneath Jesse's desk.

"Lucian has been working extensively on this project, gentlemen," Jesse said matter of fact, though his eyes gleamed with satisfaction. "I'm certain he can answer your questions about development."

The man was fucking insane. Lucian shifted in his seat, casting his friend a look of retribution as all eyes turned to him. Tally chose that particular moment to rake her teeth over the head of Dev's cock, nearly sending Lucian into heart failure. Dear God, the pleasure was streaking through his veins like comets across a night sky, only to explode in his brain. He was supposed to discuss something in this condition?

He cleared his throat. Okay, it was the first time in a lot of years, but not the first time ever that Dev had placed him in this position. He could get through this. He cleared his throat again.

Fuck! He tensed as trailing fingers of sensation shot from his dick to his head in a surge of ecstasy unlike anything he could have imagined. What the fuck was she doing? Her mouth was sucking firmly, her tongue rimming the flared head, fingers massaging taut balls with firm strokes, but she was doing something more. Pressing against the base of the cock, nimble little fingers applied pressure as the ball of her thumb rotated. He swallowed tightly, his eyes widening as he felt his release begin to build.

* * * * *

"Not yet." Tally eased the pressure of her mouth on Dev's cock, her fingers tightening on the base to delay the release she could feel surging up the shaft of tight, hard flesh. "Let's see if we can't make it better."

Dev stared at her with narrowed eyes, his breathing hard, face flushed as she reached for the glass of ice water that was on his desk. Her fingers slid over the rim, drawing a sliver of ice from the cold liquid. She saw the glimmer of amusement in his eyes and wondered if Lucian was similarly awed with her abilities.

She could barely restrain her chuckle. She could imagine the hell he was going through while sitting through that meeting with those stuffy, straight-laced government types.

Opening her mouth slowly, aware of Dev watching her every move, she laid the ice on her tongue, allowing the cold to penetrate her warm flesh as it melted quickly.

"Now we see if you can keep that control," she whispered on a small laugh as her head lowered once again to the straining flesh.

* * * * *

Lucian flinched. A strangled groan growled at the back of his throat as the pressure on the base of his cock eased, only to have the head surrounded with an icy blast of sensation a second before the heat began to return as never before. White-hot, growing, shimmering before his eyes as his balls drew up tight and hard, warning him that release was only seconds away.

"Mr. Conover?" The Major was staring at him in concern. "Are you feeling okay?"

Lucian's gaze swung to Jesse, who quickly lost his amusement in the face of whatever he was seeing. The pleasure was too intense, too destructive. Fuck. He was going to kill them.

His cock throbbed in warning, a small amount of pre-come dampening it beneath the material of his slacks.

Lucian jumped to his feet and without apology, without an explanation, stalked across the office to the private bathroom off the side. He slammed the door, his fingers shaking as he locked it with one hand and tore at the zipper of his slacks with the other.

No sooner had he managed to free the tortured flesh from its confinement than he exploded. He barely throttled his strangled groan, his head falling back as he bared his teeth and felt his semen jet violently from the head of his cock.

Hard spasms wracked his body, drew every muscle tight and locked the breath in his throat as he fought to steady himself, to rein in the harsh male shout that he knew had erupted from Dev's throat.

Son of a bitch. He shuddered with the feel of gentle lips milking the last drops of come from a straining cock before they slid away slowly. He fought for breath, his chest heaving, his composure shot now. Never, in his entire life, *never* had he known anything so fucking good, and all he'd had for his pleasure was the echo of impressions through the bond he shared with Dev.

His legs trembled; sweat beaded his flesh, dampened his shirt and did little to cool the heat raging just under his skin. With shaking hands he cleaned the sink that had been splattered with the silky jets of seed spewing from his cock moments before, then fixed his clothes slowly.

His eyes narrowed as his teeth clenched in fury. The little witch. She was going to pay, and by God, he would make sure she paid well.

He moved from the bathroom back to the office.

"Jesse, gentlemen, I seem to be afflicted by some odd virus at the moment. If you'll excuse me…"

"Lucian." Jesse stopped him as he headed for the door. "Get well quick. You and Dev have a flight in two hours. You'll be accompanying the General to Washington to lay the idea out to the committee. I hope you'll be able to make it."

Lucian stared back at them, fighting to keep his expression calm. "I'm certain it's merely a temporary affliction. I just need a few moments. Excuse me."

He nodded stiffly to the three men before he threw open the office door and stalked out to Tally's desk.

There she sat, as cool and triumphant as a reigning queen. She smiled slowly, a smug little curve to her lips that warned him of her victorious demeanor. But her gaze was hot, wild. She wasn't unaffected and she hadn't found her own release. Damned stubborn woman. He glanced at Dev, who stood furiously at the door to his office, watching her heatedly.

"Wrong move, sweet thing," Lucian told her softly, leaning close as he planted his fists on her desk and stared into her satisfied expression. "Bold. Daring. But wrong time, wrong place. You chose to pick a meeting to test your skills during office hours, business time. No quarter given. Do not make the mistake of ever asking for such, either. When I get back from this little trip you've just caused with your shenanigans in distracting me during that meeting, you better be waiting, because I intend to fuck you six ways from Sunday. Maybe, just maybe, by the time we're finished you'll be too fucking tired to cause trouble."

She rolled her eyes. He snapped his teeth together in fury at the mocking expression.

"Darling," she drawled. "I would cause trouble if I were dead. You're once again overreaching your own capabilities."

Overreaching? Lucian leaned closer, almost nose to nose, the vindictive little light in her eyes making him crazy to fuck it out of her.

"Am I, Tally?" he asked her gently. "When I get my hands on you, I'm gonna spank your tight little ass until you scream to come for me. I'm going to make you beg."

Her eyes widened. "Oh, Daddy, make it hurt so good."

She was laughing. The little vixen was having the time of her damned life. The impression hit him nearly broadside. Had he ever seen her eyes twinkle like that? Seen such joy on her face? She was torturing him and she was loving it.

For a moment, just a moment, warmth curled through his heart. Her laughter, her joy, was like an addiction, but he'd be damned if he could live through another episode such as the one he had just experienced.

"You are insane," he growled, straightening and staring down at her with a frown.

Her laughter was low, bright. "Yeah. I am," she agreed. "Deal with it."

Deal with it? He turned and glanced at Dev. Deal with it? They were so screwed.

Chapter Six

Tally knew the minute Lucian and Devril walked into the Wyman's large front room nearly a week later. Several other projects in addition to the military contract had called them out of town, leaving her alone in the office and oddly at loose ends. She hadn't anticipated how much she would miss them or the excitement that sizzled over her body whenever they were near.

But they were back now and her body was suddenly alive again. The tiny hairs at the nape of her neck lifted in some sort of primal awareness, drawing her attention away from the handsome Director of Marketing she had been chatting with.

Her head turned; rather distantly, she noticed the feel of her long, straight black hair swishing above her hips, caressing the silk of her snug bronze dress. The sensual feeling wasn't welcome. It warned her that the sexual tension between them that afternoon last week had not abated and her body was now primed and eager for their touch. It was no longer just Lucian her body lusted after, but Dev as well.

Devril had never played a part in any of her sexual fantasies of Lucian, until this past month. As she had fought for release in her lonely bed over the past week, Devril accompanied her fantasy image of Lucian, his hands playing over her body as she imagined Lucian's cock, his erection filling her mouth as his brother's filled her pussy. It had been highly erotic. It had been highly unwelcome. She was having a hard enough time keeping herself distant from one brother; she didn't need the other adding into the equation.

"Excuse me," she murmured to the young man she had been talking to, and headed for the bar for another glass of champagne. Liquid courage. She needed something to see her through this evening.

Tally had to admit she had hoped neither Lucian nor Devril would return in time to attend the small party Jesse and Terrie were throwing to celebrate the six-month anniversary of the friendly and very lucrative, merging of Delacourte and Conover electronics firms. Each company had differing strengths and areas of expertise that, when combined, would eventually make them a leader within the electronic manufacturing world. That and the government contracts that the two companies together could now pull in would push them ahead of the game.

Sipping on her champagne, Tally moved farther along to keep a careful distance between her and the Conover brothers. Damn, she just hadn't considered that they would double-team her the way they had. But she should have. It was an oversight that she had been foolish to make. She knew they were part of the much whispered about Trojans. A group of elite dominants that often enjoyed ménage sexual practices with their women.

Several ex-wives of the group had made the mistake of telling *a few good friends* about the small group and word had spread like wildfire through the small community of influential citizens. Exactly what the Trojans were, no one really knew. Sexually dominant, they were men whose extreme sexual tastes were outside of what would be considered natural.

Her best friend, Terrie, had married one of the members and Tally knew for a fact that part of her relationship with her new husband did indeed involve a third partner sometimes. It was something Terrie spoke very little of, but Tally knew the other woman had found that *something* that had always been missing in her life.

Not that Jesse wasn't extremely possessive of his new wife. He was. The love that connected the two was impossible to miss. Jesse never so much as looked at another woman. But he did sometimes share his wife.

Lucky Terrie.

Tally sighed as she wandered through the open garden doors and escaped the stifling tension following her in the house. She should have known better than to attend the party. Her emotions were too high, her control too fragile right now. She prided herself on that control and the small slips she was displaying were starting to worry her. Lucian and Dev were becoming a weakness she could ill afford.

Silently, she made her way along the rock walkway that led deeper into the shadowed expanse of flowering bushes and trees. Terrie's idea, she knew. Her friend had a green thumb that often went out of control, but the garden was a masterpiece of serenity. Nearly a square acre of lush vegetation and miniature trees.

Finally, Tally made her way to a secluded waterfall on the western edge of the gardens and the hidden padded bench beneath the shelter of a small, vine-covered iron gazebo.

The bench was wide, softly cushioned and, most importantly, private. Tally needed time to come to grips with herself before facing Lucian or his twin. It wasn't that the thought of a ménage with the two men bothered her. Tally was extremely liberal in her opinions of sexuality and completely honest with the darker side of her own sexual desires.

The fact was, there would be problems attached to any affair she entered into with Lucian, or Lucian and his brother. Her emotions were involved. How it happened, when it had happened, she wasn't entirely certain. But she knew when she stepped into that office and saw Lucian fucking Terrie she had been furious.

She had known it would happen eventually. Hell, she could have stopped it. When Jesse asked her if there was anyone who shouldn't be involved in such a situation with him and Terrie, she could have said something then. Her pride had demanded her silence, though.

It wasn't so much that Lucian had been fucking the other woman, contradictory as it sounded; it was that he wasn't fucking Tally.

"This is so stupid." She rolled her eyes at her own thoughts.

She wasn't jealous of Terrie—not really. She was just so damned consumed with the thought of Lucian, and now Dev, that she couldn't make sense of anything else. She had been ever since their first meeting at Delacourte Electronics and their mocking appraisal of her as she led them into Jesse's office.

She finished her champagne before leaning her head back against the bench and drawing in the warm night air. The steady sound of falling water, the heady scents of the night and her own weariness were about to get the best of her.

"Hiding, Tally?" Lucian's smooth, dark voice had her eyes opening in resignation.

Had she known he would follow her?

She stared up at him, seeing the halo of light around the white-blond of his hair and silhouetting the wide breadth of his shoulders.

"Well, it should be pretty evident I wasn't looking for company." She injected what she hoped was just the right amount of cool mockery into her voice. It was hard to do after their last confrontation.

He chuckled. The sound was low and wickedly amused as she rose to her feet, intent on returning to the house. He had been furious when he left the week before, he and Dev both were literally fuming over what she had done. She expected a return of that anger now.

"Tally." His hand on her arm as she moved to pass him stopped her. More from surprise, perhaps, than from anything else.

She stared up at him in the dim light, wondering at the serious cast of his expression. She had seen him mocking, sarcastic and downright furious. But she had never seen this expression on his face. Intent, his gaze shadowed with a bit of regret.

"I missed you," he whispered, his hand smoothing down her arm until he gripped her hand lightly, lifting it to his face.

Tally fought the tremor of response that started low in her belly and began to work its way through her body. His touch was gentle as he pressed her hand against his cheek. She could fight their dominance, enjoyed doing so actually. But this gentleness was destructive, weakening.

"Lucian." She stopped, attempting to clear the huskiness from her throat. She hadn't expected this. Didn't expect this tenderness, this need that stirred a part of her soul she didn't know could still respond.

"I thought of you while I was gone." He turned his head, his lips pressing against her palm. "I dreamed of you. Often."

Her hand trembled. His voice was dark and deep, stroking along her senses as the night breeze wafted over her skin. It was incredibly sensual, weakening.

"Everything ran really well at the office," she reported desperately, uncertain how to respond, how to react. "Sax had a few problems with one of the contracts…"

"Tally, I don't care about the damned office." He moved closer, his free hand cupping her hip as he pulled her closer to him. "You run that place like a drill sergeant. I have no doubt everything went just as planned."

If he had been irritated or if his voice had been snide she could have fought him, could have fought the hunger that curled through every cell of her body. Instead, a tender vein of amusement slid through his desire-rich tone and caused her chest to swell with pride. She was a damned good assistant and she knew it.

The next second, the office was forgotten completely as he laid her hand against his chest. He gripped her hips and before she could protest he lifted her to him, his lips settling at the corner of hers with heated need.

"I love how you taste, Tally," he whispered as her fingers curled against his shoulders. "So sweet and hot. I dreamed of that taste. I woke aching for it. Dev and I barely managed to get through the week without you, we ached so desperately for you."

"We?" She could barely still her groan as she felt the heat and hardness of his cock against her stomach, felt the air of tension that surrounded both of them now.

"Tell me you don't want it, Tally," he told her gently, his hand raising once again to push her hair back from her face as he stared down at her somberly. "Tell me you don't want us both touching you, holding you into the night. That you don't ache to know that either or both of us are there for you at any time you wish, willing to give you whatever you need."

"Really Lucian, you should bottle the charm. You could make millions." She swallowed tightly; the image of it had taunted her more than she wanted to admit to herself.

"Do you understand what we're offering, Tally? Do you think you can play us against each other until you choose which of us you want?" he asked gently. "It wouldn't matter, if you just had me. Or just had him. It wouldn't matter where I was on this planet; I would feel him inside you. I would feel the tight clasp of your pussy on his cock, feel the heat of your body beneath his." Her eyes widened as he continued. "That's the bond we share, baby. What I love, he will always love. What I need, he hungers for as well. And vice versa. You belong to both of us, Tally. Forever. Imagine that, baby. Two of us to torture and drive insane. Think of the possibilities."

Oh, the temptation of it. The utterly delicious carnality of the thought. All her fantasies, her desires, her dreams, rolled into two men at her beck and call. The thought was so tempting, so erotic, she wanted nothing more than to give into it.

Lucian's hand cupped the back of her head, holding her steady as his lips smoothed over hers.

"Feel that?" he whispered. "Your lips beneath mine, the heat growing between us? Dev knows that now. He can feel your lips as well as I do, feel the fullness of them, taste the sweetness of them. Just as I tasted you last week. Just as he knew your touch, you knew I would feel it as well. Open your mouth, Tally, let me truly taste paradise now."

She stared into his eyes, helpless now, trapped by the hunger and heat of his gaze.

"This is a mistake." Tally fought to keep her voice strong, to remember how fragile emotion could be and how often absent it was in the cold light of day.

"A mistake?" he asked her gently, catching one hand and pulling it down his chest, over his hard abdomen until her fingers were cupping the rigid flesh contained beneath his silk slacks. "Feel that, Tally. Is it really a mistake?"

Tally shuddered, not because she ached so desperately for what she cupped in her hand, but because of the second pair of hands and the hard warm body suddenly behind her.

It was her personal fantasy. How did a woman fight her own fantasy? Especially one that had tormented her for nearly a decade. Two men, tall and strong, dominant, determined. Both men hungry for her.

Her head fell back against Dev's shoulder as he bent to her neck. At the same time, Lucian's head bent as well, his lips covering hers, his tongue pressing fiercely between her lips to tangle with hers. It was blistering, intense. Sensation exploded beneath her skin as four male hands roamed her body, easing her, sending arcs of white-hot heat sizzling into the depths of her cunt.

She swore she would die from the pleasure. It wasn't possible that one woman could endure such a high degree of carnal excitement. It surged through her bloodstream, whipped through her womb, spasmed into the depths of her pussy.

"Soft," Dev whispered as Lucian's kiss destroyed her sensibilities. "Such heat. You're so hot, Tally, I wonder if we'll survive it."

His hands smoothed down the silk of her dress as Lucian moved one hand just below her breast. She cried out into his kiss, rising to her tiptoes, her hand gripping his neck as he held her close against him.

"I could eat you alive," Dev growled as he pushed her hair aside, his lips moving to the sensitive nape of her neck as his hands roamed over the clenching cheeks of her ass.

Tally shuddered at the touch. She could feel her juices spilling from her pussy, dampening her thong as his hands gripped the material of her dress and began to ease it upward.

She couldn't breathe and she didn't care. Lucian's tongue was an invader, conquering her mouth, swallowing her muffled screams of pleasure as Dev eased the silk over her rear and ran his fingers along bare flesh.

Her hands clenched in Lucian's hair. Pleasure tore through her body, anticipation setting fire to every nerve ending she possessed.

"Damn, you have the most beautiful ass in the world, Tally."

Lucian's lips were frantic on hers now, his tongue plunging into her mouth as she writhed in his arms. Hot male hands parted her legs as Dev knelt behind her. Tally wondered if she could possibly survive so much as another second of their touch.

As Dev's hand played with the curves of her ass, Lucian tore his mouth from hers, burying his lips in her neck as his hands pushed at the slender straps of her dress and eased them down her shoulders until the tops of her breasts were bared. She would have protested, would have worried that someone could come upon them if they hadn't struck simultaneously.

Lucian nudged the silk over one hard nipple and enclosed it in his mouth as Dev nipped at a buttock, his hard hands parting the cheeks as his tongue began to paint hot, rapid designs much too close to the puckered entrance to her ass.

"Oh God! No more." She arched in Lucian's arms and, despite her words, held him close to her breast as she felt Dev moving the narrow band of her thong from between her buttocks.

The suction of his mouth on her flesh, his tongue whipping over her pierced nipple, his teeth alternately tugging at the small gold loop, had her pussy pulsing in frantic need. She was burning, melting, and Dev was suddenly there spreading her thighs wide as his head tilted between them, his tongue a lash of excruciating ecstasy as he lapped at the juices spilling from her cunt while one diabolical finger began to breech the entrance to her ass.

Lucian gripped her leg, just behind her knee, lifting it, bracing it against his hip as Dev's lips and tongue began to torture the bare flesh of her cunt. His tongue slid inside her vagina, pumping in hard, tight strokes as she shuddered in Lucian's arms.

It was unbearable. If they stopped she would die.

Dev's finger screwed slowly, deep inside her anus, using the juices that slid from her cunt to ease his way. As her muscles adjusted to that small penetration, he added another, keeping the fiery tension alive, that small spark of pleasure/pain nearly sufficient to throw her over the edge.

"You're so hot, you'll burn us both alive," Lucian groaned at her breast as he held her still for Dev's explorations. "Does it feel good, baby? Do you like his tongue fucking you, his fingers preparing you?"

Tally shuddered, dazed with pleasure. This was too good. It was more than she had ever dreamed it would be.

"I could lift you now, Tally, push my cock up your tight pussy while Dev takes your hot little ass. All you have to do is ask me for it. Tell me you want it, Tally." His voice was strained, hoarse from arousal as he raised his head to stare down at her in the dim light. "Now, Tally."

She opened her mouth, the words trembling on her lips.

"Tally, are you out here?" They froze as Terrie's voice called out imperatively. "I have an emergency in the house. I need your help."

Like a splash of cold water her friend's voice filled her senses. Dev cursed as he quickly moved back, smoothing the material of her dress over her buttocks as Lucian raised his head and stared down at her with a hunger that speared straight to her soul.

"Tally. I need you now." Terrie's voice brooked no refusal. "I know you're out here."

"Go home with us, Tally," Lucian whispered, his fingers straightening her dress as she fought for her sanity. "I promise, you won't regret it."

"Tally," Terrie called again, closer now.

"Tally?" Lucian's voice was soft yet filled with demand. A demand that shook her to her core.

As much as she needed, as much as she knew she would regret it a second later, she also knew the price would be much too high.

"I can't." She stepped back from him quickly, watching his eyes narrow as determination stamped his features.

"Just a minute, Terrie." She knew her voice was husky, not quite even, but couldn't help it. "I'll be right there."

Silence filled the area for long seconds. "I'll wait here," Terrie called back, her voice determined now. Tally stared back at Lucian, furious with herself and with him.

"This can't happen," she told them both desperately, but knowing it was too late to ever go back. "It will not happen again. Fantasy time is over, boys. This has to stop."

"You know it will happen again," he warned her, his voice pulsing with arousal as Dev cursed again, his voice irate, husky with his own lust. "The next time there won't be any interruptions, though. Think about that one, Ms. Jaded Tally."

Her eyes widened as his words sank in, knowledge exploding through her head as she stared up at him. There were few people who knew her online persona as Jaded. So few that she could count them on one hand. Lucian should not have been one of them.

"Didn't I tell you once that your little side life would rear up and bite you in the ass one day? Consider yourself bitten, baby."

Wicked. Fury rushed through her bloodstream, white-hot and intense. He was Wicked, the online womanizing bastard! The cyber man of her dreams with a fetish for every fantasy that had ever entered her depraved imagination.

"You bastard," she hissed. "You lied to me. All that time."

"Like hell." He was in her face, nearly nose to nose as he snarled back at her. "You gave yourself away, darlin', when you started talking about Lucifer and his microchip for a brain. You should keep your online and offline insults separate if you want to hide."

She was trembling from fury. She couldn't remember ever being so angry. She had shared things with Wicked. He had been her comfort, someone to be at ease with, someone she had thought understood. Pain seared her chest even as she acknowledged the fact that she should have expected it. Had even once suspected it.

"I'll resign," she snapped. "I'll be damned if I'll continue to work for you any longer."

Lucian shrugged mockingly. "You'll be too tired to work anyway, once we're finished with you, so do what you please."

Her teeth snapped together as she fought to hold back her screams of outrage.

"I will not be your toy," she informed him coldly. "Yours or Devril's."

His eyes narrowed. "You'll be much more that that, Tally," he told her darkly. "Like it or not, the countdown starts now. Enjoy your freedom while you can. I told you, baby, you made a mistake in the office that last day. You gave no quarter, damn you, I better not hear you asking for it."

"That sounds like a threat." She fought for imperious calm but was afraid she came across as viperously snide.

"I prefer to see it as a promise," he told her enigmatically. "But you can take it however you like. We will have you, Tally, eventually."

"In your dreams." She was shaking in fury now. Fury and lust. She didn't know if she wanted to kill him or fuck him.

"Tally?" Terrie called out firmly. "Now."

Tally's lip curled insultingly as she stared at Lucian a second longer before she turned and hurried toward Terrie's voice. She was flushed, furious and just plain tired. Dealing with Terrie now wasn't something she was looking forward to.

Chapter Seven

Terrie had no emergency. Tally was almost amused when she realized her friend had followed Lucian and Dev, determined to protect her from whatever plans they had. The emergency had been no more than a ruse to get her out of their arms and back into the house so Terrie could assure herself that Tally knew what she was getting into.

She was furious, but a tiny part of her was amazed and in awe that they had managed to fool her so effectively. It had never been done before. This was a first for her. It would be funny if she weren't so damned mad.

"You can sleep here." Terrie led her into the guest bedroom nearly an hour later after a less than polite argument on the merits of Tally spending the night.

Tally would have preferred the drive home to staying in a strange bed, but when Terrie got that wounded, hurt look on her face, it was damned near impossible to say no. They had been friends for too long, had been through too much together to let a man destroy that friendship.

"I'll get you one of my gowns," Terrie said softly as Tally sat wearily on the bed. "You know where everything else is."

"Terrie, this really isn't necessary." Tally sighed. "I would truly prefer to just drive home."

"And I would prefer that you stopped hiding from me," Terrie said in that wounded voice Tally hated so much. "You've barely spoken to me in the last few months, Tally."

"Jesse keeps you pretty busy." Tally shrugged. "And we've done things. We've gone out to dinner and drinks."

Tally stared around the bedroom, avoiding Terrie's gaze. She didn't want her friend to know exactly how much she missed the late night chats and periodic sprees to the tattoo artist or piercing salon. Terrie was one of the few friends she had that could appreciate such excursions.

"All very polite and very chilled." Terrie plopped down on the corner of the bed. "Are you upset over that night with Jesse?"

Tally grinned. Now that had been fun. Seeing Jesse Wyman cuffed to the bed, so horny he was about to explode as she and Terrie tormented him, was a pleasant memory. Knowing it only made him more wary of her made it all the more sweeter. Now there was a man who understood that it just wasn't wise to tempt her fury.

"No. I'm not upset over that," she chuckled. "I actually enjoy that deer-in-the-headlights look he gets each time I remind him of it."

Terrie's burst of laughter spurred her own.

"Yeah, he's even more scared of you than he was to start with." Terrie fell back on the bed, giggling at the thought. "He dares me to even mention it."

Tally shook her head as she lay back as well, staring up at the ceiling. "That was fun," she admitted. "It's even more fun knowing he's wary now. Perhaps that's why he refused my request to stop the transfer to Conover's." She sighed, admitting she may have shot herself in the foot now.

Terrie breathed out roughly at that. "That wasn't why."

Turning her head, Tally watched her questioningly. "Then why?"

Terrie glanced at the door. "You can't breathe a word that I told you. I don't think I'm supposed to know."

Tally rolled her eyes. "Yeah, yeah, yeah." She waved her hand expressively. "Pinky promise and all that stuff. Now spill."

"Lucian made it a condition of the merger," she said softly, as though afraid the walls had ears. "I remember hearing them discuss it one evening before the wedding. Jesse was astonished at the request, until Lucian uhh…" She stifled her laughter.

"What?" Tally could feel her nerves increasing now.

"Well, Lucian informed him quite frankly that if he and Devril didn't fuck you soon, their dicks were going to rot off from lack of use." Terrie was fighting to hold back her laughter. "I thought it was hilarious. Then, Jesse made some weird comment about twins and their bonds and they began discussing the merger again. But I sensed an undercurrent there. Lucian isn't playing, Tally. He intends on sharing you with Devril."

"Hell." She stared up at the ceiling again, trying to make sense of why Lucian would go to such lengths to get her in his bed.

"Jesse isn't telling me much about this," Terrie told her worriedly. "But I get the impression, Tally, that whatever happens, it won't be with just one of the brothers. And it won't be just occasionally, as it is with the others. Jesse makes it sound as though Dev and Lucian will share you permanently."

That worried Terrie. Tally could see the concern in her friend's gaze.

"Yes, well, let them plot and plan." She shrugged as she gave her friend a smile filled with false confidence. "I can handle it, Terrie."

The thought of both men sharing her, taking her on a daily basis, wasn't nearly as worrisome as the flare of excitement and mingled possessiveness she was beginning to feel for both of them.

"Tally, can't you tell me why you've been upset with me?" Terrie asked her, suddenly changing the subject, surprising her with the question. "We've been friends for so long. I hate having this between us."

Friendships equaled complications, especially when they were as close as she and Terrie were.

She took a deep breath and turned back to look at her friend. "I'm not upset with you," she said in resignation. "I'm upset with myself."

Rising from the bed, Tally glanced at Terrie's questioning expression before pacing to the high window beside it.

"I came into the office the evening you were there with Jesse and Lucian," Tally finally said, a wry smile tipping her lips. "I was horribly jealous, you know."

"Jealous?" Terrie turned back to her at the incredulous question. "Why?"

"Because you were with Lucian," she said softly, seeing the moment that Terrie realized exactly what she meant.

Terrie blinked in surprise. "You wanted Lucian?"

Tally grimaced lightly at her own admission. "Terribly, I'm afraid," she said. "But the problem is, Terrie, I know that once I've been with him and Devril, I won't want to let either of them go. I'm a greedy person, I've told you this before. They can hurt me," she said simply.

"Oh. Dear." Terrie was staring at her in amazement. "Uhh, Tally, are you in love with Lucian and Devril?"

Tally moved to the chair beside the window and sat down heavily. "Perhaps." She shrugged. "So you see, it's becoming rather complicated."

"Pretty surprising to me," Terrie admitted as she pulled one of the plump pillows from the head of the bed and wrapped her arms around it. "What are you going to do?"

Tally smoothed the skirt of her dress slowly, watching as her fingers adjusted the hemline as though being certain she did it right. When she finally raised her gaze to Terrie she had managed to get a handle on her emotions.

"I have several applications in at a firm in New York," Tally finally admitted. "If things work out, I'll be leaving soon."

"You're running?" Terrie asked incredulously. "Tally, you never run."

Tally leaned back in her chair, assuming a careless pose of negligent indulgence. "Well, it appears I do after all," she finally said with a self-deprecating smile. "A very odd feeling, I must admit. But, I've found no other answer."

Terrie shook her head in protest. "Why fight them? If you want it, why not go for it? Holding back doesn't sound like something you do, Tally."

Normally, it wouldn't be, Tally admitted silently. She had never conceded defeat in her life. It rankled that she would now.

"In this case, holding back is the only answer," Tally said softly. "Trust me, Terrie, it would never work, and I don't want the heartache when it doesn't. It's best that I leave as soon as possible." Better for her heart definitely. As well as Lucian's safety, if he ever decided he was tired of her. She feared she might kill him if he took another woman after her.

Terrie watched her closely for long minutes as the silence deepened around them.

"I love how you lie to yourself, Tally," she finally said gently, rising from the bed as Tally watched her in surprise.

"I never lie to myself," she snapped in defense.

Terrie shook her head slowly. "I love you like I love my own sisters." She sighed. "So I can tell you, you are lying to yourself. It's losing all that hard won control that you're terrified of, not any heartache you might suffer. Lucian threatens that. You can't push him away, you can't intimidate him, so instead you're going to run." She grimaced mockingly. "Lucian won by default because you're not brave enough to see which of you is the strongest. You're afraid you'll lose, so you're giving up."

"I don't think so," Tally snapped, uncomfortably aware of the fact that often her friend saw too much. "Lucian has nothing to do with my control."

"Of course he does." Terrie laughed gaily. "He shakes it every time he looks at you. And don't even try to tell me he didn't almost have you out in the garden. I heard those moans. You're losing your edge, Tally, and you can't handle it."

Tally came to her feet slowly, her eyes narrowing on the other woman. "Not in this lifetime." She managed cool humor but she could feel the anger whipping in her mind.

"Really?" Terrie crossed her arms over her breasts, her expression mocking. "Prove it."

"Prove it?" Tally felt like snarling. "And how do you expect me to do that? There's nothing to prove."

"Isn't there, Tally?" Terrie was serious now. That was always a bad sign. "What about proving to yourself that you're worthy of love? But beyond that, there's proving that you aren't a coward. We both know how much you hate cowards."

Tally snarled. "That's playing dirty, Terrie."

"Yeah." Terrie grinned widely. "I do things like that when I see my friends tucking their tails between their legs and scampering off like puppies. Especially when they refused to let me do the same. Trust me, you'll thank me."

"I'll kill you," Tally snapped. "Right after I kill Lucian and Devril."

Terrie shrugged. "Whatever works for you, darlin'. Now I'll say good night so you can plot and plan. You're so good at managing the rest of us, Tally, let's see if you can manage Lucian as easily."

Chapter Eight

Terrie had outmaneuvered her. Somehow, somewhere, she had managed to blindside her and at the same time, ensure her downfall. It wasn't so much the challenge, though Tally thrived on a good, honest challenge; it was more the object of the challenge. Could she bring Lucian and Devril to their knees?

She had been so concerned with protecting her heart, her emotions, that she hadn't truly considered attempting to win theirs. Could it be done? They were strong, dominating men, alphas in the truest sense of the word, so it wouldn't be easy. But, perhaps it could be done. The very thought of success was enough to get her blood pumping, her excitement level rising.

They were men, she told herself as she entered her office two days later. How hard could it be?

"Tally, it's about time you showed up." Lucian slammed the upper file cabinet drawer closed, frowning as she strode calmly to her desk and stored her purse. "You're late."

"Not hardly," she informed him with cool disdain as she checked the clock above the file cabinet. "I'm a minute early, actually. Why are you in my file cabinet?"

It was one of the reasons she hated dealing with files. She could keep them in perfect order, then Lucian, just as Jesse did, could mess them up with seemingly no effort at all.

"Looking for a file, obviously," he grunted. "Where were you all weekend? I called."

And he had, several times a day.

"It's none of your business where I was this weekend. Which file were you looking for?" She arched her brows in inquiry.

"Anderhaul's." He was watching her intently now. "And I'm making it my business. You weren't at home or online. I checked."

"You wouldn't know if I was online, Lucian," she told him calmly as she opened the drawer and attempted to hide the struggle to peer into the top file as she began to search through the files. It took her only seconds to locate it. "Here you go." She handed him the file efficiently before closing the drawer and going back to her desk.

"Why wouldn't I know if you were online?" He was definitely irate.

"Because I now have you blocked." She shrugged. "I don't like liars and I refuse to talk to them." She kept her voice even, carefully modulated; she knew it was guaranteed to set his nerves on edge.

"I did not lie to you, Tally," he practically snarled. "I could have continued the charade but I didn't want that between us."

"How very decent of you." She bared her teeth when she smiled. The very thought of the things she had shared with him made her furious.

"I could give you the things you need, Tally," he told her softly. "All those dark little fantasies you try so hard to keep locked away; they could be yours."

Tally took her seat at her desk, smoothed her skirt over her legs and adjusted the cuffs of her royal blue silk blouse before raising her gaze to meet his coolly.

"You have a nine-thirty appointment with the head of security to discuss the security measures being installed in the new labs, and right after that a meeting with Jesse to discuss the homing software the design engineers are developing. I laid the files out Friday before I left." She ignored his offer, though she couldn't deny the thrill of danger that exploded through her system.

Lucian's eyes narrowed on her. "Make certain coffee and danish are available. I'll need you at the meeting with Jesse since you were aware of the early stages of the contract to design the software. We'll be working through lunch, so you might want to order in."

Great. Working through lunch. She had hoped to escape him for at least a little while.

"I'll contact Breilla's." She made a note to call one of the better establishments in the city. "Anything else, Master?" she asked sarcastically.

"Let me see those nipple rings." The request was made as easily as one for a file would be.

Tally leaned back in her chair and regarded him curiously. She didn't dare, not with the door unlocked, but how she would love to bring him down a notch or two. She lifted one hand teasingly, her fingers running over the small pearl buttons as she smiled back at him tauntingly.

It was just too much fun, teasing him and Dev in this manner. It was almost addictive.

"What will you give me?" she asked flirtatiously, her gaze dipping down to the bulge straining against his pants as she lifted her eyebrow suggestively.

Amusement flared in his brilliant green eyes and quirked the edges of his lips.

"I'll keep your teasing in mind until the minute I have you stretched across my lap, ready for the spanking I'm certain you'll deserve, and oh so enjoy," he murmured as he moved closer to her desk, staring down at her with a sudden dark hunger that had her pulse leaping in response.

She sighed expressively, lowering her eyes demurely before peeking back up at him through her eyelashes. "Promise? Until then, be a good little boss and go make yourself useful so I can finish my own chores. I'll let you know when your first meeting arrives." She dismissed him coolly, turning to power the computer up and begin the day.

Tally gave the appearance of restraining a mocking smile, though her pussy was weeping, clenching in arousal.

She was aware of him watching her for long moments and the reflective expression that came over his face as she continued to ignore him. She had no doubt that he was planning her punishment with great relish. But he had been doing that for months now.

"There are days, Tally," he finally sighed, "that it's a damned good thing I've become so fond of you. Otherwise, I think I'd find a deep, deep hole to bury you in."

From the corner of her eye she watched as he turned and walked to the open doorway of his own office. When the door closed behind him, she stared down at the slight tremble in her fingers. Fond of her? It was little enough, but it struck a chord deep inside her. It wasn't the words, but his tone. Deep, intense, making her want to believe it was conveying so much more than words spoken.

Wishful thinking. She drew in a deep breath, fought to regain her composure and turned back to the computer. She didn't have time for wishful thinking.

*****

Lucian managed, just barely, to put aside the hunger building in his cock and attend to business that morning as needed. It was the afternoon he was awaiting. His calendar was clear for the rest of the day and he intended to begin the seduction of Tally then. He knew he was courting a sexual harassment suit; hell, if he were Tally he would have likely already slapped one in his face. The only thing saving him, he knew, was that she wanted him just as badly as he wanted her.

He knew she did. He could see it in her eyes, the knowledge that he held the key to her darkest desires. He knew her as very few people did. She had given him the key to her downfall and it made her madder than hell to know it.

The meetings progressed quickly. Thankfully, there seemed to be no glitches in the present projects and everything was running smoothly. Lunch was eaten during the final meeting with Anderhaul amid discussion of the finalized contract. The meeting moved quickly and just before two, the office had cleared out of everyone except Lucian, Devril and Tally.

Not that Tally hadn't tried to escape, more than once. Thankfully, the work involved in keeping notes on the meeting as well as helping to clear the office later had kept her there.

"Tally, make a note to contact Jesse regarding the new chips we'll need for the Anderhaul project. That one should go quickly and make us a tidy little profit to boot."

"Noted." She made the addition to her notebook, tucking back a stray strand of long black silk that had fallen over her shoulder.

Lucian paused, watching her. She was small, small enough that he wondered if she could possibly handle both he and Devril taking her at once. They were both tall, broad men. Tally was delicate, exquisitely curved with full breasts and luscious hips, but tiny all the same. It never ceased to amaze him the hunger he felt for her. She wasn't the type of woman he had thought his heart would eventually settle on. She was smart-mouthed, coolly mocking, and possessed a razor-edged wit that had often left him gritting his teeth and fuming in anger. On the other hand, she made him so damned horny he could barely breathe comfortably, and he knew she did the same to Devril.

There was the crux of the matter. Unlike the other members of The Club, sharing his woman wouldn't be an occasional thing. He had learned early in life that the bond he shared with his twin would never allow for anything so conventional. The moment they set eyes on Tally, both men had known instantly what they wanted from her. She wouldn't have one lover, but two, nightly, daily, because she owned both their hearts.

Lucian glanced at his brother, sensing his building arousal, just as he knew Devril would sense his own. It was a connection they had grown used to over the years and Lucian knew he wouldn't wish it any other way. Just as he knew that eventually it might cost them the woman they loved.

His gaze returned to her, watching as she began to straighten the files scattered across the low coffee table of the meeting area. Her skirt was conservative, the black silk ending an inch below her knees. Black pumps fit over her small feet, low heeled, sedate. She exuded class and breeding, old money and genteel sensibilities. Unless you glimpsed the parts she kept carefully hidden.

Jaded. It was her Internet identity, but there were times Lucian suspected it also described her outlook on relationships and men. She was, at heart, a sexual little wildcat who had given up on the fulfillment of her own fantasies. Fantasies Lucian and Devril were determined to bring to life.

Lucian turned the lock on the office door decisively. The snick of the small mechanism had Tally tensing, her head rising slowly as she gazed back at him. Her nipples hardened instantly. He was watching for that, needed to see it.

Devril lounged back on the wide couch watching her as well, though leaving the first move up to Lucian.

"Unbutton your blouse," Lucian ordered softly as he began to advance on her. "Slowly."

"Do I look like your personal stripper?" she asked archly, amusement glittering in her gaze.

She had been expecting this. He could see it in her eyes, in the excitement that pulsed at the vein in her neck.

"If that's what I want," he said carefully. "We're about to lay some ground rules here, Tally." He watched the heat ignite in her eyes, the way her breasts seemed to swell beneath the silk of her shirt.

"Oh, we are?" she questioned him softly. "Your rules, I'll presume?"

He shook his head slowly. "Our rules, Tally. Never just mine or Dev's. All of us. We're alone now. No business, no witnesses. No more games. Come on, baby, don't you at least want to see how good it could be?" He kept his voice soft, gentle.

Tally was an expert with the comebacks. She could hold her own in any confrontation. He didn't want their relationship to be a confrontation. He wanted her sweet and wild in his arms, his name a cry on her lips.

She blinked before licking her lips in the first sign of nervousness he believed he had ever seen out of her as she considered his words.

"We can't go on like this, baby," he told her gently, watching her, letting her see the need now. "It's your choice. If you walk out of here now, then that's it. No more. We've never forced ourselves on a woman in our lives. We won't start now."

She drew in a deep, hard breath.

"And if I choose to stay?" she asked him.

"Then you get both of us. Separately, together, however we wish it, any given time when work doesn't interfere. This won't work like Jesse and Terrie's relationship, or James and Ella's. Devril and I share, Tally, consistently, regularly."

She looked around the office then. "Do you guys ever do anything sexual outside the office?" she asked.

"If the opportunity presented itself," Devril said. "Unfortunately, you were hiding this past weekend. It limited the choices."

Her gaze flickered to Devril a bit nervously.

"Come on, baby, unbutton the blouse," Dev asked her then, rather than ordering her. "We'll begin here."

Chapter Nine

Tally barely controlled the trembling of her fingers as she pulled her blouse free of her skirt. She kept each movement seductive, sedate. Excitement raced through her body, but that was no reason not to enjoy the experience. She had no idea what they intended and the jittery excitement that caused was making her uncomfortably aware of her entire body. Especially the area between her thighs. She was wetter than she could ever remember being during a sexual situation and it was close to frightening.

As the hem of her blouse cleared her skirt, she cast them a teasing look from beneath her lowered lashes. They were hot, horny. Their faces were flushed with arousal, their eyes brimming with it. She loved it. It was her greatest challenge, controlling these two men.

She began loosening the buttons slowly, watching as their eyes followed each movement, their hands clenching into fists as they fought for control of their own desires. Electrified excitement raced through her veins. Anticipation built in waves of sensual awareness as she performed the daring, taunting little striptease.

She had worn only a demi-bra beneath her blouse; the sheer navy lace did little to hide the gold hoops that pierced her distended nipples. With her shirt unbuttoned, very little would be hidden from their gazes.

They stood side-by-side now, only a few feet between them and her as the last button slid free and the edges of her shirt parted. She watched them closely, aware of the sexual tension, the blistering aura of energy that seemed to leap from them and surround her.

She had been with two brothers before, she had no fear of the experience to come, but there was something different about Lucian and Devril. Some intangible something that caressed her flesh with ghostly fingers and denied her the ability to refuse them.

She was experienced but she wasn't promiscuous. She was nearly thirty years old and well aware of her power as a woman, until it came to these two men. With them, she felt as nervous, as shaky, as a virgin facing her first lover.

"You are incredibly beautiful," Devril said as they approached her.

Tally held herself carefully still as the two men came along each side of her. They towered over her, her head barely clearing their chests, making her vulnerable, making her aware of her femininity, the weaknesses of her smaller body. It was a feeling she wasn't accustomed to.

"Come here, baby." Lucian pressed her head against his chest, holding her there as his other hand followed Devril's and pulled the side of her blouse from the swollen flesh of her breast.

Both men groaned heavily as they revealed the prize they had sought.

"How beautiful." Lucian sighed as the backs of his fingers smoothed over the curve of her breast while Devril cupped the other in his worker's hands.

The heat of Devril's palm seared through the lace of her navy demi-bra while Lucian's calloused fingers caressed the engorged nipple of the other. As the hardened little nub became more sensitive, the weight of the gold ring became more pronounced, tormenting her with the light weight of it.

She fought to keep from panting but she could feel the light film of perspiration gathering on her forehead. The tremors of arousal were becoming harder to still with each passing minute. She could feel her control threatening to crumble and fought it with every breath she took.

"So cool and controlled," Devril murmured, a shade of amusement coloring his voice as his lips lowered to her shoulder. "How long can you keep that control, Tally?"

She closed her eyes, awash in sensation, in pleasure, as Lucian adjusted his stance, his hand still cupping the back of her head, his own head lowering.

She whimpered when his mouth covered her nipple. She couldn't hold back the sound, or her own pleasure. His tongue played mercilessly with the weight of gold, his mouth drawing on her flesh deeply as Devril followed suit with the other mound. She was caught between them, a feast of sensuality to their lustful appetites.

Tally clenched her thighs tightly together as the twin mouths worked at her flesh, consuming her, feeding from hard, erect nipples, licking and sucking as she arched into their touch, her body flaming with arousal. Intense pleasure bombarded her senses with the need to be taken. Her pussy was flaming, burning with hunger, demanding fulfillment.

She shifted between the two men, searching for relief as she fought back the pleas, the deep moans of surrender. She needed to be touched, taken.

"Damn, Tally, you're killing me," Lucian groaned at her breast as Devril suddenly took the responsibility of holding her upright.

Lucian's mouth left her breast, his tongue giving it a final lick before Dev pulled her against his chest and lowered them both to the chair behind him. His hands covered her breasts, his fingers rasping her nipples, pulling on the gold rings as Lucian knelt before them.

Tally watched him through dazed eyes. Behind her, Devril was breathing harshly; his head lowered to her neck, his lips and tongue caressing her flesh with devastating results.

She fought to breathe as Lucian began to push her skirt over her thighs. Devril aided him by lifting her, adjusting her on his knees until she was spread out before Lucian like some sensual offering to his lust. His hands caressed her legs, her thighs, as he pushed the skirt to her hips, revealing the navy lace thong that covered the bare, plump lips of her pussy.

She drew in a hard breath as Devril spread her thighs with his knees, opening her for Lucian's pleasure as she stared back at him in dazed fascination. She fought to steel herself, to prepare herself for his touch, but when it came it was like a blow of hard pleasure straight to her womb.

His fingers did no more than smooth over the damp triangle of fabric as his lips parted, his tongue licking over them slowly.

"You're wet, Tally," Lucian whispered roughly.

"It would seem so," she quipped, fighting back the guttural moan rising in her chest.

He grinned, his eyes flaring with amusement at her catty tone.

"You are such a bad girl," he whispered as his thumb located the small ring that pierced the hood of her clit.

"Really?" Her breathing was jerky, her voice hoarse. "So what are you going to do about it?"

Lucian chuckled, his hot breath caressing her moist flesh with the sound.

Tally jerked in response, her eyelids fluttering closed as pleasure overwhelmed her.

"Are you going to tease me all day or do something?" She was not panting, she assured herself. Controlling her breathing was becoming more difficult by the second, though. She was growing weak, dazed. The sensual teasing of Devril's hands on her breasts, his fingers tugging at the rings as his lips caressed her neck, was bad enough. But Lucian, kneeling between her thighs, his fingers slowly removing the damp thong, was almost enough to send her over the edge.

"I'm going to do something," Lucian whispered. "I'm going to make you scream, Tally."

If anyone could, it would be Lucian, but Tally was just as determined that she would hold on to that last bit of her defenses. She had never screamed. She wasn't about to start now.

Helplessly trapped against Devril's hard body, she watched as Lucian's head lowered. His thumbs spread the plump lips of her cunt apart, revealing her swollen clit and the ring of gold that graced it.

He seemed fascinated with the piercing. His tongue played over the ring, tugging at it sensually, moving it around, up and down, until Tally was lifting to his mouth, flames leaping from her pussy to sear the rest of her body with the driving need for orgasm.

It was intense. Too intense. She could feel her mind dissolving beneath the sensual rush of pleasure, her nerve endings catching fire as the knot of sensation began to tighten in her womb.

She needed to be fucked. She needed it now. Enough of the torture, of the slow games… Her moan echoed around her as Lucian eased his finger inside the burning depths of her pussy. His tongue played sadistic games of lust against her clit as his finger fucked her with short, shallow strokes.

"Lucian, fuck me." She was panting now. Panting was okay. Damn, it felt so good, so blistering hot and exciting she could barely stand it.

"Not yet," he whispered against her soaked flesh. "Soon, baby, but not yet."

"No." She shook her head against Devril's chest as his teeth nipped at her neck. "Now. Fuck me now." She arched into his thrusting finger, gritting her teeth in an agony of need as her hands tangled in his hair, struggling to attain her release.

Devril's fingers tightened on her straining nipples, sending a hard burst of pleasure/pain streaking through her breasts at the same time Lucian added another finger to the first and thrust them hard inside her straining pussy.

So close. She whimpered, her breath catching at the intensity of the pleasure as she fought to reach that final threshold. Why were they tormenting her? She could feel Devril's cock like a wedge of steel beneath his jeans at her back, and she knew Lucian's was like a length of iron beneath his slacks. Why weren't they fucking her? Especially when she needed it so damned bad.

"Come for me, Tally," Lucian whispered against her clit, his fingers fucking her with exciting roughness as the muscles of her vagina clenched around them.

She needed more. She was reaching desperately for the pinnacle but it wasn't there.

"Fuck me." She gripped his hair tighter, trying to pull him closer, desperate now to find the release tormenting her body.

"No yet." He was breathing hard, rough. "Come for me, Tally. Now."

His lips clamped over her clit, suckling it into his mouth as his tongue flickered over it with velvet roughness. Tally couldn't halt the sob that escaped her chest. It wasn't enough. She knew it wouldn't be enough. She bit her lip, holding back the fury and the screams of disappointment as she strained against him, fighting to climax, to escape the searing knowledge that her body needed more.

It was like a splash of icy water, that knowledge that she wouldn't find her release, that Lucian and Devril would suspect the secret she fought to keep so carefully hidden. Agonized, her chest exploding with fear, she took the only option left to her. She faked it. She tightened in Devril's arms, feigning her release, working the muscles of her pussy in a spasmodic clench as she released a muttered moan of satisfaction. In this, her secret would be safe.

Chapter Ten

Lucian hid his surprise, his shock. It wasn't easy and he was well aware that Devril was doing the same. She had actually attempted to fake her orgasm. He couldn't believe it. He slid his fingers slowly from the fisted grip of her pussy, feeling the ripples of regret in the soft tissue as he retreated and fought to tamp down his anger.

He couldn't believe she had dared anything so reckless, so completely unneeded, as what she had just done. Rather than giving in to her own desires, her body's demand that she release the control she prized so highly, she had instead staged an orgasm so blatantly false that he wanted to paddle her ass for even attempting it.

Lucian raised his eyes, keeping his gaze hooded as he looked up at her. She was staring at the ceiling, her expression tense, her body taut with both unfulfilled desire and nerves.

She had a right to be nervous. His eyes met Devril's; in them he saw the same anger he could feel growing inside himself.

"Let me go now." Cool, calm, as though she hadn't just begged them to fuck her, hadn't been trembling in their arms as she fought for her release.

He nodded slowly to his brother, watching as the large hands slid away from the dusky, passion-flushed breasts they had covered. Her nipples were hard, reddened, her arousal in no way abated. She had cheated not just him and Devril, but herself as well, in such a manner that he wondered how often she had done it before. It was a practiced, well-versed move. One that a man of lesser experience might not have caught. But Lucian had caught it, and though now wasn't the time to force her past the control she was fighting so hard to maintain, he vowed that soon he would push her past that and more.

Lucian moved back from her slowly, coming to his feet as she stumbled away from Devril. Jerking her blouse from the back of the chair, she quickly pulled it over her arms. Her hands were trembling; her long hair was tangled and mussed, her cheeks flushed with both anger and need. She kept her head lowered, but from her profile he could see the emotions chasing across her face, the fear and vulnerability, the fight for control. Her and her fucking control. He'd had enough of it.

"Do you think I'm that big of a fool, Tally?" he asked her softly.

She paused in her attempts to button her shirt, freezing before him, searching desperately for explanations, he could tell.

"Don't bother lying to me, Tally." He lifted her chin with his hand, staring into those incredible brown eyes and for the first time, seeing a vulnerability he hadn't suspected her of. "Tell me why."

She swallowed tightly before jerking away from him and quickly securing the remaining buttons of her shirt as she pushed her feet into her shoes.

"I'm leaving." Her voice was husky, remnants of desire and shades of fear shadowing it. "I won't be back."

He crossed his arms over his chest as Devril moved to her.

"Do you really think running is going to help, Tally?" Dev asked her gently. Lucian could sense his brother's need for action, to ease her, to take away the pain and fear they could both see in her face.

Her head rose, fury engulfing her expression for one shattering moment before cool mockery overcame it.

"Such arrogance," she said imperiously. "I'm not running, I'm merely disinterested now. You tried, you failed. Too bad, so sad." She shrugged negligently. "No harm done."

Then she raised her head proudly and though Lucian could sense her need to make a graceful exit, she was practically running for the door.

"Tally, do you really think this is over?" He followed her, pausing in the doorway and watching as she jerked her purse from the desk.

As she turned back to speak to him the outer door opened and Jesse and Terrie walked in before stopping and staring at Tally in amazement. Dev watched fleeting horror cross her face before she rushed past them and out of the office.

"Dammit." Devril cursed furiously as he started through the door.

"Wait," Lucian cautioned him. "Let her go for now."

"What the hell has happened here?" Terrie turned from the door, anger filling her face. "What did you do to her?"

"Not nearly enough, I would suspect." Lucian pushed his fingers wearily through his hair as he turned back to Devril. "Make sure she gets home okay. I'll be there later."

"You shouldn't have let her leave," Devril snapped, his green eyes coldly furious. "Dammit, Lucian, she was in no shape to be walking out of here."

"She was in no condition to fight." Lucian sighed. "Follow her home. We'll decide what to do later."

Devril stalked from the offices and Lucian turned back to face Jesse and Terrie's concern.

"You and I need to talk," he told Terrie. "There are obviously a few details about your friend Tally that you neglected to mention in the past few months. I think it would be a good idea if you mentioned them now."

* * * * *

She had made such a fool of herself. Tally accelerated out of the company parking lot, barely missing an incoming employee as she rounded the curve and headed for the freeway.

She breathed in deeply, fighting the excess emotion straining to be free. She needed to scream or rage or something. It had never been like that. Never before had an orgasm completely eluded her in such a way. They were often not satisfying, barely taking the edge off the hunger that strained inside her, but rarely had she failed to achieve any relief at all, and with such horrifying results. They had known. Her fingers clenched on the steering wheel as fear and humiliation swept over her. They were aware that she had faked the release; that she had been unable to achieve her orgasm despite the fierce, exacting pleasure sweeping through her body.

God, it had felt so good. Their hands, their mouths, Lucian's lips at her clit, his tongue raking the little gold ring that pierced it. The pleasure had been unlike anything she had known in her life, sweeping through her, sensitizing every nerve and cell in her body until the need for release had consumed her. Yet the harder she had reached for it, the farther away it seemed.

She was burning now. Her skirt was hopelessly stained with her own juices, she knew, and horribly wrinkled. Wrinkles were a sign of sloppiness, both of mind and of appearance; the sisters of the Catholic school she had once attended had lectured that point to her constantly. Her blouse wasn't even buttoned straight. She clenched her teeth against the overwhelming urge to scream out her mortification.

Years—years of careful control, of watching every move she made, controlling every hidden impulse and presenting an appearance of unshakable calm had been destroyed at the hands of the two men who now knew her most shameful secret.

She needed the pain.

A low growl of fury passed her lips before she throttled it back and once again forcibly controlled her inborn fury. They were dominants, for pity's sake. Trojans. Part of the much whispered about Club. They liked their sex wild and rough, their women submissive and screaming, not whimpering from the gentleness of their touch. Of all the men she had thought could bring her to mind-blowing orgasm, she had thought Lucian and Devril surely could.

The drive to the upscale apartment complex where she lived was made in record time. She refused to admit she was speeding. She never broke the law. It was a point of pride for her. Just as an unwrinkled skirt, smooth hair and unblemished skin were points of pride. One's inner person was reflected in the way she carried herself, how she handled hardships. She grimaced at the thought. Why were those old, harshly worded lectures tormenting her now? The good sisters of the St. Augustine's Academy were a part of her past, or so she had tried to convince herself.

Tally, only whores wear skirts above their knees. You must rise above such hedonistic impulses. Your parents deserve so much more than such a disrespectful child…

What shame you bring to your parents, Tally. Such disgrace…

If your mind must become the Devil's playground, the least you could do is give an outward appearance of decency. Even the prostitutes that stroll the streets show more decorum…

She shook her head, parking the car and heading quickly for the cool silence of her apartment. She needed a shower. A cold shower. She needed to forget that she was different, that her needs were so depraved that even a Trojan couldn't fulfill them.

Cool silence greeted her as she entered her apartment. It was dim, perfectly neat and spotless, and so cold. Tally stared at the desert tones of the living room. Despite the warm colors, the room was cold, sterile and unwelcoming, just like her life.

Her fists clenched as she fought back the need to move something, anything. To scatter the potpourri filling the jade vase across the floor. To shatter the crystal against the wall. She wanted to destroy the very essence of what her life had become. Sterile. Unlived and unloved.

"Stop it." She breathed in roughly, pushing herself away from the door and striding quickly through the room. The dining room was no different. The heavy oak table had never known a spot of food spilled on it. She couldn't remember the last time she had used the stove in the kitchen.

The dark hardwood floor didn't have so much as a stain on it and her carpets, even after five years, appeared in flawless condition. Her bedroom… She stepped into the room and stared around it silently. There was no life here. No memories. Not even sullied ones. She had never brought a lover to her home, had never fouled her bedroom with the unnatural desires that twisted through her mind.

She had never realized how perfectly the good sisters had conditioned her. She had never known how empty her life had become until now. Until she had been forced to walk—no she hadn't walked, she had run—from something she hadn't realized she needed. Lucian and Devril.

She walked over to the bed, her hand smoothing stiffly over the white bedspread, fighting to ignore the compulsion to clench her fingers into the fabric and rip it to the floor.

Enough. She straightened her shoulders and turned, forcing herself to walk sedately into the bathroom. She undressed, stuffed the skirt and blouse into the wastebasket before dropping the demi-bra in after it.

She twisted on the cold water to the shower, watching the pounding spray run into the glass cubicle before stepping beneath it. Her breath caught as ice seemed to envelop her skin, pouring through her hair, over her face, stealing her breath. Washing away the proof of the hot tears that finally fell.

Chapter Eleven

Self-control, that much sought after, often sadly lamented virtue, should not have the destructive, unforgiving undertones that Dev had glimpsed in Tally's wounded brown eyes. It shouldn't cause a passionate, vibrant woman to deny the very heart of her sexuality, nor leave her sobbing beneath the force of a shower whose chill could be felt outside the glass cubicle she stood within. But that was exactly what it had done.

Dev and Lucian had known for quite some time that Tally Raines was unique, a challenge unlike any woman they had known in their lives. The fact that they had slowly, over the past year, fallen in love with her, wasn't the point. They had seen in her a strength of will that often mirrored their own, and a loneliness that echoed in their chests.

He and Lucian had, despite all appearances, lived a quiet, often lonely life. The bond they shared was more intense than most other twins, stemming, he thought, from the fact that they were fraternal rather than identical twins. The first years of their lives they had been largely separated by their divorced parents, seeing each other only occasionally and even then the visits had been brief. Only with the death of their mother after their tenth birthday had they finally been given the chance to know one another. From that moment on they had been inseparable.

Dev was the quiet one. The one everyone rarely paid much heed to. He preferred to watch the foibles of men and quietly learn from other's mistakes. Lucian was the more social brother. He thrived amid the high paced, often stressful career he had chosen and gloried in the challenges they presented. Dev was more content to work behind the scenes, to coordinate and see the projects through rather than forging into the fray and doing battle with competitors who would have taken the more lucrative contracts.

It was for this reason that Dev had stood aside and allowed Lucian to begin the first wave of sensual assaults against Tally. She was attracted to both of them, they had both known that from the beginning, though he doubted at that time that she was aware of the carefully plotted seduction and downfall they had arranged for her.

How easily their plans had blown up in their faces. Dev stood outside the shower, leaning against the wall, head lowered, listening to the faint sounds of her sobs. They had made her cry.

He shook his head at that thought. No, they hadn't made her cry; she had allowed her demands for self-control to cheat her out of the orgasm that had been building within her body. Those same demands had sent her running from them, sent her scrambling to pull the tattered shreds of her pride around her and retreat as quickly as possible from the two men who had seen her downfall.

He moved carefully, slowly, from the bathroom. He didn't want to alert her of his presence, that in her turmoil she had forgotten to lock her front door and had given easy access to one of the men, he knew, she considered the enemy.

He paced to the bedroom and began preparing it for her. Lucian would arrive later, but for now, Dev was in control and Tally might have figured out how to handle his brother, but she had no idea how to handle him.

He smiled at the thought as he attached restraints to the four corner posts of her bed. The soft nylon wrist and ankle cables would allow just enough freedom of movement to ensure her pleasure while holding her in place so he could assure her freedom from the strict demands of her self-control.

He put several other articles on the bedside table. A tube of lubrication gel, an inflatable butt plug and a thick vibrating gel dildo were laid to one side. Next came a set of vibrating nipple clamps and a small ball gag.

He glanced toward the door as the sounds of falling water ceased. She would be entering the room within minutes, unaware of his presence, her control shaky at best, off balance. He had a feeling that if he gave her the chance to renew that control then they would all lose. Tally wouldn't allow herself a chance to fail a second time. She would pull that cool mockery and cold demeanor around her like a cloak of protection and forever keep him and Lucian at arm's length. He couldn't allow that. He wouldn't allow that.

Taking his seat in a comfortable chair across the room, he sat back and waited. His cock was throbbing; so damned hard and engorged he was amazed he could walk. If he had ever had an erection so demanding with another woman, he couldn't remember it.

The shower door opened, closed. Minutes later the sound of a hair dryer could be heard and Dev sat back to wait. Tally's hair was long and thick, a sensuous silken skein of midnight-black that fell to her hips and made his hands itch to touch it. It had to be hell to dry, though. He would have loved to stand behind her, wielding the dryer, watching the cool strands slowly dry beneath the heat of the device. Instead, he sat and waited. The fireworks to come would be hot enough; he didn't have to tempt an early explosion.

Long minutes later the hair dryer flipped off. Dev sat up straighter in the chair, his eyes narrowing as he watched the doorway. Tally walked through it slowly, her characteristic, sensual glide a little less relaxed than it usually was. Her long hair fell down her back, caressing her hips, but the rest of her body was bare. Bare and perfect. Gold glittered at her nipples and winked at him between her perfect thighs as she came to an abrupt halt in the middle of the floor.

"What the hell are you doing here?" Her eyes nearly glowed in furious heat, her dusky cheeks flushing with anger.

Dev's brows rose in surprise. Her voice was gritty with emotion, her body fairly trembling with it. This was not the cool, self-possessed siren that had haunted his dreams for so long. This was better. More than he could have expected.

He propped his ankle on his knee, leaning back in the chair as she jerked a long, cream-colored silk robe from the smaller chair by her bed table and pulled it on with quick, angry movements. She still had yet to notice the restraints or the sexual devices on the table.

"Leave," she snapped as she belted the robe around her slender waist. "Now."

Dev sighed heartily. "I'm not Lucian, Tally. Your anger doesn't bother me as it does him."

Lucian, despite his often sarcastic attitude in the face of her normally cold temper, had that basic male trepidation when it came to prodding at an unpredictable female. Unlike his brother, it was an art Dev had perfected in his youth and had steadily applied over the years.

"Does jail bother you?" She crossed her arms under her breasts as she stared back at him heatedly. "Breaking and entering is illegal."

"The door was unlocked," he informed her, watching in satisfaction as her eyes widened in shock.

He could read her emotions as clearly as a book now. The cold mockery had been stripped away, leaving bare the woman beneath as she stared back at him with haunting, shadowed emotion.

"I don't care if it was standing wide open." She showed her teeth in a snarl that made his dick jerk in arousal. "Pick your ass up and get out."

Oh, now there was the Tally he knew existed beneath the carefully polished exterior. Vibrant, explosive, her temper was more than a match for the dominance that pulsed thick and hot through his and Lucian's blood.

He came slowly to his feet, watching her carefully.

"You honestly believe that little performance earlier isn't going to be addressed, Tally?" he asked her, keeping his voice soft, though he did nothing to hide the annoyance that throbbed beneath it. "You should have expected one of us to show up ready to do battle, if not both."

Her gaze flickered. Dev controlled the pleased smile that crossed his lips. She had expected Lucian and had been confident she could turn him away. She had obviously seen his patience as weakness instead, and thought him easier to control than Dev was.

"Poor Tally." He sighed. "You've misjudged Lucian, but you'll learn that soon enough. Even worse, you underestimated me. I won't let you run so easily. The game stops here and now."

"What is with you two?" she snapped, her voice thick with anger, her face flushed, eyes shining with emotion. Damn, he had thought her beautiful before, but now she took his breath away. "Can't you accept defeat? Can't you accept that there's a woman alive that doesn't respond to you? You tried, you failed, now leave it alone."

Her voice broke on the last word, hitching as emotion seemed to crackle like electricity within it.

"I don't think so." He stepped closer. "I was unaware that you had taken Lucian and myself for fools. That we would calmly stand aside and allow you to hide because you're too frightened to reach out for what you want. You can't keep that indomitable self-control and find the satisfaction you need, Tally. It won't work."

He didn't touch her. Not yet. He stalked around her, watching her carefully, seeing the naked nervousness in her gaze as she watched him warily. She knew Lucian much better than she did him. He had deliberately held himself away from her, stayed on the outside of her circle of friends, rarely giving her the chance to dissect him with those perceptive eyes of hers.

She did that. Watched people, waiting on them to reveal to her their every dark secret so she could use it to hold them at bay, to insure she had every weapon available to keep them from getting close to her.

"You don't know what you're talking about." She was breathing roughly, though he could tell she was fighting valiantly to control it. "I hate to prick that ego of yours, Dev, but you and Lucian may not be the walking female orgasms you think you are."

May not be. He noticed she didn't state it as a definite. His lips kicked up in a grin.

He stopped behind her, not touching her, not daring to. Her shoulders stiffened, her breathing becoming rougher still as he towered over her.

"Had you waited, you would have had what you needed, Tally." Her arms uncrossed, her hands falling to her sides and clenching at the material of her robe. He could see the hard rise and fall of her breasts, almost feel her fight for control.

"How like a man," she sneered. "Perhaps I'm frigid. Isn't that the standard male excuse?"

"Or perhaps you're too stubborn, too intent on being in control, on being the Mistress, to ever admit there could be a Master," he suggested softly. "I know what you need, Tally. I know, and I'm going to make certain you have it."

She seemed to freeze, stiffening in response, not just to the words, but also the underlying promise that came with them. When she started to run, he was ready for her. He was determined Tally was not going to run anymore.

Chapter Twelve

Tally was in shock. This was not the gentle giant she had always thought of Dev as being. This was a man in his prime, far stronger than she, and determined to have his way. He caught her as she moved to run from the bedroom, a chuckle sounding in her ear as his arms went around her, holding her close. A second later she felt her robe loosen as she struggled against him, fighting to tear herself from his muscular arms as he stripped the robe from her body.

"You bastard!" she raged as he picked her up and tossed her to the bed.

Her fingers curled into claws as fury overwhelmed her. Hot, blinding rage burned in her stomach like acid as she snarled and flailed out at him.

She gained little more than a dark laugh as he straddled her body and within seconds, to her complete horror, had her arms spread and her wrists shackled with soft, padded nylon restraints.

"Let me go." She jerked at the restraints, staring up at her wrists in disbelief as the slender chains running from the nylon refused to give way.

Instantly his weight was removed, but it wasn't to release her. She shrieked in disbelief, attempting to jerk her foot from his grip as he began to shackle her ankles. She was now spread eagle, held naked to the bed as he watched her in amusement.

"You son of a bitch!" she screamed, outraged, terrified. No matter how desperately she fought she couldn't release herself, nor could she stem the rising anger building inside her. "I'll kill you for this. I'll carve your dick from your body if you don't let me go."

"Such naughty language, Tally," he chided her in amusement as he sat down on the bed and removed his boots. "Just settle down, baby, and save your breath. You'll need the energy to scream from pleasure later."

"Oh, now haven't I just heard that one before," she sneered, jerking at the restraints that held her wrists again. "A little overconfident, aren't you, Dev?"

"Overconfident?" he mused as he stood and unbuttoned the snowy white shirt he wore. "Merely confident, I think."

Snarling, cursing, Tally fought the restraints, desperately trying to ignore the fact that Dev was undressing beside her bed. His muscular chest shouldn't have looked so inviting and when he shed his jeans and the snug boxer briefs, the hard, thick length of his cock shouldn't have caused her to catch her breath in hunger.

"Damn you, Dev, you can't do this," she denied hoarsely, knowing any chance she may have had at rebuilding her defenses was being shot to hell. "Let me go!"

He stood at the side of the bed watching her quietly, his eyes going over her body, pausing at her breasts, taking in the hard, fiery points of her pierced nipples. His gaze went lower and Tally closed her eyes in shame, well aware of the thick, glistening juices that coated the plump lips of her shaved pussy.

"Say 'shoes'," he said, smiling, his eyes coming back to her. "In every dominant/submissive relationship there's a safe word. One word that halts any further action and calls a stop to whatever's taking place. But I'm warning you, Tally, if you say it, then it's over. It doesn't matter how much Lucian and I care for you. It doesn't matter how much we need you, it's over. Say 'shoes' and I release you and walk away now. If you don't say it, then you can fight until hell freezes over and as long as your body responds, as long as you find pleasure, there will be no stopping."

The throttled growl of rage that escaped her throat surprised her, and Dev as well, if the flaring of his eyes was any indication.

"Go to hell," she cursed him furiously. "I'm not begging you for anything, you hulking Neanderthal. Kiss my ass."

"I'll spank it instead." His words had her stiffening in shock a second before she began to fight again.

He released the restraints on her ankles, quickly flipped her over and secured them once again. There was just enough length to the chains at her wrists to allow them to cross and adjust to the new position. She was panting in surprise and fury, not to mention the excitement beginning to snake through her body. But it didn't stop her from fighting as he adjusted the restraints, once again spreading her out.

"Do you have any idea how I've fantasized about spanking that curved little ass?" he whispered at her ear, his hand smoothing down her back, then over her buttock. "Watching it blush and burn, then spreading those soft little cheeks and fucking my cock up that tight little hole it hides."

Her head snapped around, her eyes widening in shock and surprise. It wasn't that she had never had anal sex. Or even a ménage. It was the tone of his voice. Rough, carnal, sinful. His expression matched the tone of his voice. He looked like a fallen angel, his black hair falling over his forehead, his brilliant green eyes glowing with lust.

"It's going to be so good, Tally." He smoothed the hair that had fallen to her cheek back from her face. "I can't wait to get my cock inside you, no holds barred, fucking you with everything I've dreamed of giving you for so damned long."

His hand landed on the curve of her ass as he finished. It wasn't a small blow, it wasn't a timid tap; it stung. It pierced into her womb, flamed through her pussy and had her gasping out in pleasure. And still he watched her, his eyes holding hers, his face close to her as he delivered a similar blow to the other side.

Tally jerked against her bonds again, whimpering as she fought to hold onto the restraint she had always prided herself on. But this was good. Too good. The utter depravity of it was enough to send her spinning into an arousal that defied reason. Lust bloomed like a conflagration, leaving her aching, hurting for release.

"Stop this," she snapped, driven as far as she could stand. Months of titillation, of teasing. She needed relief and waiting for it was not an option. "Dammit, Dev, just fuck me and get it over with."

The size of his cock would burn, it would stretch her, fill her, give enough of the heady painful intensity that she could at least have some measure of release. If he continued this course, there was no way she could bear it.

"All or nothing, Tally," he reminded her. "You'll take it all or I walk away. Lucian walks away. Are you really such a coward that your control means more than reaching out for all the pleasure you've always dreamed could be yours?"

Was she? She was. She buried her face in the comforter, breathing harshly, fighting the overwhelming need to scream out the safe word and gain her release.

"Think about it, Tally," he whispered. "Your ass is going to burn. I'm going to make you pay for even daring to consider faking an orgasm. But first, I'm going to make certain you know what you're passing up if you're thinking of whispering the word that will stop it."

He moved away from her then. Tally raised her head, turning and watching in shock as he picked up a slender butt plug and a tube of lubrication gel.

"This," he turned the device in his hand, "is an inflatable plug, Tally. Have you had one before?"

She hadn't. She could feel her heart racing now as she saw the slender pipe leading to the pressure bulb below. It was slender, but it would become larger.

"That's not necessary," she informed him, trying for haughtiness but knowing she was achieving only desperation. "I'm not a virgin there, Dev. Or anywhere else."

He smiled slowly. "Darlin', its not just for preparing your luscious little ass."

He didn't give her time to respond. Before she could draw in the breath to curse him for his arrogance, he was between her spread thighs, surprising her when he lifted her hips and pressing two of the pillows beneath her.

"Dev, you'll pay for this." She fought his hold, jerking against him as he chuckled with wicked emphasis and adjusted the pillows beneath her raised ass. "Don't do it like this."

"Sorry, baby, you lost the option to choose with that little stunt you pulled back at the office." He smacked her ass again, causing her to jerk with the sting, the pleasure derived by his calloused, broad palm. "Now you can accept what you get. Exactly the way I always wanted to give it to you."

He had exceptional timing. Her mouth opened to scream a string of expletives that would have cut him to the ground. And she would have, if he hadn't chosen that moment to run his fingers slowly through the wet slit of her pussy. Her teeth snapped together to bite off a moan. She couldn't remember a time in her life that those tender folds had been so sensitive.

"You're wet," he murmured, pleased. "Very wet, Tally. I think you like this more than you're letting on."

He swirled his finger around the tightly clenched pucker of her anus as she tried to breathe through the incredible pleasure. She was restrained, she should be screaming, fighting, cursing. She knew exactly what he intended. He wanted to strip her of control, make her beg. How disappointed would he be when it didn't work? She couldn't lose control. She would freeze up. She would lock down inside until no sensation could ignite the spark that would send her careening into orgasm.

Her hands clenched the comforter as her breath hitched in fear. She didn't want this. She didn't want the humiliation as she saw the searing knowledge in Dev or Lucian's eyes.

"Dev..." The safe word was ready on her lips when his finger pressed against the tight pucker of her anus and eased inside.

Her breath caught. How long had it been since she had felt that tiny pinch of fire, the exciting knowledge of the hot, streaking pleasure to come? She bit her lip, her breath hitching as fear and need began to war within her.

"You don't have to control yourself, Tally," he whispered seductively. "You don't have to do anything or pretend to be something or someone you're not. Just be yourself. A creature of pleasure, an exquisite form of energy and sexuality, that's all you have to be. No demands, no expectations. And no reprisals. None, baby."

His finger slid deeper, spreading the cool essence of the lubrication he used while parting the delicate, sensitive muscles of her anus.

"I can't." She kept her face hidden, her shame covered. "You don't understand. I'll freeze up. I can't let it go."

He smacked her ass. A burning slash of pleasure ripped through her body, arching her back as a strangled moan tore from her chest.

"You freeze up and I'll make your ass burn so bright you won't sit for a week," he snapped, his voice determined, firm, as his finger slid quickly up the tight passage.

She writhed against the pillows. The heat of that abrupt thrust struck the depths of her pussy like a well-aimed bolt of lightning. A second later she bit her lip, whimpering in regret when the thick presence eased free of her tiny entrance and the tip of the lubricating applicator slipped inside. The gel eased inside her, filling the passage with cool relief for but a second. When he removed it, she felt the head of the butt plug pressing against the entrance instead.

Okay, she knew how to do this. She'd had anal sex before. It was easy. She relaxed her muscles, biting back a moan as the slender device was worked inside her. It was only five inches long, not really thick but pliable. When it was fully lodged inside her she breathed out slowly. She doubted the inflation would be much; it didn't look large enough to actually inflate to a size that could test her control.

"So calm." Lucian's voice at her side had her gasping in shock.

Her head turned as he sat down beside her, his hand smoothing her hair back from her face as he stared down at her.

"This won't work," she whispered regretfully. "You're only going to hurt all of us by letting him continue."

"You know the safe word?" Lucian asked her gently.

"Yes, but..." She stopped, her eyes widening at the sudden pressure in her anus.

Slow, insidious, the plug began to lengthen, thicken, filling her in ways she had never expected. Her breath caught in her chest as her muscles began to stretch, the nerves protesting, burning, as Dev continued to inflate the device.

"She was a very bad girl today, Dev." Lucian never broke eye contact with her as he spoke. "I think she needs to be spanked while that plug fills her little bottom. What do you think?"

Dev's answer was a light blow to one of the soft curves, then another. And another. Tally trembled as the fire beneath her skin began to build, the pleasure and pain combining in a conflagration that began to spread through the rest of her body. Her clit was swelling, the small ring encircling it barely containing the torturous little nub of flesh as the butt plug continued to swell within her, even as Dev's hand brought a fiery blush to her ass.

"Lucian," she whimpered. She had never known anything so incredibly arousing, so destructive to her senses. "Help me, Lucian. Please. Please don't let me freeze..."

Chapter Thirteen

The plug was fully inflated, filling her ass, creating a pressure that held her on the edge of a sharp, painful pleasure. The cheeks of her ass were so sensitive that the slightest caress had her gasping; laying on them was an exquisite torment when Lucian and Dev adjusted her restraints once again and spread her out on her back.

Her pussy was incredibly wet. She could feel the thick layer of syrupy juices that lay along the swollen lips and coated her tortured clit. The arousal was so incredibly blinding she wondered if she would survive it. But Dev and Lucian gave her no mercy.

Lying on each side of her, the two men slowly began to torment her already over-sensitized body. Lucian's kiss was drugging. His tongue filled her mouth, playing slowly with her own, never giving in to the wild need that had her reaching desperately for a hotter, harder kiss.

His lips sipped at hers, his tongue moving with languid ease along the curves before slipping back into her mouth as she moaned harshly into the kiss. Dev was making up for his gentleness at her breast, though. His teeth were rasping the hard, brutally receptive point with devastating results. His suckling mouth ate at her nipple; his tongue tugged at the little gold ring piercing it.

She writhed beneath them, her hands curled into fists, her feet flat on the bed as her hips plunged upward in fruitless need.

She was sweating. She never sweated, but she was now. Her flesh was soaked with it, her hair damp as she strained between them, agonized mewls of pleasure echoing from her throat as Lucian's lips moved to her ear.

"Are you ready, baby?"

"I'm going to make you pay for this," she snarled. The excess emotion and demanding responses in her body had her senses careening.

"I can't wait," he murmured in satisfaction. "Until you're free and able, though, I have something else for you to enjoy."

Dev's lips began to move down her body, his tongue painting lascivious trails of near ecstasy across her abdomen as he moved between her thighs. Lucian moved from her side, pressed a pillow beneath her head and leaned forward. His cock, engorged and heavily veined, neared her lips. The flared head was nearly purple in color, the size of a plum and throbbing with lust.

"Suck me, Tally. Make it good, baby, and we'll see if Dev can't make that pretty pussy feel just as nice."

She opened her mouth eagerly. She needed relief. She was at the point that she didn't care if it was only minor relief, as long as the excruciating need eased. His cock slipped into her mouth, thick and hot, as her lips closed on it, his groan echoing around her as Dev's tongue began to play demonic games with the ring piercing her clit.

"Yes, sweetheart," Luc hissed hoarsely. "Take me deep, baby, straight to your throat."

Dev's hand held her hips still, refusing to allow her to thrust her tormented flesh firmer against his lips, though Lucian moved closer to her mouth, groaning heavily as her tongue stroked down the shaft, the engorged head sinking deep.

She suckled his flesh like a woman starved and, clearly, she was. Uppermost in her mind was the desperation to achieve the orgasm that lay just out of reach, tempting her, taunting her. Dev's mouth was a sucking, licking demon of pleasure as he lapped at the juices spilling from her vagina, suckled her engorged clit or used his teeth to pull at the little ring and cause desperate mewls of need to echo around Lucian's cock.

"Ah, sweetheart," Lucian groaned, a grimace of sublime pleasure twisting his face. "Perfect. Fucking perfect."

She took the rigid flesh to her throat, swallowing, caressing the throbbing head while her tongue worked against the ridged shaft as she strained closer to him. The plug in her ass was a heavy pressure that only tormented her further, reminding her of the sensations that could arise should one of her lovers thrust the thick length of his cock inside her instead.

The thought of such brilliant arcs of sensation had her working her mouth hungrily over Lucian's erection, moaning at the lash of Dev's mouth on her tormented cunt as she suckled the hard flesh.

She was shaking, her body wracked by shudders of arousal as she strained toward Dev's mouth. She wasn't going to make it. She could feel her body rebelling, her mind rejecting the demands of her flesh.

Tally tried to scream around Lucian's cock, fought the final humiliation as tears filled her eyes and she felt the building pressure in her womb begin to dim.

"Suck it." Lucian's hands gripped her hair as his voice hardened, his cock suddenly fucking rougher between her lips as the sharp tingles of fire raced across her scalp. "I'm going to come, Tally. Right down your sweet throat, baby."

A hard convulsive shudder wracked her abdomen as her womb clenched in a sudden burst of renewed heat. Dev's teeth raked her clit with an exciting roughness a second before they clenched the ring and tugged and two fingers plunged inside the gripping, ultra tight depths of her raging pussy.

A strangled scream echoed around Lucian's cock as her eyes widened, her vision darkened. The inflation of the plug had done more than create a heavy pressure up her anus, it had made the already snug depths of her pussy that much tighter.

"There," Lucian groaned as his hips increased the strokes of his cock between her lips. "Suck it, Tally. Deeper, baby, I'm going to come."

She took his cock to her throat, swallowed, her tongue flexing against the sensitive underside of his erection as it spasmed and exploded. His hands tightened in her hair, holding her still as hard, hot jets of semen shot down her throat. Swallowing convulsively, aware of the caress it would be to the sensitive head of his cock, she accepted each powerful stream of thick fluid.

Seconds later he pulled back from her lips, his cock still hard, heavy with arousal as she felt Dev's fingers pulling free of her as he rose between her thighs. She was sweating, shaking, her pussy pulsing with the frantic rush of blood thundering through her system. Then Dev's hand landed hard and heavy on the pad of her pussy.

Tally screamed, thrashing against the bed as violent sensations of pleasure tore through her body. No one had ever dared to strike her pussy. Another blow landed, directly over her clit and her back arched, her head grinding into the mattress as the breath locked in her throat. Explosive arcs of pleasure/pain tore through her pussy, her womb, spreading along her body as her mind shut down. There was no control.

The next blow destroyed her. Her eyes flew open as an orgasm, her first true, decadent, explosive orgasm, shattered her senses. A thin, high wail escaped her throat as she tried to fight off the nearly violent tremors sweeping through her body, but once he had pushed her over the edge, Dev wasn't content to let her attempt any sort of control again.

His cock, fiery hot, thick and steel-hard, pushed inside the spasming entrance of her pussy. Her muscles gripped him, locking tight as she fought to come down from the shattering release.

"Take me, Tally. Now. All of me." Dev's voice was hard, dangerously male, as he began to work the shaft inside her with strong determined thrusts.

Inch by inch her flesh gave, inch by inch the coil of heat that had exploded through her pussy began to build again. The plug, still inflated in her rear, left little room for the thick width of his erection, and Dev made little concession to the extremely tight grip of her cunt.

"Oh yes, baby…so fucking tight…so fucking good around my dick…" He gasped, his erection pistoning forcefully inside her saturated pussy.

She was going to come again. Oh God, it would kill her. She couldn't bear another explosion so violent, so destructively powerful. But she knew it was going to happen. His cock sent bolts of excessive pleasure/pain slashing through already sensitized nerve endings as he stretched the unbearably snug channel of her cunt to accommodate his strokes.

"No. No more!" she screamed wildly as his cock pistoned hard and deep, shattering her nerve endings. "No more…"

"Come for me, Tally," Dev groaned. "One more time, baby. One more time. Let me feel you come on my cock, baby. Look, Tally, look how sweet and wet you are. Just one more time."

Her eyes flew to the point where their bodies connected. His hands held her hips away from the bed, his erection plunging in and out of her, wet and hard, gleaming with her juices as he pulled back, his flesh slapping wetly against her as he thrust forward.

It was too much. Too much pleasure, too much sensitivity. He fucked her hard and deep, separating the soft tissue, the clenching muscles, as she threw her head back, her neck arching, her body tensing until she felt she would shatter. And then she did. She couldn't scream, she could do nothing but allow a lifetime of recessed needs, lust and emotions to pour from her soul, spilling with the hard wash of climactic juices that rushed from her pussy, mixing with the powerful jets of Dev's semen.

Tally was only distantly aware, long minutes later, of Lucian and Dev releasing the restraints on her wrists and ankles. She floated, languid, relaxed, on a cloud of satisfaction unlike any she had known before.

She moaned in low protest as she felt the deflating of the anal plug from her rear, but as it slid free of her body a shudder of pleasure coursed over her. Exquisite. She wanted more, but she couldn't seem to rouse herself to do more than try to breathe.

"Come here, baby." It was Lucian who pulled her in his arms as he lay down beside her. Behind her, she was aware of Dev as he settled into the bed as well. Warmth surrounded her. Lucian's arms as he held her close, Dev's chest at her back.

"Can I keep you?" She was only barely aware of the thought that drifted through her mind, unaware that she had spoken the words.

"Forever, Tally. Keep us forever," Lucian whispered as he kissed her brow, Dev kissed her shoulder and darkness enclosed her.

Chapter Fourteen

For the first time in more years than she cared to remember, Tally made no effort to make certain she was presentable before she slipped from her apartment. Escape was the only thing on her mind.

Dressed in one of her few pairs of jeans and a bronze silk blouse, she pushed her feet into leather sandals and practically ran out the door to her car. Lucian and Devril were still sleeping when she left them in the bed after awakening. Getting from between them wasn't easy and had only been accomplished with a promise to return within a few minutes.

Thankfully, the spare bedroom held older clothes that she rarely wore and possessed a small bathroom. After a fast shower she had dressed, leaving her hair damp, and ran. Like the coward she was, she all but raced from the apartment.

So where the hell was she going to go now? It was barely daylight on a workday, her hair was wet, she wasn't wearing makeup and she was trembling like a leaf as she headed the car to the outskirts of town.

This was all Terrie's fault, she decided in panicked desperation. If she hadn't let Jesse choose Lucian as the third in their little ménage, and if she hadn't had it right there at the office, then Tally would have never walked in on them. She would have never seen him, or been overcome by lust. She wouldn't have seen his cock, thick and hard, fucking someone other than her. Her possessive instincts would not have been aroused, and therefore, her control wouldn't have been lost. Her calm wouldn't have been shattered. She wouldn't be driving down a nearly deserted country road with wet hair soaking one of her best silk blouses.

She felt lost. In her heart and in her mind, she had lost something that had kept her centered over the years, something that went further than control. If this was what love did to you, then she wasn't certain it was worth it. She was drowning now in her own fears and her own demons.

"Damn you, Terrie." She swiped at the tears that trembled on her lashes as she cursed her friend. Perverted, depraved wench that Terrie was, she had to allow Jesse to share her with one of the men Tally had staked out for herself.

It was Jesse's fault. Every bit of it. She snarled silently at the thought. He knew she didn't want him to invite Lucian into that little threesome. He had at least suspected it, otherwise he would have never asked her that day in the office if there was someone he shouldn't consider. He should have chosen someone else.

Her eyes narrowed as she took the turn to the Wyman property. It was all their fault so they could share in the misery.

She pulled into the curved driveway of the Wyman home and threw the neat little Lexus into park before moving quickly from the car and heading to the front door. She pressed the doorbell hard. Once. Twice. She took her fist and pounded demandingly on the wood panel.

"Dammit, Terrie, I don't care how good a fuck he is. Open the damned door." The longer she thought about it, the longer she stood there, the madder she got.

"Tally?" The door flew open, but it wasn't Terrie greeting her, it was a nearly bare-chested, obviously ill-tempered Jesse Wyman.

"You and your friends are a threat to society." She poked him in that bare chest, between the edges of his unbuttoned shirt, hard, feeling no end to her satisfaction as his eyes widened marginally and he jumped back from the sharp nail of her finger.

"Uhh, any friends in particular?" He gave her clear berth as she stomped into the entryway.

Her eyes narrowed on him. He was staring at her a bit too amazed, a bit too smugly.

"Any friends in particular," she mimicked him. "Try the son of a bitch who helped you screw your wife. Him and his perverted brother, you, James…the whole damned lot of you are a menace. A danger to every sane woman who ever walked this planet. All of you should be locked away."

She was yelling at him. She ignored the slowly dawning knowledge in his eyes, the way his gaze went over her in near shock as well as the compassion that suddenly filled his face.

"Tally, Terrie will be down in a minute." His voice softened as she stood before him, her fists clenched, her breathing rough and heavy. "She was in the shower."

"Don't you dare pity me." Her hands fisted at her sides, fury enveloping her as she faced him, knowing by his expression that she would never regain the respect he had once watched her with.

"Tally?" He was saved from answering by Terrie's incredulous voice as she came down the stairs. "Tally, your hair is still wet and you're wearing jeans?"

Tally turned to her, seeing the concern, the worry in her friend's face and fought back the tears that suddenly clogged her throat. She was shaking. God, she hated the feel of the nervous tremors shuddering through her body.

"Tally." Terrie's eyes were wide as she glanced at her husband, then back at her friend as she stepped to the landing. "Hon, what happened to you?"

Tally swallowed tightly. "I really need a drink. Something strong."

She turned and moved quickly for the bar in the large living room. The forest green and cream toned room was unlit, the faint glow of the rising sun outside the only illumination she used to light her way.

"A drink?" Terrie exclaimed as she rushed in behind her. "Tally, its barely six-thirty in the morning. You never drink before evening."

She pulled the whisky decanter from the back of the bar, grabbed a shot glass and was preparing to pour when Jesse caught her hand. She stilled, swallowing tightly, fighting the overwhelming urge to attack.

"Tally, this won't help," he said gently, setting the decanter back on the bar as he pried the glass from her other hand. "Whatever happened can't be that bad."

She stilled the snarl that trembled on her lips, though her teeth snapped together in fury. Rounding on him, she clenched her fists in the edges of his shirt as she jerked at it hard, watching his eyes round in surprise as he bent to her involuntarily.

"I can still hurt you, Jesse," she snarled into his narrow-eyed expression. "I am to be feared. In all ways. At all times. Is this understood? You are not safe from me. Never think you are."

Jesse had suffered through tar thick coffee, stale doughnuts, mouse traps in his desk drawer, thumb tacks in his chair and any number of nasty little surprises for attempting to put her in her place in the past. His arrogance had been a complete pain in the ass. Training him had not been easy and she would be damned if she would lose ground with him now.

"Of course, Tally." She saw that worried little glimmer in his eyes even though his attempt at sarcasm was sufficient to fool his wife.

Nodding sharply, she released him but didn't return to the liquor. She needed a clear head to get through this.

Breathing in deeply, she fought to still the tremors in her stomach, the nerves that caused her hands to shake and made her heart beat a frantic rhythm within her chest. Terrorizing Jesse always seemed to help restore her balance. If she could master him, surely she could master Dev and Lucian. Couldn't she?

"Tally, are you forgetting that's my husband?" Terrie asked her, though laughter lurked in her voice as she watched the byplay in interest.

Tally breathed in deeply. "Yeah, well, he was my problem first," she reminded her. "I have years of his torture to make up for. He could have scarred me, you know, working for his depraved ass."

"Scar you?" Jesse snarled from behind her. "My depraved ass? At least my brother has his own wife."

"And you brought in Lucian when you knew I disapproved." She turned to him sedately, her voice cool, sarcastic. Now here, she was on even ground. "You, my friend, deserve pain. But I'll be nice since Terrie is a friend of mine."

Yes, that returned her sense of generosity. See? She told herself soothingly, all hope was not lost.

Jesse snarled silently, glancing at his wife as she fought her laughter. "Deal with this crazy woman," he snapped, pointing his finger at Tally as she arched a brow imperiously. "I'm going to shower. I want her gone when I get back."

He stomped from the room and up the stairs, his muttered curses drawing a small smile to Tally's face.

"I love it when they fear me." Tally sighed in satisfaction. "It just seems to make my day better."

"I take it Lucian and Dev weren't too frightened of you?" Terrie asked as she headed for the kitchen, motioning to Tally to follow her.

Tally frowned at her friend's back. That parting shot had to be in return for reminding her husband of his place in the scheme of Tally's Perfect Order. There was no other explanation.

"I need coffee if I can't have whisky," Tally said, following her. "Then I have to leave. I just know those two think they can handle me now," she sneered, thinking of the satisfaction that filled them as she had screamed beneath Dev's thrusting cock the night before. "I'm certain Jesse called them as soon as he escaped. I knew he couldn't be trusted."

Chapter Fifteen

Lucian disconnected his cell phone slowly after the brief discussion with Jesse. At least he knew where Tally was, knew she was safe. His jaw tightened in irritation at Jesse's furious refusal to discuss her, though.

"If you want to discuss that viperous little witch then call my wife," he had snarled. "Maybe she can talk about her reasonably." Which meant Tally was there, at least. And evidently, she had once again struck the fear of Tally into Jesse's heart. She was one of the few capable of it.

Across the room, Dev stared out into the steadily growing morning, silent, pensive.

"The woman is a pain in the ass," Dev finally snorted. "You would make us fall in love with a control freak with commitment issues."

Lucian winced, but grinned. He wasn't pleased with Tally right now, to say the least, but he wasn't exactly worried either.

"And she thinks we're depraved perverts with sharing issues," Lucian reminded his brother with a laugh. "At least she's rational and safe. We can deal with the rest."

He controlled his laughter as Dev turned back to him with a frown. "That woman is never rational," he grunted. "Snide, mocking, psychotic maybe, but never rational."

"And we are?" Lucian was having a hard time containing his amusement. "Maybe it takes someone just slightly off center to appreciate the relationship she's stepping into here, Dev. Give her time, she'll be her normal self soon."

"Yeah, that's what worries me." Dev tucked his hands into his jeans and shook his head in exasperation. "Hell, she almost scares me."

Lucian laughed at that. Tally terrified damned near every man she knew. She could cut them off at the knees with a look, or unman them with a few carefully chosen words. She would challenge them, amuse them, infuriate them to no end and he found himself looking forward to it, as he did nothing else.

"Let her get her bearings." Lucian finally shrugged. "A day or two and she should begin to see that the loss of control isn't as big an issue as she thought it was. She'll want more then. Tally's adventurous, Dev, and she's had a taste of satisfaction now. She'll be back."

Dev hesitated as he moved from the window, heading to the doorway. He looked over at Lucian with brooding reflection as a grimace crossed his face.

"Yeah, but which one of us will she hurt when she does?" he grunted. "She likes Jesse, admits she does, and she has him terrified of her. That's not a good sign, Lucian."

Lucian laughed at this as he slapped his brother on the shoulder and they headed out the door. "No, simple pain would be too easy for her. Castration would be more Tally's style. Maybe we should hide the knives for a while."

"Or keep her restrained," Dev growled. "I liked her much better tied down and at *our* mercy. Being at Tally's mercy would be scary."

Lucian restrained a shudder . "Don't even think like that." He couldn't imagine the horror of it. "Hell, I'm going to work. Let her pout it out and come looking for us. I'll be damned if I'll chase after her any further."

Dev grunted. "Yeah, with a knife. Watch my back, brother, and I'll watch yours; otherwise, we could both end up sacrificed to sweet Tally's fury."

"Or her lust," Lucian murmured, and that was part of what he was fighting for. They had her love, he knew that to the bottom of his soul. All they had to do now was ensure the surrender she had made the night before.

Going to their respective cars, they pulled out of the parking lot and headed back to the large house they owned outside of town, but in the opposite direction of the Wyman home. There was plenty to do while they waited on Tally to accustom herself to the events of the night before. Jesse suggested going after her, giving her no time to regain her balance or her strength. But Jesse was uncharacteristically wary of Tally. He swore she would make an excellent serial killer. There were times Lucian almost agreed with him.

* * * * *

"So, are you going to let them get away with it?" Terrie's voice was amused yet filled with all the loving concern of a true friend.

There were few people Tally allowed close enough that she called them true friends. Terrie was one of those people, unfortunately. True friends knew your past, your secrets, your foibles and faults. Most of which had been revealed through more than one night of drunken revelry after the death of Terrie's first husband.

Tally propped her chin on the palm of her hand and regarded the other woman seriously. "Sister Redempta said vengeance is a sin," she reminded her lightly.

The good sister had a face like a prune with squinting, hard hazel eyes that sent shivers of dread chasing down the spines of all the good little girls at St. Augustine's Academy.

Terrie snorted. "I remember your reply to that one, my friend."

Tally cleared her throat and affected an innocent look. The sister had been rather offended when Tally informed her that since she was Satan's spawn, Vengeance could be her middle name and she would practice the art on the nuns of the academy the minute she came into her full power.

Not that Tally had gone unpunished. That damned wooden ruler with its metal sides had lashed her bare butt for what seemed like hours. She had then been locked in her room for a total of two weeks, during which time the nuns who brought her food and took her to the showers were forbidden to speak to her.

"She broke me." Tally sighed. "I didn't think she had, but she did."

She ignored Terrie's surprised look.

"Tally, you're the strongest person I know." She shook her head in confusion. "How could you ever imagine you didn't win over that old bat?"

Tally sighed somberly. She lifted the cup, playing for time as she sipped from the warm brew and gathered her courage to face things she had only just realized herself.

"I never truly orgasmed until last night, Terrie," she finally said, lowering her head to avoid her friend's gaze. "I would freeze up, lose the intensity, but it always ended the same. I could get off, but I couldn't orgasm." She knew her friend could understand the difference between the two.

"Until Lucian and Dev?" Terrie asked. "It's different when you're with someone you love, Tally."

Tally swallowed before licking her lips nervously. Yes, it was different when you loved, when you felt loved. For all their dominance and rough play the night before Tally had felt the difference in Lucian and Dev.

"Everyone I've ever loved has been horrified by me." She tried to smile as though unconcerned, but she felt the warning tremble of her lips. "The sisters told my parents about catching me with what's-his-name." She frowned, trying to remember the boy's name and couldn't. It didn't matter, she remembered the event well enough. "They still remind me of their shame at being called into Sister Redempta's office and being informed that I was caught allowing *some nasty little boy,"* she affected the sister's tone, "to put his mouth in my private places and daring to beg him to do other disgusting things to me."

The truth was, she had been begging him to push his finger deeper up her ass as his tongue whipped at her clit. Damn, she had been close when that evil old bat had thrown the door open to the gardener's shed and interrupted them.

"You parents are prudes, Tally. You've always admitted that," Terrie said softly. "How did that break you?"

"Because, they allowed the sisters at the academy to punish me as they pleased."

She shook her head. The whippings had been the worst, the lectures, the silence from the other girls because they were forbidden to talk to her. She had endured nearly a year of it before she was able to leave.

Looking back now, Tally realized that her defeat had begun long before that day. Slowly, insidiously, the academy had wreaked havoc on her growing sensibilities; turning her into the mocking, cold-hearted bitch others accused her of being.

It wouldn't have been such a terrible thing if she hadn't already been uncertain of her emerging sexuality. The need for stronger sensations, that edge of pain and extreme sex that had been growing within her, was frightening in itself. Sister Redempta's harsh, derogatory lectures had only made it worse.

"Tally." Terrie sighed deeply. "You always feel so strongly about things, and fight so hard to hide it, to appear uncaring, cool and aloof. It was bound to catch up with you someday. You've denied the very heart of who you are because you were afraid those you loved would look down on you for it, shame you for it. Hon, haven't you realized yet? You've gravitated to a group of friends who are marrying the Trojans, for pity's sake. That should tell you something."

"It should," Tally drawled in amusement. "But I won't be participating in a single ménage or even a few with Luc and

Dev," she said, her voice growing softer. "I want them both, Terrie. Forever. And that terrifies me. No one has ever wanted *me* forever. Besides, after I get back at them for what they did last night, they might not want me anymore, period." She sighed regretfully.

Terrie shook her head in confusion. "But I thought you enjoyed it."

Tally leaned back in her chair, her eyes narrowing. "I did. But it gives them the upper hand. You know I can't allow that."

A hint of worry entered her friend's expression. "You're plotting. Oh hell. Tally, Lucian and Dev are not men you can just mess with at will. They're more dominant than even Jesse is."

Tally frowned over at her friend. "Marriage is making you soft," she accused her archly.

An incredulous laugh burst from Terrie. "Tally, I rather enjoy keeping Jesse comfortably happy. The benefits are incredible. I'm not getting mixed up in one of your schemes."

Tally smiled over at her confidently. Terrie so loved to play hard-to-get when it came to getting in trouble. "He might spank you harder next time."

Terrie's eyes sparked with reluctant interest.

"I bet he's let up on the punishment side of the benefits." Tally sighed regretfully. "Men do get so confident after a few months of marital bliss. Why, I bet he thinks you're so well trained now that he doesn't have to do more than give you a sweet little love tap here and there, instead of a nice spanking, to remind you of the pleasure."

Terrie's eyes narrowed dangerously. "That's not nice."

Tally shrugged. "But true. Yes?"

Terrie leaned back in her chair. "You've never been married," she stated. "How do you know?"

Tally arched her brow mockingly. "I'm not exactly a virgin, sweetie. Just because I have an orgasm issue doesn't mean I don't know how men work."

"Orgasm issue, huh?" Terrie said drolly as she played with her coffee cup. She stared down at it for a second and Tally knew she had her.

"So." Terrie raised her head, anticipation lighting her eyes. "What did you have in mind?"

Tally smiled slowly, confidently. "It's really a very simple plan," she assured her. "All I need you to do is help me sneak into The Club tonight." She ignored the incredulous horror that filled her friend's eyes. "I'll take care of the rest."

"Oh man, Tally." Terrie shook her head as amusement suddenly overcame her. "We're going to go to hell, aren't we?"

A satisfied grin shaped Tally's lips in reply. "Well, if we do, we'll definitely be roommates. Wonder how hard it would be to sneak in the ventilation system?"

Their laughter echoed through the kitchen, a reminder of the nights spent laughing and crying, philosophizing and generally creating mayhem before Terrie's marriage. Mayhem is in the eye of the beholder, though, Tally thought in satisfaction. Tonight, she would remind Lucian and Devril Conover of just that fact.

Chapter Sixteen

"Are you sure you want to do this, Tally?" Terrie paused at the closet, her hand reaching inside as she looked over her shoulder and met Tally's gaze.

Tally refused to fidget or to chicken out. This was the rest of her life. It wasn't a scheme, it wasn't a game, it wasn't a titillating little adventure. It was the final break with a past that should have never affected her the way it had.

"I'm sure." She nodded firmly. She was. Certain.

Until Terrie pulled the clothes from the closet.

Clear plastic protected the garments and hid nothing from the eyes. They were innocent. A simple red plaid skirt that would have ended at Tally's knees when she was much younger but would rise to mid thigh now. A short sleeved white cotton shirt. A very proper Catholic girl's school uniform. It struck a chord of fear in her chest so strong that she nearly trembled in the face of it.

It was just clothes, she told herself realistically, but she knew her subconscious saw it as so much more.

Terrie laid the outfit out on the bed. It was over ten years old and should fit in the manner that Tally required. She needed to exorcize the ghosts the good sisters of the academy had placed within her, and what better way to do it than to take this first step into a new life, dressed as the person she had been so long ago?

"It will be shorter," Terrie warned. "And snugger. But it should fit you okay."

Tally swallowed tightly. "It will work perfectly."

She stared at the clothing laid out as though it were a snake, coiled and ready to strike. In many ways it was.

"Tally, you don't have to do this," Terrie said. "You know Lucian and Dev love you..."

"This isn't about Lucian and Dev." She shook her head slowly, still staring at the innocent articles of clothing. "This is about me. I need white stockings. The ones that go just over the knee," she told her friend faintly. "Do you have shoes that will work? I don't dare return to the apartment yet."

"I have everything you need." Terrie nodded as she smoothed her hand over the plastic. "I wish we had schooled together, Tally. Perhaps I could have made things easier."

Tally shook her head shortly. Nothing could have made it easier; nothing could change the parents who never knew how to love the wild little girl they had given birth to.

"It's really shouldn't be that big a deal," Tally said softly. "I'm a grown woman, Terrie. Not a child. I should have faced this a long time ago. I don't know why I've fought as I have."

"Perhaps because nothing was worth the risk until now," Terrie suggested gently. "You've changed since going to Lucian's office, Tally. You're like this bright flame; where before you once glowed, now you sparkle. Love changes you. I told you that before. Perhaps, Lucian and Dev merely gave you the strength you needed to face it."

Tally smiled rather mockingly. Was that true? At this moment, she had no idea. All she knew was that suddenly nothing mattered more than changing the course her life had taken.

The empty, cold apartment. The loveless life. The chill she felt when darkness fell and she realized how empty her bed was. When she realized she could only envision two men within that bed with her. Lucian and Dev.

"They'll be there tonight?" she asked Terrie quickly rather than replying to her previous statement.

Terrie nodded, a smile of conspiracy crossing her lips.

"I just talked to Jesse a few minutes ago. He's meeting them for drinks this evening after work. He's been doing that a lot lately." She frowned. "What the hell do they do there anyway?"

"Fuck each other's wives?" Tally asked her with an amused grin. "As I understand it, the married Trojans can only fuck their own women there, never anyone else's. House rules." She rolled her eyes at the thought.

Not that she wanted Lucian and Dev to ever touch another woman. She would have to commit murder if that ever occurred, but the rule seemed designed to keep the married members in a constant state of lust while within the hallowed halls of their cherished Club.

Terrie snorted at that thought. "Jesse better never suggest such a thing. I don't think he could stand it himself."

"He doesn't share you any longer?" Tally knew she was desperately delaying the moment she would have to uncover that damned uniform.

Terrie frowned. "Not in a while. He threatens to." She shrugged. "He seems to enjoy it. But he's been busy I guess..." Her voice trailed off.

"Men get complacent, I told you," Tally warned her distantly.

"Hmm. We'll see about that," Terrie said thoughtfully, though her eyes were glittering with the light of battle.

Score another for Tally against Jesse, she snickered silently. So far, she was still ahead and Jesse was far, far behind her.

"Tally?" Terrie's quiet voice drew her gaze from the uniform and back to her friend.

Terrie watched her with an edge of compassion, of concern. Tally could see the worry in her eyes now, the knowledge that Tally had to gather her courage to even touch the clothes, let alone put them on.

"I must really love them," Tally mused with a self-deprecating little smile. "Because only love could get me in those clothes." She looked up at Terrie, arching her brow mockingly. "What do we do if the clothes get ripped off me?"

Terrie shrugged in unconcern. "I would consider it a worthy sacrifice then," she laughed. "The uniform has no meaning to me, Tally. Burn it when you're done if you need to. Consider it a wedding present."

Wedding present. Tally swallowed tightly. "One step at a time here," she breathed in deep and hard. "One *slow* step at a time here."

Chapter Seventeen

"You're so fucked!" Jesse took a seat at the small table on the far end of The Club's main room and stared at Lucian and Dev in sublime amusement. "You know, I would feel sorry for you if I didn't think you had brought it all on yourselves. Didn't I warn you about her?"

Lucian finished the drink he had ordered earlier and shot his friend a brooding look. Beside him, Dev grunted in obvious ill temper. Tally hadn't shown up at work and hadn't answered the message they left on her machine or the one they left with the cell phone's messaging service later that day. Neither man was in the mood for Jesse's mocking laughter.

"Don't you have better things to do than harass us?" Dev asked him. "I thought you had a wife to keep fucked. Go home and do your job."

Jesse laughed softly at that. "I've had mine today, have you had yours?"

Lucian gave him a look filled with the promise of retribution.

"What the hell are you doing here anyway?" Dev growled. "Marriage suddenly staling on you?"

Jesse laughed again as he shook his head. "You two are like bears with a sore paw. I have it on the highest authority she's going to be home later tonight. You should go back and teach her a lesson. The right lesson this time. She won't be so eager to make trouble then."

He was clearly delighting in tormenting them, Lucian thought. Jesse was no more a hard ass than any of them were. Though, sexually, they were all well aware of his hold on Terrie, and hers on him.

Lucian stared morosely around the room. Was it their sexuality that had caused Tally to run? It wouldn't be an occasional ménage; it was a lifetime commitment to two dominant males. Two men who were, defined by society, sexually depraved. Their every sexual desire hinged on their woman's ultimate fulfillment, whatever that may be. They encouraged their women to relax all their inhibitions, to give in to even the most exacting pleasures.

"Jesse, you're getting on my nerves tonight," Lucian finally said with the barest hint of a smile. "Your marital bliss offends me."

"Well, having your woman threaten my life this morning didn't do a whole hell of a lot for me," Jesse informed him with a disgruntled frown. "And I was trying to be nice to her, too."

"That will teach you," Lucian grunted, still uncertain exactly where they had gone wrong with Tally.

Jesse was clearly enjoying his smug amusement at the brothers' expense. Lucian made a mental note to return the favor at the first available opportunity.

"Have you two thought that maybe you pushed her too far?" Jesse asked, his voice sobering.

Lucian sighed as he shook his head and leaned back in his chair. It was a question he and Dev had been asking themselves all evening.

"Hell, Jess," Lucian finally sighed wearily. "The woman takes control to a whole new level. I'll be damned if I haven't given up on understanding how the hell her minds works."

"I could have warned you of that," Jesse grunted. "Why do you two think I let her believe she has me under control?" he asked them seriously now. "Tally functions at peak efficiency when she's in control. You can't conquer that woman. You have to gentle her. That's a whole 'nother ballgame from the one you've been playing."

"Jesse, go away." Lucian sighed. "I distinctly remember you forgoing advice with Terrie; now we'll do the same thing."

Jesse smiled at that. "Well, she surprised me too. Having her bring Tally in the bedroom scared the hell out of me. You don't want to be restrained with Tally in the room."

A frown snapped over Lucian's brow as Devril seemed to growl beside him.

"Forget that night ever occurred, Wyman," Dev snapped. "Amnesia could be a good thing."

Jesse chuckled at the ire in Dev's voice as he leaned back in his chair and regarded the two men with a striking absence of compassion.

"Have you two ever considered that breaking all that control at once could unleash a monster?" he asked them curiously. "In all honesty, I think I'd be scared if I were the two of you. Hell, I didn't have anything to do with it and now I'm scared of her."

Lucian narrowed his eyes on his friend. Jesse was offering little in the way of solutions and much in aggravation. He glanced over at Dev and shook his head as wry amusement tilted his brother's lips. They weren't frightened of her. They were more frightened of losing her.

Lucian finally sighed roughly as he dragged his fingers through his hair in irritation. Hell, he was horny, half drunk and less than pleased with the world in general today. He didn't need Jesse's amusement adding to the mix.

"It may have been a miscalculation," he finally admitted. "Not unfixable, but a miscalculation all the same."

Jesse snorted. He would have said something more but a commotion in the outside hall had all their eyes widening at the sound of the precise, furious female voice that echoed from there.

"You put your grubby little paws on me again, you little twit, and you'll be carrying stubs."

"Terrie!" Outraged alarm filled Jesse's voice as they all jumped from the table and rushed to the entrance hall.

There she was. Lucian blinked at the vision, not certain he was actually seeing Terrie Wyman exactly as she was dressed.

Skintight, soft cotton black shorts accentuated the long line of her legs. The matching sports bra-type top barely concealed the full curves of her luscious breasts. Her flat stomach with its gold belly ring looked like the finest silk tanned a soft, golden brown.

Her hair was held securely back from her face in a tight French braid and she wore black sneakers on delicate feet.

"Cat burglars are dressing fine this year," Lucian murmured behind Jesse as he held back his snicker.

Jessie took a brief moment to cast him a fulminating look before facing his wife once again.

"What the bloody damned hell were you thinking?" he snapped as her eyes widened then narrowed at the incredulity in his tone.

"That I was looking for my husband?" she replied with mocking sweetness. "You spend so much damned time here I was starting to wonder exactly what was going on. And the goon at the gate wouldn't let me in."

"Did he know who you were, darling?" Jesse's voice was dark, but smooth as silk, a clear indication that his patience and his temper were being tested.

A slender graceful shoulder shrugged as Terrie's lips tilted in a sultry smile.

"Well, I didn't mention any names," she drawled sweetly. "Where would be the fun in that?"

Silence reigned for a full minute before Jesse turned to Lucian. His gaze was filled with amusement, though, rather than anger.

"I'll warn you, Lucian," he said mildly. "Only one person could have talked Terrie into such a stunt."

Lucian's eyes narrowed as Dev cursed behind him. Tally. It was a well-known fact that only Tally Raines could convince Terrie Wyman to get into any type of trouble.

"Come on, wife." Jesse's voice hardened when he turned back to his wife and her less than innocent smile. "I think it's been too long since your last spanking."

Lucian would have commented on just that lack of threat if someone behind him hadn't let out a low whistle and a muttered prayer for strength.

"Have mercy!" one of the members muttered from the doorway to the main gathering room. "I've been a good little boy after all, because here's a glimpse of paradise."

Lucian turned slowly and moved to the doorway. And there she was. The definition of carnal, insatiable lust. This wasn't sin. This was an angel of pleasure. Every good little boy's wet dream come to life.

Terrie had warned them that Tally's years at the girl's academy hadn't been pleasant. It was obvious Tally was out to exorcise some ghosts.

She was dressed in a mouthwatering, skintight, make-your-cock-stand-up-and-take-notice Catholic girl's uniform.

The red plaid skirt showed off her gorgeous thighs and legs. The short-sleeved white blouse was open just below her breasts, giving a peek at a black lace bra as tempting as sin itself.

Delicate feet were shod in demure black leather shoes, while deliciously shaped legs were crossed at the ankle, covered by over the knee white stockings. He knew how perfect the flesh above the elastic lace of the stockings would taste and it made his mouth water.

Her long black hair was pulled to each side, braided and fell over her breasts. She was the perfect picture of decadence. She was the Tally he dreamed of day and night.

She was leaning against the bar, a drink in one hand, as the bartender stared at her with a bemused expression. Thom was clearly entranced.

"Good evening, gentlemen," she greeted them in a low, sex-filled voice that had every cock in the room jumping to instant attention. "Nice place you have here."

Lucian could hear the panting from behind him. He could sense Dev's possessiveness rising to the fore as well. All those damned men, their dicks and their eyes trained on that luscious flesh was just too much for their already testosterone-overloaded bodies.

"Back off, asshole," Dev turned and snarled as one of the men tried to push forward.

Tally wasn't helping the situation. A perfect, brilliant red fingernail rimmed her glass as she watched the crowd gathered at the door. Matching lips quirked into a smile as dark eyes lowered drowsily to gaze back at the two men ready to battle every man in the room over her.

"I've heard quite a bit about your little Club," she continued in that throaty voice, causing their cocks to jerk, the blood to beat hard and heavy through their veins. "Wasn't it Stanton's wife who related the complete orgy she had here for a honeymoon?" Her gaze sought out Drew Stanton as she tsked lightly. "Such bad little boys you are. You should all be spanked."

A collective sigh of ecstasy sounded behind them.

"Somebody should be spanked," Drew muttered from the back of the crowd.

"Tally, my love." Lucian shook his head as he felt the heat of over a dozen men behind him lusting after her. "I wouldn't tempt fate if I were you."

She arched a perfect black brow mockingly. "Are you going to share me with them?"

"Not fucking likely," Dev answered her, his voice grating, rough with lust and male possessiveness.

"Shit, Dev, give us a break," Sax groaned. "What the hell sort of club do you think you're a member of?"

"Wanna die, Sax?" Lucian snarled, not even bothering to look behind him as he advanced into the room.

Tally's head lifted, her gaze seductive, her expression erotically knowing.

He could sense Dev's wariness now; they were both aware that this was one game Tally had to play out. No pressure, no dominance. Not yet. She had to assert her authority, reaffirm her sense of strength, or she would never trust them enough to give her control back to them.

"Tell me something, do all you fine gentlemen bring your wives or lovers here for the communal orgy?" She lifted the glass to her lips and sipped lazily as her husky voice wrapped around each man in the room. "Or is there a criteria to being part of your little club?"

"There's definitely a criteria, sweetheart." Lucian crossed his arms over his chest as he watched her with simmering lust and a large amount of incredulity. "How the hell did you sneak in here anyway?"

A mysterious little smile played at her lips as she cast him a sultry glance. Come hither, sweaty sex and wickedly knowing. Her look was a temptation that had his cock aching for relief.

"So. What's the criteria?" She ignored the last question in favor of the first as she glanced around her, her gaze stopping on the shackles that fell from the wall at the other side of the room. "Have you ever tested your play pretties out on yourselves?"

"Fuck!" Dev growled behind him as a dozen other men shifted uncomfortably.

Lucian drew in a hard, deep breath. Surely to hell she wouldn't ask that?

"No need to," he drawled softly. "We've made a lifestyle out of control, sweetheart. We don't need the added help.

What about you? Which of us do you truly think would give in first?"

She glanced up at him through the veil of her lashes, and he wondered if she was aware of how delicate and sweet her hard, pierced nipples looked beneath the thin material of her shirt and bra, if she was aware that her breasts were swollen, their up thrust curves making his and Dev's hands itch with the need to touch them.

She arched a black, wing-tipped brow with curious mockery. "Which of us will be restrained?"

"No restraints," Dev growled. "Don't worry, baby, we'll let you lose fair and square."

Soft, amused laughter whispered from her graceful throat as she set her drink on the bar, her dark eyes watching them with lust and emotion. The emotion drew them both. They could feel the soul clenching fear that glistened for a second in the depths of the tobacco-brown orbs.

"Or *you'll* lose. But here I am, you can spank me now. I've been a very bad girl," she warned them with sultry heat as she straightened from the bar, one hip thrown forward as she spread her hands out to her sides, showing that luscious body in a pose so mouth wateringly sexual that Lucian was afraid he was about to drool from the effect of it.

"Oh hell. This is going to be one of those look-but-don't-touch deals," one of the men behind them moaned. "Hell's fire. I knew I was going to pay for my sins somehow. But this is too cruel for words."

"Touch and die," Dev grunted as he and Lucian began to advance on the siren slowly.

Her breathing increased; her breasts rose and fell with excitement, her nipples becoming harder, the little rings surrounding them becoming fainter as the stiff little points grew more erect.

"Be sure, Tally," Dev warned her as he moved behind her, not touching, allowing her to feel only the heat of his body as he leaned close to her, his hands moving to her braids, loosening the thick ropes of silk.

Lucian stopped in front of her, staring down at her broodingly, lust eating him alive.

"Here or upstairs?" Lucian gave her the choice, though he had the feeling she had already made her choice.

She cocked her head, regarding him with an amused, aroused gaze.

"Do you need privacy?" she asked him, her expression reflective, her gaze lighting with excitement at the thought of an audience. She didn't want to just bring them down, break their control; she wanted everyone in The Club to know who owned them. Just as they had made it known who owned her.

"Privacy isn't needed, baby," Lucian said as his blood began to boil in his veins and his cock seemed to engorge further than it ever had before. The hard-on from hell, and it was demanding relief. Where he would find the control to hold off for more than five minutes before fucking her blind, he had no idea.

"You can stop this at any time, baby," Dev whispered to her as he leaned closer to her, his breath feathering the hair over her ear.

Lucian watched her eyelids flicker in pleasure. Her gaze clashed with Lucian's, held, the steady build-up of excitement shadowed only by her fear. "Do your worst, Wicked."

Lucian grinned, a slow, amused curve of his lips as he thought of all the wicked things he and Dev could do to her, for her.

His arm lifted, his fingers glancing over her cheek as Dev's hands settled on her waist. She shivered at their touch; he forced back a shiver himself at the feel of her skin, so soft, so warm.

"You're safe with us, Tally," he whispered then, for her ears only, feeling her shudder against him as the heat between them began to rise. "Always. But tonight, you will beg..."

"Or you will."

Chapter Eighteen

Tally's head turned, her teeth locking onto Lucian's thumb, her tongue swiping over it, hot and teasing as her head fell back against Dev's shoulder, her body arching to Lucian as Dev's tongue traced her ear.

Tally could feel the other men watching, taking their seats within the room, all eyes riveted on them. It wasn't the first time they had driven a woman crazy in front of the other Club members, she knew. Terrie had given her what information she had, though that had been sketchy at best. She knew what happened tonight would be her choice. Knew that in taking this step, she was making herself a part of Lucian and Dev's life in a way she could never take back.

"Do you have any idea how arousing this can become, Tally?" Lucian asked her softly. "All eyes are on you, watching you, waiting to see that one moment when you can no longer stand the pleasure and everything inside you explodes. That's what The Club is all about, baby. That's who we are. What we are. What we long to be. The trigger that transforms a woman's climax into an explosion unlike anything she's ever known. Her darkest desires, her deepest needs. We long for nothing more than to be the fulfillment of them."

She wanted to cry out at the declaration, wanted to alternately rage at them for being so accepting of her, and whimper in submission. That need to whimper shocked her back to reality. She would take control here. Not them. They would learn that she could be just as dominant, just as aggressive, as any Trojan ever born.

She leaned away from Dev, licking her tongue slowly over her crimson lips as her hands slid up Lucian's arms. His eyes narrowed on her. Oh yes, she liked that. He wasn't certain what to expect, what she would do. She allowed her fingers to smooth over his chest, curl around the parted edges of his shirt.

A quick jerk and buttons scattered. Behind her, Dev groaned, his hands clenching on her hips as her lips moved to the wide expanse of muscular flesh. Her tongue circled a flat, hard male nipple as her other hand moved lower, her fingers curling around the rigid length of Lucian's cock swelling demandingly beneath his slacks.

"Fuck!" His hips bucked against the sudden caress as his hands gripped her head, his lips lowering to hers.

She met him with her teeth. A hard nip at the hungry curve had him drawing back, staring down at her, his face flushing in arousal.

"Bad boy," she snapped, then moaned, a low drawn out sigh of pleasure as she felt Dev's teeth at her neck. Scraping, warning.

Lucian smiled dangerously. "Two of us, one of you," he reminded her darkly.

"True." Her fingers moved to his belt, loosening it with deliberate flicks of her fingers. "Next time, maybe I will use the restraints on you."

A second later Lucian's cock was free. Tally didn't give him time to retaliate. She bent at the waist, her buttocks pressing into Dev's thighs as her mouth covered the wide head of the flesh straining from Lucian's body. He filled her mouth, stretching her lips, burning her tongue with the heat of his cock.

"Tally," Lucian growled as her tongue rimmed the mushroom shaped flesh, flickering as her mouth suckled him deep, moving over the tip of his erection with steady strokes as she felt Dev's hands slip under the hem of her dress, drawing it upward.

They were all panting now. The air in the room was growing warmer, a dozen male bodies heating up as they watched the show being played out before them. As her mouth sucked at him, she allowed her fingers to stroke, beguile. Her nails scraped delicately along the shaft that wasn't covered by her mouth, trailing to his heavy scrotum, caressing, scratching lightly, causing him to jerk in response.

Tally was fighting shudders, though. Dev was diabolical, his hands easing her thong from her hips, then her thighs, his lips moving over the curves of her buttocks with precise movements as his tongue dampened her flesh. Kissing, licking, making her pussy heat with the nearness of his mouth.

Lucian's hands tightened in her hair as her lips slid from his cock and she began to lick down the hard shaft. She alternated the movements of her tongue with light, gentle nips and suckling pressure; she used the fingers of her other hand to torment the throbbing head.

"Take those damned clothes off, Tally," Lucian said as one hand moved to the lace of her bra, struggling to get beneath it to the swollen curves of her breast. At the same time her mouth slid back up his cock, her tongue finding the ultra sensitive flesh beneath the flared tip of his erection as her mouth began to suckle at it lightly.

He tensed, the hand in her hair tightening as she felt the warning pulse just beneath the stretched flesh.

"Like hell," he groaned.

He attempted to draw her head back. Tally's nails tightened warningly, her lips moving to cover his cock again, draw it into her mouth and catch the hot, liquid drops of fluid that pulsed from it.

Behind her, Dev spread her thighs further, his breathing harsh and rough against her as his lips came steadily closer to the soaked flesh of her pussy. She tensed in expectation, trying to steel herself against the caress coming. If she could steal Lucian's control then she would be satisfied. Just one of them.

The odds were against her, but surely one of them would give before her.

As she suckled at Lucian's cock her hand lowered, fingers spearing between her thighs into the thick length of Dev's hair as she pulled him closer, rubbing her cunt over his suddenly licking tongue as he insinuated himself between her spread thighs.

She rose then, releasing Lucian's cock as she jerked at the buttons of her shirt, parting the material further, revealing the swollen globes of her breasts, the hard dark nipples rising from them.

"Oh hell, spank her or something," one of the men watching groaned in despair. "Spank that bad girl, Lucian."

Lucian groaned as he gazed down at her hungrily. His head lowered, her lips met his and she cried out from the pleasure. How would she endure it? How would she survive both of them pushing her steadily closer to the final limits of her control?

She forgot about their audience, forgot about anything but each touch, each sigh, the feel of their lips taking her, tongues fucking into her. Lucian at her lips as Dev did the same at her cunt. Her body was a meal and they were greedy in their hunger. But no greedier than she.

The battle was one she knew she was ultimately doomed to lose. But she wouldn't beg. She wouldn't give in first. Even as her body screamed out in release, her pussy riding Dev's thrusting tongue as her mouth accepted every hard thrust of Lucian's, she swore she wouldn't.

"Give in," Lucian growled as his lips trailed to her neck. Desperate kisses, hard little nips testing the border between pleasure and pain, had her gasping at the sensations.

His hands covered her now bare breasts, his fingers tugging at the rings piercing them, sending shocking waves of pleasure searing through her, adding to the sensations piercing her womb as Dev ate from her pussy.

"You give in." Her fingers stroked his cock from base to tip, milking the thick flesh as her lips went to his shoulder, her teeth scraping over it as he did the same to her neck.

Dev was groaning heavily between her thighs, his tongue licking from her clit to the entrance of her vagina, then sliding in deep and hard and thrusting in a series of shattering waves of pleasure.

Tally could feel her knees weakening, feel the currents of energy building in her womb, tightening, begging for release.

Lucian eased a bra strap over her shoulder, as his lips lowered to her breasts. Her fingers slid to the base of his erection, where the rock-hard shaft met the tightening flesh of his scrotum. Her thumb moved slowly, in sensuous circles until it pressed into the small indention there. She felt him tighten, heard a groan tear from his chest as his lips covered her nipple, his body jerking in response as she felt for, then found, the sensitive spot she had been searching for.

Her teeth nipped at his ear, her other hand twining through the strands of hair at the back of his neck as she felt Dev's fingers exploring the area around her anus while Lucian's teeth scraped her nipple.

The voracity of their passions began to heat the air around them. Sweat stood out on Lucian's flesh; Dev's hand tightened on her hip as a finger found the entrance to her anus. The digit, slickened by her own juices, pierced the tiny opening as Tally's hand stroked upward, her thumb finding and caressing the sensitive spot just beneath the flared head of Lucian's cock.

Twin male groans echoed around her as her own thin cry pierced the atmosphere. The caress of a dozen gazes wasn't helping the rapidly building tension.

"Give in," Lucian growled as Dev's finger stroked in and out of the snug entrance of her ass. "Now, Tally."

"You give in," she panted, her legs shaking, perspiration coating her skin as she forced him away from her breast, leaned forward and nipped at his nipple.

Lucian's hands clasped her head as her lips ran down his rock-hard abdomen, her tongue seeking and finding the damp head of his cock.

"Damn you, suck it," he ordered heatedly as her tongue rimmed the thick knob. "Now."

She moaned against the grip he had on her hair, pleasure and pain streaking through her scalp. She refused the harsh demand, though. Her tongue continued to lick firmly, arousingly, relishing the beads of semen that formed on the head of his cock as her hips writhed against Dev's demanding tongue.

Pleasure seared every cell in her body as she fought to maintain control, to push Lucian past the brink of his own boundaries until they gave her what she desperately needed. Not just the loss of control, but the heady, ultimate knowledge of her strength as a woman. She wanted to be taken, no holds barred, no attempt at tenderness, not caring of who controlled what. She needed to be taken hard, fast, to a point where the pleasure and pain combined and she knew that the men she loved were as deeply enmeshed in the pleasure as she was herself. No restraints. Neither physical nor mental.

Her tongue flickered at the head of Lucian's cock; her mouth sucked firmly, once, twice, then halted so she could lick at him again. His thighs were corded with the strain of holding back, his breathing harsh, broken.

"Now." His snarl surprised her.

Primal excitement shuddered through her body as he gripped her hips, lifted her. Dev quickly rose, parting her thighs; the hard, thick column of Lucian's cock surged hard and fast inside the snug depths of her pussy.

Tally's scream echoed around them. Nothing could have surprised her more.

"You fucking win," Lucian growled as she arched in his arms, pleasure streaking like lightning through every cell of her body as he stumbled to a barstool, bracing himself in the seat as his hips surged, driving his cock inside her with hard, deep strokes.

"Oh God! Lucian," she screamed as her own control shattered.

Behind her, she felt Dev moving in closer, lubricating the sensitive channel of her anus as Lucian drove her insane from the hard thrusts in her pussy. He stretched her, filling her to capacity as she shuddered in his grip.

All question of control—who owned it, who gave it—was gone. There was only the pleasure now. Pleasure unlike anything she could have known, could have imagined.

As she fought the building tension in her womb, the curling heat and static energy, Lucian stilled, holding her tightly to his chest, his breathing rough as he tilted her head to him, his lips taking her in a kiss that stole her need to breathe. At the same time, Dev moved against her, his cock pressing at the entrance to her ass, spreading the tightening muscles there, working the slick head of his erection inside the narrow channel, sending bolts of lava-hot sensation streaking through her nerve endings.

Her cries were smothered by Lucian's lips, but there was no hesitation in her acceptance of the pleasure/pain that destroyed her mind. She was a creature of sensation, of sensuality. A figure of electrical impulses, gasping cries and liquid heat as the silken, steel-hard length of Dev's cock surged into the tight recesses of her ass.

There was no fight to make it last now. Hunger, gripping and primordial, filled them, connected them, bonded their bodies in a way Tally knew she would never be free of. Hard, driving strokes filled her over and over again. The border between pleasure and pain widened as each sensation built upon itself until she tore her mouth from Lucian's, her head falling back against Dev's chest as her scream of release ripped from her soul.

Her orgasm ruptured inside her womb, raced through her body, tightening every straining muscle to the breaking point as they fucked into the clenching recesses of her body, their groans and hoarse male cries joining her scream as they found their own release.

Hot, rich semen jetted into her clenching pussy, her hot ass, filling her, marking her in a way she knew would change her forever.

Long minutes later she collapsed against Lucian's heaving chest, trusting in the hard arms that wrapped around her, the lips that caressed her cheek, her shoulders. Whispered, fragmented words blended around her as they claimed her, their rough voices demanding, firm, despite the weariness that now dragged at all their bodies.

"Mine..." They said the words together, and she accepted them as one.

Chapter Nineteen

Tally awoke early the next morning, despite the fact that as soon as Lucian and Dev arrived at their secluded home they had taken her straight to the bedroom and *punished* her exquisitely. She had to pay, they had laughed, for daring to slip into The Club and break their control in such a manner.

Hussy, Dev had called her as he restrained her to the bed. *Wanton,* Lucian had laughed as he smacked her ass, watching as she drove her hips upward, seeking more of the erotic stimulation. They had kept her on the edge forever as she begged, pleaded, demanded they fuck her into oblivion. Which they had done, quite well, she had to admit.

Stiff, aching in places she had never known could ache, she dragged herself over Dev's prone body, ignoring his irritable grunt as she slapped his well-defined ass.

"You're late for work," she informed him as she pulled Lucian's shirt on over her bare body. "And I still have to go home and get dressed." She picked her shirt up and frowned at the jagged holes where buttons had once been. "You ruined my clothes."

"They were illegal," Dev grunted.

"I agree. Ripping my clothing should be a killable offense." She cast him a mocking look. "I'll punish you tonight maybe."

He opened one eye, staring at her balefully. "Go back to sleep."

Back to sleep? She had never felt so energized. She pushed at his shoulder, chuckling as he groaned but still rolled over. His cock was erect, tenting the sheet, a thick invitation to pleasure as she straddled his hard abdomen and stared down at him warningly.

"I hope you were serious last night," she said softly, aware that Lucian had rolled closer as she felt his lips at her knee, his hand running down her calf. "Try to get away from me and I promise you, I'll become your worst nightmare."

She had read about stalkers. She was fairly confident she could do a wonderful imitation.

Dev reached up to tuck trailing strands of her hair behind her shoulder. His smile, normally wicked and provoking, was soft and gentle with emotion.

"Every word," he told her softly. "Both of us, Tally. Forever."

Tally swallowed tightly. She was giving so much of herself to these two men. She looked over at Lucian. "What if one of you wants someone else later?"

He looked at her in surprise. "Tally, you're *our* heart. You don't seem to understand, baby, we're two sides of the same coin. You can't have one without the other. And we've waited too long for this—for you—to even want or need anyone else."

How could she not believe them? They watched her, their brilliant eyes filled with their love, their promises.

"What about children?" she finally whispered. "If we have children?"

Lucian shook his head in confusion. "Well, it would be nice." He smiled slowly. "But what about them?"

She cleared her throat delicately. "You won't be certain, you know." She waved her hand expressively. "Who the father is for sure."

A quick frown on both their faces was leveled at her. But it was male displeasure rather than the regret she thought she would see.

"Any child you have, Tally, is our child. It will never matter which of us fathers it, we'll both know that possessiveness, that love for a child that is ours. That's part of our bond, baby, and part of our gift to you." Dev's voice was low, deep, filled with emotion as Lucian's hand caressed her flat abdomen almost reverently.

They took her breath, stole her fears, and for once in her life she believed. Believed that she was loved and that the needs that haunted her, tormented her, would be accepted. She loved them both. Slowly, overwhelmingly, both men had moved into her heart and filled it to overflowing.

"Good." She glanced down at Lucian, swallowing past the lump of emotion in her throat. Grinning back at her wickedly, he pushed at the bottom edge of her shirt.

"Stop that." She slapped at his hand and before either of them could stop her, she was off the bed and padding to the bathroom. "I have to get ready and go home before I can go to the office. I'm going to need coffee if neither of you minds. I hope you have a cappuccino machine." She closed the bathroom door behind her, a pleased smile crossing her face. Life was definitely beginning to look up.

Dev glanced at Lucian as he rolled from the bed, staring at the closed door with a less than pleased glare.

"We're fucked," Lucian said simply. Dev knew he wasn't referring to the act, but rather the state of dominance they could see would evolve during the less sexual moments of their lives with Tally.

"Hell, let her have fun." Dev scratched his chest lazily. "She gets too far out of hand and we'll tie her to the bed again."

Lucian glanced at his brother mockingly. "Oh, you have no idea the monster we're going to create." He shook his head warily. "We're fucked, brother. Plain and simple."

He didn't sound displeased.

"I'm waiting," she called out from the bathroom. "Who had back washing duty this morning?"

Lucian looked at Dev as his brother met his gaze. They glanced at the door, each other, and the race was on. They could share during the best of times, but that damned shower didn't have a chance of holding all three of them. Unfortunately, they both reached the door at the same time.

They sighed together. "Bigger shower for sure," Lucian said with a grimace as Dev managed to push him back and, smiling smugly, reached the shower first.

Lucian leaned against the doorframe, smiling as Tally's laughter echoed from the stall. The shadows of his brother and their lover twisted, turned, hands touched, lips met. Arousing and starkly possessive, Dev pressed her to the wall and proceeded to show her who was boss—at least, in the shower.

Life would definitely change for them all, but they had her now, their jaded little consort, ripe for loving and willing to accept the pleasures they could give, the adoration they had saved just for her.

Like the Trojans before them who had found that perfect woman, they would hold her, hide her when they could, watch her in pride when they couldn't, and protect her as long as they drew breath. Their wicked intentions had paid off when they set their sights on her. And now their hearts, their very souls, would forever bask in the glow of Tally's smile.

Epilogue

"Easy, Red. Fuck yes, baby, there we go, take it all." Red, or Kimberly Madison as she was known to the political elite in Washington D.C., lay back on the walnut table, her hands tied to the straps attached to the sides of it, her legs elevated by Sax as he slowly fed his cock up her tight, well lubricated ass.

Her head thrashed on the hard surface; beads of perspiration dotted her face, her full luscious breasts and peaked nipples. It ran in rivulets down her waist, a small amount pooled in the tiny indention of her belly button and her thighs glistened with it and the added mixture of thick juice that accumulated from her bare, flushed pussy.

Sax had her thighs spread wide, bracing them with his muscular arms as he slowly fucked the petite little redhead while she screamed and bucked against him, begging for release. It was a sight Jared Raddington was certain would be burned in his mind forever.

Long, fiery red curls fell over the side of the table, strands of thick silk that would have caressed her hips but brushed the floor instead. Hair that dared a man to touch, stroke.

"Please, Sax," she screamed as she fought the bonds. "Let me go. I can't come like this. Please."

Dark male flesh glistened with sweat as the hard thrusts increased, the bronzed length of his cock powered up the snug little channel in driving strokes, parting the exquisite curves of her ass and filling her with every inch of his dark, steel-hard erection.

Jared rose from his chair in the secluded corner he had chosen hours ago when he entered The Club. His first night there he wanted to get a feel for the place and the members, but he hadn't expected the shocking scene that had unfolded.

Kimberly had walked in as pretty as you please, ordered a drink and stepped over to the tall dark engineer for Delacourte Electronics. For the first time in the year Jared had known her, she was without makeup, her expression displaying honest, bare emotion, even if it was lust, and the thin veneer of cold haughtiness she presented to the world was gone.

"Harder. Please, Sax, please." She was nearly in tears now, begging for release. She strained against the bonds that held her, her hips writhing against the hard penetration of a thick dick tunneling up her ass in increasing strokes.

Her clit was swollen, peeking desperately above the folds of flesh that protected it, the little knot of nerves red and glistening in hunger.

"What's with her?" Jared finally questioned one of the other members sitting close to him.

"Red?" Lucian Conover's voice softened as he glanced at the scene. "Too much stress usually. She shows up about every three months, usually after the forced physical to prove she's still a virgin, and lets off some steam. She's a good kid."

Kid? She was twenty-four years old and screaming now for release, begging another man to fuck her ass harder, deeper. If it went much deeper she'd be giving the bastard a head job as it came up her throat. She was tiny, barely five four, delicate and as fragile as a fairytale princess. Or so he had thought. No fragile princess could take a cock up her ass like that and beg for more.

"Forced exam?" he finally found his tongue long enough to ask.

Conover grimaced. "That's Senator Madison's daughter. Her mother's will stipulated the she had to be a virgin on her wedding night to collect whatever the hell her inheritance was. Evidently Daddy dearest wants it," he sneered. "He had a judge order the quarterly exams to prove she was still eligible to inherit upon her wedding, whenever that may be. Should she fail the test, the good ole Senator collects it all."

Jared clenched his teeth at the information. He knew Madison was a bastard, but even this was more than he had expected from the man.

"Damn you, Sax," she screamed. "I can't stand this."

"She needs clitoral stimulation," Lucian sighed. "Sax will have to delay it until he gets her to the point that he can get her off easily. The only members here today, besides him, are married." There was a thread of amusement in his voice. "Except you."

Jared stared back at her. She was bucking, begging, as Sax fought his own release.

"What does she need?" he asked then, knowing he was damning himself.

"Not much." Lucian shrugged. "Smack her pussy a little and she'll come like the fourth of July. After that, she'll have a drink, play a few hands of cards and take a room for the night to sleep."

Jared rose slowly to his feet. He would slap that pretty little pussy, for now. But his cock was raging for more. Soon he would fuck it just as hard.

As he crossed the room, Sax looked up; the strain of holding back was clearly reflected on his dark face.

"Help her," he panted. "Fuck, I'm not going to last."

"No. No. Don't stop yet. Please..." Her voice trailed off as Jared rounded the table.

Her eyes widened, her face paled then hard, violent shudders began to wrack her body as she suddenly exploded, Jared's name a keening cry on her lips as Sax suddenly thrust inside her hard and heavy, before pausing, his expression twisting with his own release.

Jared leaned close, one large hand framing her face as she gasped for breath.

"Next dick up your ass will be mine," he swore forcefully. "No more, Kimber, not without me. Never again..."

SACRIFICE

Dedication

And as always, dedicated to my loving husband Tony who has taught me the meaning of true love and acceptance.

Chapter One

"Easy, Red. Fuck yes, baby, there we go, take it all." Red, or Kimberly Madison, lay back on the walnut table, her hands tied to the straps attached to the sides of it, her legs elevated by Sax as he slowly fed his cock up her tight, well-lubricated ass.

Her head thrashed on the hard surface; beads of perspiration dotted her face, her full luscious breasts and peaked nipples. It ran in rivulets down her waist, a small amount pooled in the tiny indention of her bellybutton and her thighs glistened with it and the added mixture of thick juice that accumulated from her bare, flushed pussy.

Sax had her thighs spread wide, bracing them with his muscular arms as he slowly fucked the petite little redhead while she screamed and bucked against him, begging for release. It was a sight Jared Raddington was certain would be burned in his mind forever.

He hadn't expected this when he accepted membership with The Club, and he sure as hell hadn't expected it when he left the Madison estate, furious that Kimberly had left before his arrival. She had been making a habit of it in the past six months, disappearing just before he arrived.

Why he had taken such an overwhelming interest in her, he wasn't certain. She wasn't the type of woman who normally attracted him. She was smaller, barely five four to his six two. She was rounded rather than model slim with full breasts, lush hips and a delightfully rounded little tummy. He could imagine the pale curve of her stomach decorated with a jeweled belly ring, perhaps emeralds to match her beautiful green eyes. And above all else, he could see her in his bed, his dick tunneling up her ass rather than Sax's, his hand spanking the soft curve of her buttocks, her voice screaming his name rather than the other man's.

Long, fiery red curls fell over the side of the table, strands of thick silk that would have caressed her hips but brushed the floor instead. Hair that dared a man to touch, stroke.

"Please, Sax," she screamed as she fought the bonds. "Let me go. I can't come like this. Please."

Dark male flesh glistened with sweat as the hard thrusts increased, the bronzed length of his cock powered up the snug little channel in driving strokes, parting the exquisite curves of her ass and filling her with every inch of his dark, steel-hard erection.

Jared felt every muscle in his body tighten at the primal demand in her voice. She was poised on an agonized peak of need, a peak he wanted to push her over. The sight of another man's cock up her ass, stretching that little entrance, tormenting her with the pleasure/pain of every thrust was driving him crazy. Would she enjoy a ménage with the same brutal hunger?

Jared rose from his chair in the secluded corner he had chosen hours ago when he entered The Club. His first night there he wanted to get a feel for the place and the members, but he hadn't expected the shocking scene that had unfolded.

Kimberly had walked in as pretty as you please, ordered a drink and stepped over to the tall, dark engineer for Delacourte Electronics. For the first time in the year Jared had known her, she was without makeup, her expression displaying honest, bare emotion, even if it was lust, and the thin veneer of cold haughtiness she presented to the world was gone. This wasn't the ice princess he had come to know. This woman was wild, fiery hot, a witchy temptation no man could resist.

"Harder. Please, Sax, please." She was nearly in tears now, begging for release. She strained against the bonds that held her, her hips writhing against the hard penetration of a thick dick tunneling up her ass in increasing strokes.

Her clit was swollen, peeking desperately above the folds of flesh that protected it, the little knot of nerves red and glistening in hunger.

"What's with her?" Jared finally questioned one of the other members sitting close to him.

He thought he knew her, had thought that seducing her into his hungers would take time and finessing. He had been wrong. But he suspected that the woman he was seeing now wasn't the total picture of who and what Kimberly was, either.

"Red?" Lucian Conover's voice softened as he glanced at the scene. There seemed to be an odd note of affection in his voice, distant, sympathetic. "Too much stress usually. She shows up about every three months, usually after the forced physical to prove she's still a virgin, and lets off some steam. She's a good kid."

Kid? She was twenty-four years old and screaming now for release, begging another man to fuck her ass harder, deeper. If it went much deeper, she'd be giving the bastard a head job as it came up her throat. She was tiny, barely five four, delicate and as fragile as a fairytale princess. Or so he had thought. No fragile princess could take a cock up her ass like that and beg for more.

"Forced exam?" he finally found his tongue long enough to ask.

Conover grimaced. "That's Senator Madison's daughter. Her mother's will stipulated that she had to be a virgin on her wedding night to collect whatever the hell her inheritance was. Evidently Daddy dearest wants it," he sneered. "He had a judge order the quarterly exams to prove she was still eligible to inherit upon her wedding, whenever that may be. Should she fail the test, the good ole Senator collects it all."

Jared clenched his teeth at the information. He knew Madison was a bastard, but even this was more than he had expected from the man. The tension in the Madison household was always elevated when Kimberly was there. She had rarely spoken more than a few words in his presence, and was more often than not arriving late and leaving early to whatever function she showed up for. Why his mother had married the bastard he still hadn't figured out. And though he knew about the exams, he hadn't been entirely clear on why.

"Damn you, Sax," she screamed. "I can't stand this."

Jared barely controlled his own flinch. Her voice echoed with a dark hunger that he knew the other man would never quench.

She was being tortured with her own sexuality. He could hear the dark cravings in her voice, the carnality that made his loins tighten with his own hunger.

"She needs clitoral stimulation," Lucian told him, his voice low. "Sax will have to delay it until he gets her to the point that he can get her off easily. The only members here today, besides him, are married." There was a thread of amusement in his voice. "Except you."

The Club wasn't a brothel. It was just as the name implied, an atmosphere where men whose base desires went deeper than most. The married men there had never been known to touch another woman, but the unmarried men were often thirds in occasional ménages with the other men's wives. They were drawn together because of their need to dominate their women's sexuality, to bring them the ultimate release, the ultimate pleasures. It was a men's club, but one created as a support base for those whose desires often crossed the line of acceptable depravity.

It wasn't a swinger's club. The married members of The Club, so far, had no desire for any women other than their wives. Fidelity was one of the cornerstones behind The Club's existence. Just as female pleasure was.

Jared stared back at Kimberly then. She was bucking, begging, as Sax fought his own release.

"What does she need?" he asked then, knowing he was damning himself.

"Not much." Lucian shrugged. "Smack her pussy a little and she'll come like the Fourth of July. After that, she'll have a drink, play a few hands of cards and take a room for the night to sleep."

That might have been what she usually did. Tonight though, her schedule was about to change. He would slap that pretty little pussy, for now. But his cock was raging for more. Soon he would fuck it just as hard.

As he crossed the room, Sax looked up; the strain of holding back was clearly reflected on his dark face.

"Help her," he panted. "Fuck, I'm not going to last."

The other man was panting, so close to his own release that his expression looked pained. Between Kimberly's thighs his dick powered hard and thick inside her. Thankfully, it was condom-sheathed. Jared was honest enough with himself to admit that he didn't want another man's seed inside her body, anywhere. Not yet. Not until he decided who would be the third in the relationship he was determined to build with her.

"No. No. Don't stop yet. Please…" Her voice trailed off as Jared rounded the table.

Her eyes widened, her face paled then hard, violent shudders began to rack her body as she suddenly exploded, Jared's name a keening cry on her lips as Sax suddenly thrust inside her hard and heavy, before pausing, his expression twisting with his own release.

Jared leaned close, one large hand framing her face as she gasped for breath. He could smell the scent of her lust, wild, sweet and subtle, making him long to get closer, to taste every spicy drop of her need. And he would. Soon.

"Next dick up your ass will be mine," he swore forcefully. "No more, Kimber, not without me. Never again…"

Chapter Two

A rare, unknown rage gripped Jared as he released Kimberly from the wrist restraints and pulled her quickly from the table. He managed to stay silent, just barely, by clenching his teeth and jerking her robe from a nearby table.

She was pushing him though. Before he could wrap it around her shoulders, she jerked it from his hands and shrugged it on with deliberate provocation. A slow, teasing move that made him want to growl with the need rising like a hungry beast in his loins.

"Well, well, well, and here I thought the saying 'farmers like it dirty' was just an old wives' tale," she said with cool mockery. "Shame on you, Jared. Just think how disappointed Daddy will be."

He was aware of the silence of the room, the eyes that watched them. Under different circumstances, he really wouldn't have given a damn, but this wasn't sexual. To be honest, he felt like turning her over his knee and paddling her ass in a way that had nothing to do with pleasure, and everything to do with asserting his control over her.

"Considering my daddy helped found this little home away from home, I can't say he would be disappointed," he quipped as her eyes widened in surprise. "But I doubt yours would feel the same."

Her eyes narrowed then, the dark green color sparkling with a surge of anger as he gripped her arm and began to pull her from the room. Reminding her of her father wasn't guaranteed to garner any points in his favor, but at the moment, he didn't give a damn. He had played her game for a year now, and it was time to change the rules, as well as the balance of power.

"I'm not one of your stupid cows," she snarled as she tried to dig her bare heels in and fight his hold on her. "Let me go, dammit!"

"Even my stupid cows know better than to argue with the bull in charge, Kimber." He tightened his fingers around her slender wrist and headed for the stairs. "Keep balking back there and I might show you *why* they know better."

She paused for just a second but seemed to resist a little less until he crossed the threshold to her room and slammed the door behind them. God help him, he was in such a state of arousal it was all he could do to keep from throwing her to the bed and fucking the hell out of her now.

A fucking year she had danced just out of his reach, her teasing green eyes laughing at his attempts to corner her, her pouty lips curving into a smug "dare you" smile every time he warned her that he wasn't going to let her escape him forever.

The smile was gone, the laughter in her eyes was dimmed by the anger, and the freckles across her cheeks and nose were readily apparent beneath the pale flesh of her face.

"You have no right to drag me around like that." She faced him with her hair falling in disarray down her back, the spiral curls tempting his fingers to clench in them, to drag her to him…

Wrong direction, he chastised himself. Thoughts like that would get him zero answers and likely end up hurting his cause right now, more than helping it.

"I took the right," he growled, crossing his arms over his chest to keep from touching her. "Like I should have taken a year ago."

Her upper lip lifted in a silent snarl that had his cock reacting with a fierce throb of hunger. She had kept him so damned hot over the past months that the hard-on was almost constant.

"Oh, get over yourself, Jared." She waved a hand negligently before tightening the belt of her robe with a controlled jerk. "The he-man attitude is long out of style. Didn't you know that?"

He could see the anger trembling through her body though, the glow of it in her eyes. Just as he could see the hard little nipples beneath the silk of their covering and the flush of arousal on her face. She might be pissed, he had no doubt, but she couldn't hide the lust now, either.

"That never goes out of style, Kimber," he reminded her with deceptive gentleness. "Otherwise, sweet little ladies like yourself would have no place to let off all that steam."

He locked the door slowly, watching her carefully as it clicked securely into place. The pulse beat with sudden, renewed speed in the side of her neck, as her pupils dilated just enough to assure him that she wasn't unaffected. She wasn't frightened in the least; he could see that in the sudden, stubborn set of her chin. She was excited though. Her breasts were rising and falling at a faster rate, her face flushing a soft, delicate blush that entranced him.

Damn if she wasn't pretty as hell. Not really beautiful, but damned pretty with her pert little nose, slanted cat's eyes and all that glorious red-gold hair falling around her shoulders. She faced him like a little enraged goddess, certain of her own power and her determination.

"My 'steam' as you call it, is my business," she reminded him with an attempt at her past icy hauteur. "I don't need your interference."

Of course she didn't. From what he had seen downstairs, he was a weakness she was determined to keep to herself. But he had seen the heat, the hunger—hell, the lust that glowed in those brilliant green eyes when he caught her unaware, fighting for her release. He had been the trigger. The hunger had been for him. The need whipping through her body had been for him.

Jared wasn't untutored in either the ways of lust, or of women. He had known since their first meeting a year before that Kimber was different, special. At least to him. She had drawn him as no other woman had, despite her shield of aloof disinterest; he had known something was there. He was certain of it now.

"You needed my interference downstairs," he pointed out as he pushed his hands into his pants pockets.

His palms were itching with the need to touch her, to pull her against him and taste the silky texture of her skin. The desire was raging through his blood, tensing his body and reminding him just how long it had been since he had taken any other woman. The need for this one had surpassed even the interest in taking another.

"You surprised me." She shrugged in an attempt to hide her earlier reaction. "It turned me on. We are after all, family."

She cast him a wicked, mocking look tinged with a bitterness that ate at his soul. He wanted to wrap her in his arms. Wanted to shield her from the pain he could see in her eyes. The sudden urge to protect her, rather than fuck her, was overwhelming.

Jared snorted. "Be damned glad we're not family, Kimber," he warned her. "Because if we were, I'd be breaking more than one damned rule before this night's over."

Something flashed in her eyes then. Regret? Pain? It was so fleeting he couldn't quite pinpoint the cause of it.

"You won't be breaking any rules, Jared." Her voice firmed, the edge of steel that always dared him to see how far he could make her bend, echoing in her voice. "Whatever thrill you got downstairs will be all you get from me."

There was the pain. It was almost hidden, nearly overshadowed by the cold edge of purpose. She wasn't willing to give an inch. Jared smiled with slow, easy confidence. That was okay though, because he had a hell of a lot more than an inch to give to her.

"Oh, I don't think so, Kimber." He advanced on her then, narrowing his eyes as she swallowed tightly and began to back away. "You see, baby, I've waited almost twelve full months to figure out exactly where your weaknesses were and how to use them to my own advantage. I found them tonight, and I'll be damned if I'll let you run from me now."

"Stop, Jared." Something in her voice had him doing just that. He stopped no more than a foot from her, staring down at her silently. Waiting.

"This can't happen," she told him then, trying to cover the regret in her voice with steely demand. "You have to understand that. What you saw downstairs, that's all I want. All I need. Whatever you're offering, I can't accept, I won't accept. You don't have a choice but to let it go. Now."

Jared shook his head as his lips tipped mockingly. He stepped to her, backing her into the wall she had retreated against as his hands framed her face. It amazed him, how small and delicate her catlike face was beneath his hands. His fingers slid into the sides of her hair as he held her still before him, the tips relishing the cool, silken texture.

"There are choices, Kimber," he told her. "And then, there is determination. You may as well stop fighting, because I won't let you go now. My name was on your lips when your body bucked in release. I saw the hunger in your eyes and felt it in the shudders that racked your body. You can't hide from it anymore than I can."

"No." Her hands gripped his wrists as she stared up at him, her eyes no longer filled with anger, pain or regret, only weariness, and the weariness pierced his heart. "I can't, Jared. Even if I wanted to, even if what you say is true, I can't accept it. Because if I do, I lose everything. There is nothing or no one worth the risk I would be taking."

Her father. Jared wanted to curse the man for his unjust treatment of his daughter, for the pain, the anger and that damned weariness. But she was going to have to learn that there was more to dreams, more to needs, than the empty satisfaction she was allowing herself.

"I won't let you go," he told her again.

Before she could respond, he lowered his head, taking her open lips in a kiss that surprised them both. Flames shot through his body at the speed of light, making his muscles draw tight in hunger as his erection threatened to burst the zipper that held it at bay.

And Kimberly wasn't unaffected. After her first surprised gasp, her nails bit into his wrists, but her tongue met his with a speed and hunger that had him throttling a savage growl. His fingers threaded into the long curls of her hair, feeling them twine around his hands as he tipped her head back further and began to drink from the passion erupting through her body.

It was like a narcotic, ambrosia, it was the most sensual, most erotic dance of lips and tongues that he had ever known. They ate each other, both ill-prepared for the sudden fires erupting through the other.

She could spout her denials until hell froze over, but here, she couldn't hide. Beneath his lips she couldn't lie, couldn't refuse the pleasure that burst through their bodies like a firestorm of the senses. And he wouldn't let her if she tried.

Jared forced one hand free of her hair, lowering it to her back and lifting her against him as he pressed her into the wall. Instantly, her knees clasped his hips, a startled cry erupting from her throat as he pressed his cock against the hot, wet pad of her pussy.

"Feel that," he snarled against her lips, staring down at her fiercely. "You're so damned wet you're soaking my slacks. So hot you burn me alive. And you expect me to take no for an answer?"

Shocked, drugged with passion, her eyes widened as he ground his erection against her.

"No." She swallowed tightly, shaking her head in denial despite the flow of heated liquid that damped his pants. "I can't, Jared..."

"Oh, but you will," he assured her darkly. "I'm warning you now, baby. The next dick that slips up that tight little ass will be mine. The next man to touch you, taste you, hold you, will be me. Only me, Kimber. Until you admit to the fever burning us both alive, no other man will touch you."

Her fierce shove against his chest had him stepping back. Reluctantly, he released her, seeing the simmering fury pulsing in her gaze as she faced him now.

"You do not own me." She was fighting to even her breathing, to still the desire pulsing hard and hot inside her, as it was him. "I won't let you dictate to me this way."

"Oh won't you?" he asked her, almost wincing at the dark, rough tone of his voice. "Too late, sweetheart. I know your weakness, and I know your hunger. And Kimber..." he watched her closely now. "I know your secrets. Don't think for a minute I won't use every weapon I can find to have you. That would be a mistake you don't want to make."

She drew in a deep, hard breath, the flush of arousal receding as she realized that now, he most likely knew far more than she had ever wanted him to.

"I'm still a virgin." She drew herself stiffly erect as a little painted smile of mocking triumph curved her lips. But her eyes were dark with pain. "And unless you're into rape, you won't win, Jared. You or Father."

The bitterness in her tone tugged at his heart. He could see the suspicions in her eyes, the fear that he was somehow working to aid her father's triumph. Nothing could be further from the truth.

"Your father can go straight to hell. And no, Kimber, I'm not into rape," he finally said gently. "But I will be into you. Sooner or later, one way or another, that I can promise you.

You can keep your virginity, but I'll be damned if you'll continue to run. Not anymore."

He turned away from her, knowing if he didn't leave now, then he may do something both of them would end up regretting. His control was shakier than he had ever known it to be, his hunger deeper than he could have imagined.

"Jared, this won't work," she warned him again as he opened the bedroom door, pausing in the doorway. "You have to forget what you saw tonight."

He turned back to her, smiling with a bit of mockery himself now.

"Do I, Kimber?" he asked her, his tone musing. "Tell you what, when you can look at me and not let me see the memories in your eyes, then we'll discuss whether or not I can forget. Then we'll discuss just how the hell I'm supposed to fucking let you go."

Because despite the obstacles he suspected he faced in possessing her, Jared had a feeling he would never manage to push her out of his head now. And if he did manage that, how was he supposed to break the threads weaving around his heart?

Chapter Three

"She's going to make me crazy. A year. I've chased the woman for a blasted year and still she's running from me."

Jared pushed his fingers restlessly through his short hair as he paced the length of his mother's kitchen two days later, uncomfortable under the eagle-eyed scrutiny of his too perceptive mother, Carolyn Raddington Madison.

He couldn't get Kimberly out of his head. It was frustrating, aggravating, driving him insane with the liquid heat pulsing through his bloodstream and keeping his cock in a constant state of readiness. But even more was the ache in his arms to hold her. Fuck, he just wanted to hold her close to his heart, to shelter and protect her from the pain he had glimpsed in her shadowed green eyes. He wanted to see laughter there. Wanted to see warmth and passion and naked need, and happiness.

He couldn't sleep for the image of her lying across that table, fighting for her orgasm. And he knew, deep in the darkest hours of the night that it wasn't the orgasm she was reaching for as much as it was a sense of freedom and escape. It was her escape. As extreme as it was, coming to The Club and baring her tempting little ass for a fucking was Kimberly's way of escaping the pressure, hopelessness and needs that had not as much to do with the sexual, as it did with the emotional.

"Really, Jared, as you say, she's been running for a year. What has you so upset over it now?" Carolyn's voice was lightly amused and more than a little curious.

Jared stopped his pacing before turning his head to look at his petite, conservatively dressed mother. Her soft graying brown hair was upswept and held at the back with a silver clasp his father had given her for their tenth anniversary. Around her neck she wore pearls he had bought her for a birthday. She wore a plain wedding band on her left hand; on her right she still wore the simple engagement ring and thicker band she had worn as Judge Victor Raddington's wife.

She was still a beautiful woman, one of the most beautiful Jared had ever known. With her pretty features and dark blue eyes, she wasn't classically beautiful, but there was an air of calm stateliness about her that always comforted him. At least, at most times.

"I'm tired of this," he finally sighed roughly as he turned back to her and paced over to the light oak kitchen table and returned to his seat. "I can't get her out of my head. I can't let her keep running like this."

She was destroying herself. He had seen that much, had glimpsed the bitter rage that filled her the moment before he kissed her. And that kiss. He breathed in deeply, still affected by the sensations that had swept through him. It was wildfire. It was an explosion of the senses, too intense to fight, too deep to ever let go.

"And how do you intend to stop her, Jared?" His mother lifted her coffee cup to her lips, but he saw the grin edging her lips. "Kimberly is a grown woman. You can't force her into a relationship with you. Those days have long since passed, son."

She was amused. Hell, had there ever been a time when she hadn't been amused when he and his father displayed what she called their "male quirkiness"?

He leaned back in his chair, watching her silently for long moments. She was married to Senator Madison, and though she didn't appear deliriously happy, she did appear content. The shadows still lingered from her first husband's death, though. That veil of sadness that he knew would never completely lift.

Her relationship with Victor Raddington had been tempestuous, passionate and, he knew, deeply loving. He had been raised in the shelter of their love, and later, after his adult years, in the unspoken knowledge of the fact their sexuality wasn't what others would consider "normal".

His father had helped found The Club. The secretive membership of highly public figures that had created the group had done so out of a need of privacy and protection. A judge, a governor, a vice president hopeful. Their sexuality would have been a smear on their public images.

"What do you know about this Trust her father's holding over her head, Mother?" He finally asked the question eating at his mind. There had to be an answer to this, though after his meeting a few hours before with Senator Madison, it wasn't looking as though it could be answered in his favor.

Carolyn glanced back at him with some surprise before a glimmer of understanding entered her gaze.

"She told you about it?" she asked curiously.

Jared shook his head. "Not in so many words, but this is Washington, you forget—there are few secrets."

She sighed in acknowledgement. "It was established generations ago. It states that she must marry a man her father approves of and that she must be a virgin to inherit Briar Cliff, the estate that has passed down in her mother's family for generations." She held her hand up when Jared would have protested. "It's entirely legal, Jared, I checked this myself. Her father enforces an exam every three months to ensure that she's fulfilling the terms of the trust. It's all entirely legal and unbreakable. In five years, the conditions of the Trust will become null and void. If there is no female child, or the female child has lost her virginity and not married with the approval of the father, signed and notated before the Trust lawyers, then Briar Cliff reverts completely to the oldest male heir or to the father. If neither father nor surviving male heir is in existence, then and only then, does it revert to the female child unconditionally. Daniel is determined that she will marry a man who can restrain her passions, not someone who will encourage them."

Rage tightened his chest, clenched his jaw as he stared back at her. The bitterness in her gaze, the pain in her voice was beginning to make sense now. He had hoped, hell, prayed that the information he had been given at The Club had been wrong. Though he had suspected it wasn't.

"Why did you marry this..." he bit off the words with a snap of his teeth, "...person?"

A soft smile curved her lips as he covered the more explicit terms he would have used.

"Really, Jared, my marriage to Daniel has nothing to do with his relationship to his daughter. Though I was unaware of the conflicts between them at the time." She shook her head as she wrapped her fingers around her cup, staring into the remains of her coffee pensively. "It pains him, the distance between him and Kimberly, but he does what he feels is right. And the terms of the Trust were not his doing. It was done five generations ago by a strict, straight-laced mother who entirely disapproved of what she called the 'unnatural' desires of the females of her family. She was determined that her ancestors would comport themselves with all respectability, and she made it stick."

Jared breathed in roughly as he began to suspect the obstacles that now stood in the way of possessing the woman his heart seemed attached to.

"If it pained him, he would do something to right the situation, such as allowing her to marry someone she cares for rather than someone he chooses." He restrained the fury burning in his gut. "Are you aware he considers me unacceptable as a husband to his daughter?"

Why he had bothered to approach the Senator that morning he still wasn't certain. He hadn't formally stated an intention to marry Kimberly, but he had been curious as to the qualifications the Senator approved.

Carolyn's lips thinned with carefully controlled anger. The news didn't sit well with her any more than it had with him.

"I understand why he feels that way," she surprised him with her statement. "Wait, Jared." She shook her head when he opened his mouth to argue. "As you said, this is Washington, there are few secrets that aren't told in glistening detail. The rumors of The Club, the Trojans, and their lifestyle have been prevalent in the past year or so. Your name was linked to it no sooner had you joined. Daniel considers The Club and its members, the epitome of what he's determined to save his daughter from."

Jared rubbed his hand over his face wearily. Some people couldn't keep their mouths shut if their lives depended on it. In this case, a bitter divorce and a less than sober ex-wife had broken the secret of the exclusive men's club to a society that soaked up the rumors.

"His daughter's sexuality isn't his business," he growled.

"No more than yours is my business," she pointed out. "Yet, I've fielded questions concerning your membership there for several months."

There was no censure in her voice, only the acceptance he had always known from her.

"I'm sorry." He could only shake his head wearily. "I won't apologize, I knew the risks."

Carolyn sighed deeply. "Tell me, are the rumors concerning Kimberly's membership there exaggerated, or true?"

She picked up her cup as though the question wasn't dropped like a bomb.

Damn! The leak was worse than he had been warned it was. They were going to have to find the person or persons responsible for it.

Jared watched her carefully. Anything between them, he had no doubt, would stay between them, but this was Kimberly's secret to bear, not his.

"You're so like your father," she chuckled then. "I will assume she is, and I will assume that your temper this week is due from learning of it yourself." She leaned forward somberly then, her blue eyes dark and intent. "Jared, that estate means everything to Kimberly. Everything. Her mother's last words were a plea for her to stop the cycle that the women of her family have endured for over five generations. If she loses her virginity, her father gains control of the estate, the house, everything that has been passed down, mother to daughter, for so very long now. In each case, the mother was forced to wed a man chosen by her father, one deemed capable of restraining her passions and her sexuality. The cycle is destroying her and, in many ways, Daniel as well."

"He can break it," Jared pointed out, aware that the anger pulsing inside him colored his voice as well. "He's destroying her."

"He believes he's saving her."

"For God's sake." He came out of his chair in a surge of energy born of the fury pulsing inside him. "When did we return to the Middle Ages, Mother? She's a woman, not a child."

"Jared, you can't fight this," she said softly, regretfully. "I've discussed this with Daniel until I'm blue in the face. He won't relent. It's the only conflict we've had in our marriage in a year now. He believes he's right. He believes Kimberly should marry a man of restrained passions, one capable of controlling what he considers her 'wild inclinations'."

"He's a self-righteous prig," he snapped.

"Why do you care?" she asked him, frowning now as he paced the room. "I understand your desire for her, Jared, but there have been other women you've desired and couldn't have as well. What makes her different?"

"She makes me crazy," he growled, pushing his hands into the pockets of his slacks as he hunched his shoulders against the tension invading them. "She makes me want to throw her over my shoulder like a damned caveman, and at the same time I want to wrap her in cotton and protect her from anything and everyone who could hurt her. I want her happy."

His voice, his body, vibrated with that need, with the complete certainty that he could make her happy.

"And you think marrying her will do that?" she questioned him with a shadow of mockery. "Jared, Daniel will never allow Kimberly to marry a man as sexually intense as you so obviously are. And she'll lose everything she's fought for to this point if she accepts you."

"She's mine." He winced as the words tore from him. "Damn, didn't that sound arrogant enough?" He laughed with an edge of self-mockery.

But he couldn't escape the claim he had just made. As the words came from his lips, the knowledge wrapped around his heart. She was his, even if he couldn't have her. He had seen the pain in her eyes, the sexuality that tormented her, the ache that shadowed her eyes. And so much more. He saw the need to be touched, to be held, to let go and share the passion, the heat that built within her.

"Do you love her, Jared?" his mother asked again, her voice firm now, demanding.

He stared back at her, meeting her gaze with a determination of his own.

Did he love her? He sighed with weary acceptance. Yeah, he loved her, more than he had thought it possible to love a woman.

"More than you know," he finally said, his own need echoing through his body. "More than you could ever know, Mother."

For a moment compassion filled her eyes. She had waited years for him to find the one woman he felt he could spend the rest of his life with, and settle down into a relationship that fulfilled him, as much as her marriage to his father had fulfilled her.

"Then you have a choice to make," she said gently. "All her life Kimberly has been forced to choose, and always it's been a choice that's ripped another wound in her soul. Can you ask her to add your heart and your needs to her burden?"

He stared back at her, restraining the fury erupting inside him. Swallowing tightly, he shook his head with a rough, negative movement. He couldn't force her to make such a choice, and they both knew it. But he didn't know if he could force himself to let her go, either.

Carl Stanton had a lot to pay for. It had been the nasty divorce with his wife that had spurred the first of the rumors. Kia Stanton had wanted out of that marriage, and when Carl had refused, she had let the first rumor free. But Kia was no longer associated with the membership there, so how had the rumors of his and Kimberly's membership leaked out? Even more worrisome though, was the threat that his father's previous association would be revealed as well.

"Does Madison know about Father's connection to The Club?" he asked her then. "Is this causing you problems?"

He would kill the bastard if he had dared to abuse the petite, fragile woman that Jared knew his mother was.

She smiled mirthlessly. "You forget Jared; this is a marriage of convenience. But as far as I know, Daniel hasn't heard any rumors he shouldn't have. But if he did, it would serve him no good. He can't harm me with it. But that isn't the point. What will you do now?"

What else could he do?

"Let her go," he whispered bitterly. "The only thing I can do."

Chapter Four

She could have been a spy, Kimberly thought, but the additional training didn't go hand in hand with enforced chastity. There was always modeling, but Kimberly always thought that doing without pizza and losing that extra fifteen pounds that tormented her would have just been too painful. And being a rich man's mistress was just out of the question; there was only so much shopping one could do before it became rather boring. Besides, just like being a spy, it would require the loss of her virginity. Everything else was just boring, so she joined the Police Academy instead, going from there to several security agencies that specialized in protection.

The work wasn't really abnormally dangerous, and she got to wear a gun. She liked that part. Especially when the assignments required her to be in close proximity to arrogant men with more testosterone than good sense. Those assignments were few and far between thankfully, but occasionally they reared their ugly heads. Then there were those assignments that just sucked. The ones that she knew were going to test her patience and her training. This was one of them.

She stared back at her boss and one of her dearest friends, dumbfounded, restraining her disbelieving laughter. This one was just too bizarre to be real.

"Could you repeat that?" she asked carefully, certain she had to have heard wrong.

Richard Decker's thick gray brows snapped into an instant frown.

"You heard me, Kimberly," he said with careful emphasis. "You will be assigned to Raddington's team, despite the alert that your welfare could be on the line as well. You will stick close to Raddington, and the team will surround you for the duration of time it takes to ascertain if the threat is real or imagined. You'll head out to the Raddington Farm tonight, and you will stay there until this assignment is over."

Kimberly stood stiffly before him, breathing in carefully through her nose as she gritted her teeth with the effort it took to restrain her sarcastic reply. This was a farce if she had ever heard of one. How in the hell had it happened?

"Richard, I don't believe this is a good idea…"

"It isn't your place to make that determination," he said coolly. "The order has come down from the Capitol itself. There is no other option."

Another deep breath. Deep breaths, she reminded herself. She could control the explosion building at the top of her head; all she had to do was breathe. At least, that's what that arrogant, soft-spoken martial arts expert had told her.

"Then I'll resign." It wasn't a threat. It wouldn't be the first time she had resigned from an agency, and she doubted it would be the last.

"You could do that." Decker nodded his head slowly, watching her dispassionately as she stood before him. "You're a big girl, Kimberly, you can do whatever you want to. If you want to keep running. Or, you can face the fact that there will be times you'll have to knuckle down and accept the inevitable. Especially if your father is chosen as the vice presidential hopeful in the next election as is rumored."

So the rumors were true. Just what she needed.

"I don't consider it running…"

"Well I do, dammit," he growled. "I put my ass on the line to hire you, if you remember correctly. I didn't think I was bringing on a damned quitter."

She almost flinched. He didn't raise his voice, but Richard Decker didn't have to, his dark brown eyes could slice you in half when he felt the need.

"It's a trick," she argued, dropping the pretense of subordination as anger fed the resentment that had been building within her for weeks. "It's not his first, it won't be his last," she said as she spoke of the father she had given up on years before.

She shook her head, fighting the need to confide in the only person who had reached out to her in years.

Richard Decker wasn't just her employer; he and his wife had become friends of hers. They had supported her need for independence from her father, and had provided her a quiet, peaceful retreat in their home when she had needed it. Turning him down ate at her soul, but the risks were too great.

"If you walk away from this assignment, then you can kiss your future in security work goodbye. You'll never get another decent agency to hire you. And you know it." He leaned back in his chair, his arms lying comfortably on the sides as he regarded her. "Is that what you want?"

She resisted the urge to clench her fists. "You know it isn't," she said heatedly. "But this is insane, Richard. There's no more a threat to Raddington and myself than there is to you. It's another of his asinine little plots, nothing more."

"And we can't be certain of that," he retorted. "Until we are, you will take this assignment Kimberly, and you will do it to the best of your ability. If for no other reason, than for me. I really don't relish the ass chewing I'll get from my boss if you pull out."

Emotional guilt. She hated that and he knew it. He knew it and he was using it against her anyway.

"That's low," she snarled.

"But effective." He leaned forward once again. "You'll take Matthews, Adams, Lowell and Danford with you. They'll take shifts patrolling the main grounds while you stick close to Raddington. Stay with him. Just until we're certain."

Stay with him, close to him, be in the same house with him. Kimberly wanted to groan miserably at the thought. The past week had been hell already, the arousal that normally taunted her was turning into a torment. She dreamed of Jared, craved his touch, his kiss. The emptiness that echoed between her thighs seemed to echo through her soul now.

He wouldn't take "no" for an answer for long. He would have what she had denied every other man at that club, and she knew it. In the process, he might very well steal her heart. She couldn't afford to let any man touch her heart.

She breathed out wearily. She was tired. Sleep was getting harder and harder to attain and she knew she was going to deal with the exhaustion claiming her soon. Another trip to The Club was out of the question. After the last episode with Jared she had a feeling the relief she had found there would be nonexistent now.

"Fine," she finally muttered, knowing she was making a mistake, feeling it so deep in her soul that it reverberated through her body. "We leave tonight. Anything else?"

Richard's eyes narrowed thoughtfully.

"Is there something you're not telling me, Kimberly?" he finally asked. "Something that could affect this assignment?"

Yeah, she wanted to fuck the client so damned bad that even now, her vagina wept with the hunger of it.

"No," she answered instead. "Other than the suspicion that Senator Madison is playing yet another of his games, I can't think of anything."

"Would Jared go along with it?" She could see the automatic need to protect her in his eyes. Richard and his wife had been lifesavers in the past few years, but as she had told him before, there was nothing anyone could do to save her from her relationship with her father.

"I doubt Jared is involved in any scheme he would hatch up." She finally shook her head at the question. "I don't even think his mother knows all the details. The Senator wouldn't want to ruin his good image." It was all she could do not to sneer in contempt.

"Even I don't know all the details," he grumped. "Does anyone?"

She smiled mockingly. "The Senator and myself, and as far as I'm concerned, that's two too many."

Richard's gaze was compassionate, but it did little to still the demons raging within her.

"I would pull you out of this if I could," he told her softly. "You know I would Kimberly. But it's not my call."

She nodded bleakly. "I know Richard. Don't worry, I won't mess this up. We'll leave tonight."

He nodded slowly. "I'll keep in touch with any new developments. As I said, at this point, the threat is only suspected based on intel coming through Homeland Defense. Your father's a dirty son of a bitch, Kimberly, but he's working wonders in Washington in national defense. That makes him a target, and it makes you and Jared a target. You can't get away from that."

"There are a lot of things I can't seem to get away from," she bit out fiercely. "Doesn't mean I have to like any of it… I'll get ready to leave now, if there's nothing else."

Richard sighed heavily. "No, there's nothing else, Kimberly."

She nodded shortly and turned and left the room. She managed to hide the fine tremble in her body until she reached her jeep, but as her fingers wrapped around the steering wheel, she felt the small shudders that reverberated inside her.

Jared. She stifled a moan as she laid her head against the wheel for long seconds and fought for her composure. For some reason, it seemed fate was out to destroy her. She could be strong away from him, but how the hell was she supposed to hide the hunger that ate at her soul for him, if she was forced into such proximity with him? And why was she suddenly wondering if the fight she was embroiled in with her father was even worth losing out on so much as a minute in Jared's arms?

* * * * *

Jared stood on the back porch of his home staring into the twilight of a Virginia summer evening. He remembered, long ago, watching his father stand here as he debated some problem, staring into the surrounding forest with a frown on his dark brow as though the answers he sought were to be found there.

"The fact of the matter is, it's Kimberly's life in jeopardy, Jared," his mother continued to speak behind him. "I've managed to convince William Lance, the head of the Secret Service, of my plan. He in turn has convinced her father that this is the only course they can take in protecting both of you. I didn't think you would want this left to strangers."

The mist was rising along the mountains now, he noticed distantly. Like gentle wisps of fairy dust, easing along the ground. Soon, they would enshroud the land as night took over, bringing an eerie comfort to the darkness.

"How high is the risk?" he finally asked her, keeping his voice carefully even.

"They aren't certain yet. But you know how these things are. It could be rumor; it could be fact. I didn't think you would want to take the chance with her life, though."

Never. There could be no risk.

"How many are on the team with her?" he asked her quietly.

"Four, though two of them are iffy. I attempted to get them pulled, but when William approached her father with the idea he was vetoed out of hand. Their records aren't as good as I would have preferred."

He nodded slowly. "I have several of the men who were with me in the Forces working here. I'll pull them in to the house and set up safeguards. As for the men on Kimber's team, I'll need their records as well as any intel on them."

"I have everything with me," she said, smiling back at him gently as he turned to face her. "Do you have any idea how much you remind me of your father when you stare off like that?" she asked him fondly. "He solved his most difficult problems here on this porch."

Her voice echoed with the memories.

"He solved most of mine out here, too," he sighed. Damn, he could have used his father's advice now.

Jared rubbed his neck tiredly. He had returned from Texas that morning to find his mother awaiting him with the news that Kimberly's safety could possibly be in danger and the plan she had set in motion to protect her.

"Does Madison know you're behind William's brilliant plan?" he asked her suspiciously. He had a feeling the Senator only knew what Carolyn wanted him to know.

She smiled serenely. "Daniel might not approve of you marrying his daughter, but he's very well informed of your qualifications to protect her." Not exactly an answer, but he knew that tone of voice well. He wasn't going to get any more out of her.

"And how much does Kimberly know?" he asked her.

"That she's to protect you, the team is to protect both of you. It's simply a matter of protecting two birds with one shield so to speak. You are aware of the budget crunch the government is in the middle of, dear. Cost effectiveness is a major consideration."

He snorted at that one.

"When does she arrive?" He needed time to go over the information his mother had brought with her and get his own plans in place.

"She's leaving D.C. this evening. They should arrive here at the farm by morning. Kimberly is less than pleased with the assignment as I understand it, but I'm certain she'll settle in nicely."

Jared cast her suspicious look. "Are you sure there's nothing you're leaving out here, Mother?" Carolyn Raddington was as sharp as a dagger when the need presented itself, and he could clearly glimpse the sharp edges in the cultured, cool tones of her voice.

She watched him with a gleam of laughter in her eyes as her lips curved at the corners in a sedate smile. "I've told you everything I know, Jared," she said soothingly, causing him to wince. Damn, he knew there was something she was holding back now. The only thing he was confident of was that it would be personal information, rather than anything he needed to keep Kimberly safe.

He faced her, resignation filling him now. He had stayed away from Kimberly, just as he had known he should, and now, for some reason, they were being thrown together in such a way that keeping his distance would be impossible.

The need for her was eating him alive. He tasted her kiss on his lips, could smell the sweet scent of her on the air around him. And at night, when he should be sleeping, he was stroking the tormented length of his cock instead, fighting to ease the hunger racking him. He hadn't been back to The Club, even though he had a job to do there. He didn't think he had enough control to restrain himself if he found Kimberly there again.

"Are you staying all night?" he asked her as he opened the kitchen door for her and stood aside.

"Not this time," she said, her voice soothing, compassionate. "I need to get back to D.C. by morning. I have a luncheon I can't miss."

He shook his head. His mother had her fingers in too many organizations and charities for him to keep track of. She was a political dynamo, and he hoped Madison realized the gem he had in her. If Carolyn had her way, she would see the Senator standing in the Presidential wings. He just hoped she knew what the hell she was doing.

He escorted her to the front of the house and out to the limo awaiting her. Kissing her cheek, he saw her into the back of the car and watched as she rode away. She had brought the seeds of his destruction with the information on Kimberly and the threat endangering her. God help them both, he didn't know how the hell he was going to keep his hands off her.

Chapter Five

"Matthews, you and Adams have days, Lowell and Danford can take nights," Kimberly informed the four men as they were escorted by Jared's housekeeper to their individual rooms. The men were downstairs, Kimberly was upstairs. Right next door to Jared.

"Will do, Kimberly." David Matthews nodded his dark head solemnly, his puppy dog eyes smiling back at her. "Lighten up, we shouldn't be here long. Raddington doesn't seem the type to really like company."

Kimberly snorted. Jared had stopped just shy of rude when they drove in that morning.

"What the hell an ex-Special Forces soldier needs us for, I have no idea. He didn't look like he had grown lazy," Tim Adams grumped as he tossed his suitcase on one of the two double beds that filled the large bedroom.

The agents' rooms were connected, two to a room, at the back of the house. The rooms were airy and comfortable, but not exactly homely. Jared evidently wasn't one to encourage overnight guests.

"He'll get used to it." She shrugged as though unconcerned, but it bothered her as well.

Jared was considered one of the best soldiers in the Special Forces when he retired after his father's death. His record was impeccable, his mission successes rated at ninety-nine percent. He could take out all five of the bodyguards sent to protect him, and likely take on a full assassination team with the advanced notice he had been given.

She focused instead on the four men she had been assigned. She was aware that Jared had approached her father in regards to what he considered suitable for a husband for Kimberly. Senator Madison had been extremely derogatory when he relayed that information to her.

As though I would consider him, he had told her, derision thickening his voice. *You need restraint, Kimberly, not a man as deviant as you more than likely are yourself.*

Deviant. He had no idea, she thought in smug satisfaction as she wondered if he had any idea how effectively she had sidestepped the Trust's conditions. Anal sex might not be the most satisfying act, but it eased the fury and the tension that drove her.

But he knew Jared's interest in her now, and she knew how the Senator worked. One of the men with her was sent, not to guard anything, but to report back to the Senator instead.

"Keep your eyes open and keep me updated," she told the four as they watched her now. "I'll get unpacked and meet you back down here for dinner. The housekeeper said it's five sharp, no later. Let's try not to disturb his routine too severely."

She actually preferred to make certain they didn't disturb Jared at all; he hadn't looked pleased with their presence.

Taking a deep breath, she moved down the hall to the back stairs and climbed them quickly to return to her own room. It was on the far side, a small suite with a large queen bed that looked so damned inviting she wanted nothing more than to sink into it. She had spent nearly a week with little sleep and it was making her sluggish. She couldn't afford not to have her wits about her on this job.

She closed the door behind her, locking it automatically as she moved through the small sitting room and into the much larger bedroom. The deep forest green carpet cushioned her feet as she kicked her sneakers off her feet and moved them to the side of the door.

Her suitcase sat on the large rosewood trunk at the bottom of the bed, opened invitingly, her gown lying on the top of her serviceable clothing. Closing the lid to the case, she stared around the room silently. The dark cherry wood furniture made the room seem warmer, comforting. This room was meant to pleasure, to soothe, and it did that far too well.

"Do you like the room?"

Kimberly jumped in surprise as she turned, facing the door on the opposite side of the room that Jared had managed to open without a sound.

Her breath caught at the swift punch of desire that contracted her womb and sent heat spreading through the vulnerable flesh between her thighs. She could feel the thick, warm juice spilling along the folds there, preparing her for him, making her ache all the more.

He looked good enough to eat. Leaning against the doorframe, his muscular arms crossed over his chest, his gaze somber as he watched her. His gray eyes were stormy, the color flowing and ever-changing as tension thickened the air around them.

"It's beautiful." She cleared her throat, hiding her grimace at the thick huskiness of her voice.

She was so weak. She pushed her hands into the pockets of her jeans as she fought the need to touch him, to taste his kiss again. Her heart was racing out of control, the blood pumping furiously through her veins and echoing in the swollen bud of her clit.

Drawing in a deep breath, she swallowed tightly as she watched his eyelids lower sensually. She could see the sexual tension moving through his body. Darkening his eyes, swelling the front of his jeans.

"You know this won't work," he growled the words at her. "You, here, in this house. I couldn't even keep from putting you in the room beside mine, how much longer do you think it will be before I have you in my bed, Kimber?"

Images too hot to escape flashed through her mind. His hard body bare, perfect, muscles gleaming with sweat as he came over her, his powerful thighs moving between hers…

"I didn't want this. Not for you, nor me." She shook her head fiercely, fighting the temptation. And it was a temptation. The need to go to him, to accept him and to forget the vow she had made so long ago.

She remembered his kiss, dark and intoxicating, the sensations whipping through her system as his lips dominated hers, his tongue forging past hers to take possession of her mouth.

"I know you didn't. And I know what we're both risking." He straightened from the doorframe. "It's why I've stayed away from you. It's why I jack off at night instead of kidnapping you and tying you to my bed where I can fuck you at will. It's why I think this is one of the dumbest things I've ever done in my entire life."

He gripped her shoulders, ignoring her gasp as he pulled her against him, his head lowering.

She was caught. Helpless. God, he tasted too good. Too hot and seductive. Her hands gripped his hard waist, her lips opening for him as his tongue pressed past them, a groan vibrating from his chest as she met it with her own.

This wasn't a kiss. It was a possession. It was a hunger, a temptation and an addiction. And she couldn't get enough. She wanted to wrap around him, to lose herself in the pleasure and the heat that was Jared.

"God help us both," he growled as his lips tore free of hers, only to string nipping little kisses across her jaw, along the line of her throat.

His arms were wrapped around her, holding her still as he bent to her, his lips burrowing beneath the opened neckline of her blouse to run his tongue over the smooth, swollen curves of her upper breasts.

Her head fell back, helpless against the pleasure, her muscles unable to hold her neck upright now as streaking delight seared through her.

"Jared." She arched to him, to his touch.

Her nipples ached, throbbed for the touch of his mouth. This was insanity. It was too much temptation, but it was unlike anything else she had known. This wasn't an urge, nor was it an exercise in controlling the fury that sometimes built within her. This was a firestorm taking over her body and her mind. Heat and lightning and a demand that he only fed as his tongue licked over the lace edge of her bra.

"You taste as good as I knew you would," he groaned roughly. "Like sweet honeysuckle and summer heat. God help us both, Kimber, I don't think I can control the need to touch you, to taste you."

She had a week to remember this. A week to regret, to need, to ache for even the simplest, smallest touch.

"Jared." She fought to find her breath, to speak past the clawing, brutal arousal rising in her body.

She couldn't speak further, couldn't make anything more intelligent than a long, drawn out cry of blistering hunger escape her throat as his lips managed to push the cup of her bra aside enough to allow his tongue to rake the hardened point of her breast.

She went on her tiptoes then, her hands holding his head, pressing him closer, harder to her.

"More," she gasped as he licked again. She wanted to feel his lips closing over her, drawing on her, sucking the tight point into his mouth.

"I was going to stay away," he muttered gutturally. "I wasn't going to taste. To touch…"

He lifted her against him, moving her to the bed, laying her back against the comforter as he moved quickly to her side. His lips covered hers again and the storm inside her body fed on the growing hunger of his kiss.

Kimberly was only distantly aware of his fingers at her blouse, tearing the buttons from their holes; his calloused hands were sensually rough, demanding as he pushed the material aside and quickly loosened the catch of her bra.

She couldn't fight them both. She was starved for this. This something that his touch held that no others ever had. As though a stroke of his finger alone was a narcotic to her senses.

"Son of a bitch, I'll go to hell for this for sure." There was no pausing between her lips and her pierced nipples.

Kimberly's back bowed, arching tightly to him as a cry tore from her throat. His lips covered one aching tip as his fingers went to the other. Nimble and hot, his tongue rasped over it as his mouth drew on her, tugging at the little gold ring that pierced the center of the elongated tip.

His fingers plucked at the other. Pulling at the gold ring, sending shards of desperate, fiery heat flowing through her body as her fingers gripped the fabric of his shirt, pulling at it, eager to feel his skin against her.

This was the stuff of her dreams. Jared overtaking her, forcing the pleasure from her body, giving her no time to think, to fear.

"I want to touch you," she moaned, shuddering from the exquisite sensations ripping through her body. "Let me touch you, Jared."

He growled back at her. She didn't know if it was a yes or a no.

"Now." She bucked against him, pulling harder at the shirt.

"Fuck no." His head rose from her reddened nipple as his hands gripped her wrists, jerking them above her head and holding them with one hand as he stared down at her, his gaze dark, sexual. "Don't touch me, Kimber. Not now. Not like this. I'll end up doing something we'll both regret."

Kimberly fought for breath.

"You can have me," she whispered. "Like Sax..."

She couldn't deny him, not any longer. She was too hungry, too wild for his touch. She had thought she could hold herself aloof. Thought she could deny her need and his lusts, but she knew now it wasn't going to happen. This wasn't just a need. It was a craving, an addiction.

He stared down at her, his chest rising and falling as quickly as hers, his face flushed with his arousal, with his lusts. She could see the battle waging in his eyes, the desperate need for anything she would offer, the knowledge it would never be enough.

"It's all I have, Jared," she whispered painfully. "All I can offer." But it wasn't. Not really. She had the heart she was terrified he already held.

His head lowered, his forehead meeting hers as he stared into her eyes.

"Such a pretty little rear you have," he whispered, his voice suggestive, dark with lust. "Do you know how many nights I've dreamed of you, Kimberly? How often I've lain awake hungry for you?"

She licked her lips, weakening desire washing through her body.

"I'm here," she whispered.

His hand rose to her face, his fingers smoothing over her cheek with a touch as soft as a whisper.

"Here you are," he agreed. "And yet you're further away than you ever were."

Kimberly watched in confusion as he loosened her wrists and forced himself from her. And he did force himself. She could see it in every line of his body, in the tight, angry grimace of his mouth.

"What do you mean?" She shook her head, pulling the edges of her shirt together as he rose from the bed and stood staring at her from beside it.

It broke her heart, needing him as she did and knowing she could never have him and keep the vow she had made to herself and to her mother. A vow that was weighing down her soul more and more by the day.

He shook his head shortly. "I have to get the hell out of here before I take something you don't want to give. And that would only hurt both of us."

Before she could speak, he stalked through the connecting doorway, closing the door firmly between them.

"But I do want to give it to you, Jared," she whispered bleakly. "More than you know. More than you will ever know."

Chapter Six

He should have stayed the fuck away from her, just as he had intended. He shouldn't have gone into her room and he sure as hell shouldn't have touched her. But he had. Helpless against the need to taste her, to touch her. She was like a narcotic to his senses, wrapping around him, a siren's call of lust and heat that he was helpless to deny. He craved her.

Jared couldn't remember a time in his life when need had struck him so hard, so imperatively. No other woman had ever affected him this way; no other had ever tested the control he had fought to preserve over the years.

A good woman is worth any sacrifice, son. The memory of his father's words washed over him as he stared into the darkened forest from the back porch. She'll soothe your soul even as she makes you burn inside and out. That kind of woman is worth dying for, but even more, she's worth living for.

He knew his parents hadn't had an easy time of it together. Their relationship had been hampered by her parents, and by Victor Raddington's extreme sexuality.

Jared still remembered coming home that first time when the knowledge hit him. He had been in college, nearly a grown man and had returned home unexpectedly. He had walked in on something that even now, simply because it was his parents, he wished he never had walked in on.

He hunched his shoulders against the uncomfortable memory. But the thought of it was enough that it brought Kimberly to mind. How erotic it would be, holding her, watching as another man touched her, fulfilling all her most sensual fantasies.

She was a highly sexual creature. He had seen that at The Club, and the information he had learned later had only reinforced that impression.

Her requests when it came to sexual conduct with the club members were simple. She didn't want foreplay, she didn't want to be kissed or held; she had only wanted to be fucked. And she had enforced those demands herself. Because they made her weak. They made her want. And Jared knew he made her want those things she could never have more than others.

And now she was here. A part of his home, of his life. He had no choice but to stay close to her, to protect her, and to shield her from the plant Madison had placed within his home to watch Kimberly and to report any sexual misconduct.

He shifted uncomfortably as he leaned against the wide post, wishing he could ease the pressure in his jeans just a bit. His erection was killing him. Walking away from Kimberly was the hardest thing he had ever done in his life, but God help him, he was dying for her.

"You can have me...like Sax..." The words whispered through his mind as his eyes closed in tormented desire.

Like Sax. He could have her anally.

Fury pulsed inside him as he clenched his teeth against the need to have all of her. He wanted everything, and the fact that he couldn't fight the shield placed between them enraged him.

He could fight another man, or any danger that raised its head to threaten her. He could seduce her, if it was only her stubbornness, out-argue her if it was her anger holding them apart. But it was something out of their control. Something that would destroy her if he forced her to choose.

So he had to choose. Because he couldn't bear the pain he saw in her eyes, and the need he felt shuddering through her body. He couldn't still the need to hold her, to show her, if only with his touch, the love he had for her. A love he knew would destroy him eventually, because he couldn't fully have her. Not now. Not ever.

"You're not here to advise me on this one, Dad," he whispered as he stared into the mountains his father so loved.

He missed the man whose advice he had so come to rely on throughout his adult years. His death, five years before, had left a hollow spot in his soul that echoed with regret in times like this.

His father had raised him with solid values, with a sense of family and honor, one he refused to break now. Fact was fact. He couldn't fully possess the woman he loved with every beat of his heart, but he could give her a time without pressure, without demands. A time to hold to their hearts in the long, lonely years that would come.

He lowered his head, his hands gripping his forearms as he crossed them over his chest and nudged at the side of the support post with the toe of his boot. There was nothing else he could do.

"You know, it's not real bright to stand in full view like that when you could possibly have a terrorist or other unknown assailant waiting to pop your ass."

He grinned as Kimberly spoke from the back door, her voice irritated and still shadowed with arousal. He wondered if she knew how that husky little sound made him crazy to fuck her.

He turned, glancing back as she stepped outside, watching him warily.

"Sorry, some days my control is not what I would want it to be," he grunted with an edge of self-mockery. "So much for my Trojan status, huh?"

"The Trojans." She shook her head at the title that had been given to the eight men that Stanton's wife had identified as being part of the exclusive men's club. "I imagine you're more like them than either of us wants to admit to right now.

But it doesn't change the fact that you aren't indestructible. You shouldn't be out in the open like this."

"My neck's not itching. I'm not worried," he told her, wondering at the pleasure that just the sight of her brought him.

He wanted to see her clothed in nothing but moonlight, reaching for him, her body shimmering with moisture, her eyes glazed with need. His hunger for just that rocked him to the very core of his being.

"Oh Lord, another man whose neck itches," she grumped. "I'll tell you the same thing I tell my boss—they make salves for that sort of thing."

A surprised chuckle escaped his lips. She was daring and sharp as hell. He loved that about her. He had missed her blistering little retorts, her teasing laughter. He hadn't realized how much until now.

She moved closer to him, the scent of her, clean and fresh, with just a hint of peaches enveloped him, making him hunger to taste her again. He wanted to spread her legs wide and lick up all the sweet cream her body had to give. To gorge himself on her passion, her cries and her sweet release.

"Come here." He pulled her into his arms, ignoring her slight, indrawn breath at the intimacy of the act.

It was one of her taboos, he knew. No cuddling, no foreplay. Those rules he could and would break.

He was surprised though, when after a second's stiffness, she relaxed against him, her hands settling cautiously at his waist as he rested his cheek against the top of her head. His hands smoothed down her back, fingers working at the muscles there, a smile tipping his lips as they slowly eased.

"I'm sorry," she finally whispered. "I don't want to make this harder for either of us than it already is."

He smiled against her hair. If he got any harder he would burst right out of his jeans.

"Just let me hold you," he finally whispered deeply, responding to the need to feel her against him, the ache to shelter her like a knife through his soul. "Just for a minute, Kimber. Let me hold you."

The night wrapped around them, quiet, soothing. The sound of the frogs in the pasture pond, the hoot of a faraway owl, a whippoorwill in a tree in the backyard. The night enveloped them, hid their fears, their hungers, and for those few precious minutes, brought a measure of peace to them both.

Chapter Seven

He didn't come to her bed that night as she expected. Kimberly lay awake, long into the night, listening for him, her body sensitized, ready, aching for him. She watched the connecting door until her eyes finally closed in exhaustion and sleep claimed her as restless dreams haunted her.

The next morning she sat bleary-eyed and irritable over a cup of coffee, listening to Matthews and Adams as they discussed the reports from the previous day. No sign of intruders, not a whisper of danger. Other than a deer munching the grass in the backyard, there was nothing to report.

"I'll cover the inside today," Matthews said thoughtfully. "Adams will take the outside. I gather you're stuck with Mr. Dark and Gloomy Raddington," he snickered at her.

Kimberly lifted her brow mockingly. "Dark and Gloomy?" she asked him curiously.

"Yeah, he came down earlier for breakfast looking like a thundercloud before retreating to his office. Barely said two words to us."

At least he spoke to them.

She lifted her shoulder as though unconcerned. "Maybe he just doesn't like company."

Tim Adams snorted. "Maybe we're the wrong company. From what I saw last night, he liked you pretty well."

She looked over at him slowly, careful to keep her expression blank.

"Excuse me?" she said carefully, her body tensing at the implied insult in his voice.

He stared back at her, his gaze condemning.

"I saw you on the porch with him last night," he sneered. "Getting a little close and personal weren't you?"

"Getting a little nosy aren't you?" she snapped back.

"I would say too nosy." Jared's voice was dangerously soft as he walked into the room. "Should you have an opinion on how close I am or am not, with my stepsister?" he asked the bodyguard softly as he moved to the table.

Kimberly took one look at him and came to her feet quickly.

"Geez, is there enough testosterone in this room?" she growled irritably. "What the hell is with you guys?" She turned back to Tim Adams. "What I do is none of your damned business. And you," she poked a finger in Jared's chest demandingly, fighting to hold back a shiver as those steel-cold gray eyes turned on her, "are not my keeper. I don't need anyone to defend my honor or whatever the hell you think it is you're doing."

This was just great. She was pretty certain she knew who her father's plant was. Tim Adams was as moralistic as they came. His views on women and what they should or shouldn't do was as rigid as the Senator's.

Jared's expression didn't change. It remained hard as stone and more dangerous for it as his gaze turned back to Adams.

"I'll call your superior myself," he said flatly. "Until then, stay the hell out of my sight, or you'll regret it." He snagged Kimberly's wrist as her eyes widened in surprise. "And you, I need to talk to."

Before she could stop him, he was pulling her along behind him, again. Dammit, she was getting tired of him dragging her along like medieval chattel.

"Jared, has anyone ever told you that you're a pain in the ass?" she snarled as he propelled her into the study and slammed the door behind them.

"Has anyone told you that you'd test the patience of a saint?" he retorted shortly. "You should have let me kill him. I would have enjoyed it."

She rolled her eyes at his bloodthirsty tone.

"He's a moron. If you killed all of them, there wouldn't be any men left to continue the species," she informed him sarcastically. "What the hell is your problem anyway?"

"The bastard was sneaking around my house all night," he snarled. "If I had caught him listening at either of our bedroom doors again I would have killed him."

Surprise widened her eyes as she stared back at him.

"Just what I need," she sighed roughly. "Ignore him. It won't do any good to have him taken off the assignment, because I suspect at least two of them were sent here deliberately to watch me. It's the Senator's favorite sport, having me spied upon."

His lip lifted derisively. "I won't give you my opinion on the Senator," he bit out. "I can't believe my mother married that bastard."

Kimberly had a hard time believing it herself. Carolyn was a warm, caring person, besides being smart as hell. It was one of the most unlikely matches that she had ever seen.

"Is that why you're so pissed this morning?" She moved over to the couch and sat down wearily. Damn, she needed a few more hours sleep, or a pot of coffee to herself.

"I'm not pissed," he informed her rudely. "I'm pure mean mad. I don't like people sneaking around my house listening at doors, Kimberly. I'll take him apart the next time I catch him."

Kimberly sighed at his snarling voice, her fingers smoothing back the stray curls that had fallen from her thick braid.

"Take him apart then." She shrugged negligently. "It's your house, not mine."

He grunted at that, moving to stand over her, staring down at her as his eyes went from cold steel to stormy gray.

"Take your hair down," he ordered softly. "Slowly."

Her breath caught in her throat, her womb clenched with instant arousal. A quick glance to his thighs showed that he wasn't in a bargaining mood. He was fully erect, his cock straining the zipper of his jeans as he watched her.

"What about the ears at the doors?" she asked him breathlessly.

"Let him listen," he snapped. "I'm not going to take your virginity, but I'll be damned if I'll leave that sweet mouth of yours innocent much longer. Tell me, Kimberly, is it true you've never been taken there? Never felt the hunger to have a hard cock straining between your lips, pulsing with the need to fill your mouth?"

Oh God. Her mouth was watering with the need now while her lips were drying with nervous excitement. She licked over them quickly, her breath hitching as his eyes darkened at the movement.

"I haven't." She shook her head, entranced by the shifting color of his eyes.

She never had. Had known no desire for it, until now. Her hand gripped the cushion beneath her, her nails biting into the fabric as the bulge inside his jeans seemed to get larger.

"I won't follow your rules," he growled. "You'll share my bed. I'll touch you, hold you, kiss whenever I damned well please. If you can't handle that, Kimber, then you better get the hell off my farm now. Because I'll be damned if I'll fight the need knowing how hot and hungry you can get."

She lost her breath. Sitting there, staring up at him, fire exploded in her body, washing through her veins and sending the juices spilling from her desperate pussy. She couldn't contain the whimpering moan that whispered past her lips, or the sudden, overwhelming urge to experience every touch, every sensation he had painted on the canvas of her imagination.

"Undo that fucking braid," he growled. "Now."

The braid? She blinked up at him for a second in confusion, her mind so entranced with pictures of them entwined, his arms wrapped around her, his larger body shielding hers, possessing her, that for a moment she wasn't certain what he meant. Then she blinked as it connected, her hands raising, pulling the length of her hair over her shoulder as she pulled at the stretchy band holding the braid in place.

Within minutes her hair was spread out over her shoulders, the long, fiery ringlets falling around her in wild disarray.

"God, that's so pretty," he whispered, his voice thick with longing as she pushed the mass over her shoulder nervously.

"Now, stand up. I want to watch you undress. All the way, Kimberly. Let me see that hot little body I've been dying for."

She could hear the raging hunger in his voice; see the lust glittering in his darkened eyes. She rose slowly to her feet, her hands going to the buttons of her blouse as she fought to stand steady.

He towered over her. She had never noticed that before, not really. How tall and broad he was, how much stronger and heavier. He would cover her like a living blanket; shield her from even her own fears.

"I'm scared," she suddenly whispered, though her fingers never paused as she finished with the buttons. "I've never done this before, Jared."

Not like this. Before, at The Club, she had known the rules, known what was coming. She showed up, undressed and prepared herself in the privacy of her room before donning a robe and heading to the bar area. There, she would order a whisky over ice, down the liquid courage and turn to whichever member awaited her.

There were few preliminaries before she was bent over a table or pulled onto a hard, willing cock. There were no kisses, no foreplay, no breathless anticipation.

His fingers paused as he unbuttoned his own shirt. Stepping closer, his hands framed her face, his gaze holding hers hostage as he whispered a kiss over her lips.

"I'm going to eat you up," he warned her sensually. "There won't be a place on your body that doesn't know my kiss, or a single cell that isn't crying for my touch. There's no reason to be scared, honey. No reason at all. All I'm going to do is love you."

Chapter Eight

She could drown in his kiss. Kimberly whimpered beneath the lustful demand as Jared held her against his half naked body long moments later, his hands roaming over her back and hips as his lips and tongue possessed her with an assurance, an ownership she knew she could never deny.

Her hands buried in the thick, short strands of his hair as she arched closer, trying to feel every inch of him, every hard muscle and strong contour of the fierce male body she was plastered to. She couldn't get close enough, couldn't feel him deep enough inside her skin.

Every breath she took was filled with his scent, with his passion, until she felt consumed by him.

"Good, baby," he groaned roughly as he tore his lips from hers long moments later, his hands pushing her blouse from her shoulders before his lips slid down her neck, finding the creamy, swollen curves of her upper breast as she arched to him. It was heaven and hell. Ecstasy and agony.

"You're killing me," she whimpered, feeling his fingers on the buckle of her belt, releasing it quickly before he attacked the snap and zipper of her jeans.

Within minutes he had everything stripped from her except the damp, violet thong she wore. Her juices spilled from her pussy, wetting the small triangle between her thighs as Jared slid the backs of his fingers over the soft fabric.

"I'm going to make you scream for me," he warned her, his voice husky, deeper, darker than she had ever heard it before. "I'm going to make you burn, Kimber, in more ways than one."

She shuddered in pleasure from his voice alone. The gravelly tone rasped over her nerve endings and made her ache in ways she had never ached before. She had never known this overwhelming compulsion, this craving for another person's touch.

"Jared, it's killing me," she panted with the excess sensation, trembling as his lips teased the tip of her nipple, his breath wafting heatedly over it, his lips barely smoothing it, toyed with her.

"Then you'll surely die before it's over if it's killing you now." She could hear the wisps of amusement lingering at the edges of his passion. "Just relax, Kimber. You don't have anything to worry about here. Nothing to fear. I'll take care of you, baby."

She jerked, crying out as his lips snagged the small gold ring that pierced one of her nipples and tugged. She could feel the pleasure whipping through her body, bolts of it spearing into her womb as her hands fell to his shoulders, her nails piercing the hard muscles there.

"Mmm," he murmured softly. "How responsive you are. Let's see what else you like now."

His tongue curled around the tip as his mouth covered the peak of her swollen breast, sucking it inside the wet heat of his mouth as a strangled plea erupted from her throat.

She couldn't bear this. Her head fell back on her shoulders, her eyes closing helplessly as he moved her back to the couch, laying her full length upon it as he came over her. His mouth never broke its fierce suction; his tongue never paused in its tormenting flicks of ecstasy against the gold ring that pierced her flesh.

He lay over her, his chest bare, his hands stroking the fire that raged through her bloodstream as he caressed her. The calloused warmth of his fingers stroked over her side, her hip, her thigh, growing steadily closer to the agonizing ache between her thighs.

When he cupped her there, Kimberly arched to him, her shattered plea breaking from her throat unbidden.

"Oh God, Jared," she cried out. "Please, I hurt…"

She wanted to cry from the overwhelming pleasure, the hollow, never-ending ache that seemed to grow more intense with each touch.

"Easy, baby." His lips whispered over the shell of her ear. "I'll make the ache go away, Kimberly. Eventually…"

His fingers moved more firmly against the damp mound of her pussy, his hand pressing on her tortured clit and sending brilliant explosions of white-hot heat racing through her bloodstream.

Eventually? At this rate she would dissolve from the electric pleasure before he ever got around to easing it. But she couldn't protest, couldn't deny the intense sensations he was building within her body.

"Damn, your pussy is so hot you're scalding my hand," he growled, his voice tortured with his own arousal now as his lips moved back to her breasts then lower.

Kimberly's breath caught in her throat as she felt his lips travel down her stomach, her abdomen, his tongue licking her flesh, the heat of his lips searing her skin.

"Do you know what I'm going to do, Kimber?" he asked her softly as they came to the band of her silk panties.

She whimpered at the warning tone of his voice.

"I'm going to do what no other man at The Club has dared to do. I'm going to eat your sweet pussy until you're screaming to come. Begging me to ease the ache that's going to consume you."

"I'll do it now," she cried out, certain there was no way she could bear the additional pleasure. "I'm begging now, Jared."

He chuckled against the silk over her clit, causing her to flinch at the sensation. She wouldn't be able to bear it. Already her body was honed to a fever pitch of excitement.

"Then," he continued. "I'm going to turn you over and I'm going to spank that pretty ass until it turns a bright, fiery red, for making me wait so damned long for you."

She shuddered, her womb convulsing as she nearly climaxed from that threat alone.

"You like the thought of that?" he asked her, his voice too gentle, too deep to be anything other than a warning. "I can tell you do, baby. Your panties are so damned wet now they'll be dripping soon."

Her hands tightened in his hair as his fingers slid beneath the elastic band and began to lower the material. Slowly, so slowly, until the silk revealed the swollen, bare folds to his gaze.

He paused then, his body tensing above her as she watched him with drowsy heat.

His face was flushed, his lips swollen and sensual; his eyes were like thunderclouds, swirling with more shades of gray than she thought existed. Then his head lowered.

Suspended on a rack of torturous pleasure, Kimberly could do nothing but shudder violently as his tongue swiped over the cream-slick flesh of her cunt before insinuating itself into the narrow slit and slicing through it with devastating results.

It was humiliating to climax so easily. She should have had enough control to at least know the orgasm was coming. Instead, the height of excitement, the heat of his tongue, and the explosive pleasure undid her.

She arched to him, her cry shattering the silence of the room as everything inside her detonated at the lick. Her clit throbbed, pulsed, her vagina spilling the slick essence of her release.

"I'm sorry," she cried out, shame eating at her even as the storm within her body stole her reason. "Oh God. Jared. I'm sorry."

Her panties were ripped from her thighs and discarded as he moved lower, pressing her legs further apart, his hot breath like a whiplash of sensation against her sensitive pussy.

Kimberly shuddered with the excess of sensation still surging through her, as well as the hunger. She couldn't control the need, the fierce throb of desperation or her own gasping cries. Despite her release, she needed more. So much more.

"Shhh, baby, we're not done yet," he soothed her, his voice tight, a harsh growl that eased her, that assured her that her pleasure had only pushed his arousal higher. "It's okay, Kimberly. Now, I get to build you back up. I'm not done with you by a long shot."

Chapter Nine

She was being tortured. He was a cruel, black-hearted sadist to do the things he did to her.

Lying between her thighs, his mouth worshipped, his tongue alternately soothed and enflamed the swollen folds of her cunt. His tongue pressed inside her vagina, sending her into an orgasm that had her screaming for mercy. She twisted against his hold, fought the hands that anchored her to the couch and begged, pleaded with him to ease the storm riding mercilessly through her body.

When he finally rose from between her thighs, his eyes were black with lust, his face flushed with it. Kimberly shuddered with exhaustion, with her own needs and the blood thundering through her body. How she could even conceive of the need to climax again, she didn't know. But the whipping, pleasure-induced flames that licked over her body assured her that she was more than ready for more. Ready and willing, hungry and eager.

Her breath stopped in her throat as his hands went to the buckle of his belt. She licked her lips, her eyes lowering with the excess passion surging through her body and watched as he slowly unbuckled it. The wide leather fell to the side and his hands were loosening the metal buttons that strained to stay closed over his erection.

"I wish you could see your face," he whispered. "Flushed and damp, your lips swollen and red and so very, very fuckable. It's my turn, Kimber. Are you ready for me?"

His turn. She wanted to whimper at the knowledge of what was coming. Instead, she watched in eager anticipation as he lowered his jeans and the snug boxer briefs, revealing the thick length of his erection to her gaze.

Her womb convulsed in painful arousal as her mouth watered at the sight of the dark flesh. Thick veins pulsed with blood, the flared head glistened with pre-cum, flushed a ruddy red and eager for attention.

"Sit up," he growled. "I want to watch you take me into that sweet mouth of yours, Kimber."

She sat up slowly, her eyes trained on the demanding length of male flesh as it came closer, closer, to her mouth. Within seconds, it was nudging at her lips as a harsh, male groan wrapped around her senses.

Her lips opened, her tongue reaching out to smooth over the glistening head of his cock, tasting the wild, salty essence of him. A low moan came unbidden from her chest as her hands rose, the fingers of one wrapping around the lower portion of the shaft as the other tentatively touched the taut spheres below.

"Sweet Heaven," he groaned, his hands threading through her hair, clenching the strands until small darts of pain began to flicker along her skull. "That's good, baby. So good."

She stared up at him dazed, poised on a pinnacle of arousal she had never known before. Her entire body ached for release, though she had spent the past hour experiencing one orgasm after another. She couldn't seem to come hard enough, long enough though, to still the flames raging through her body. She only became hotter…hungrier.

"God yes," Jared hissed as her mouth opened and she took the head of his cock inside its heat.

She closed her lips over him, her tongue stroking him as her hand moved on the steel-hard flesh. She watched, entranced, as ecstasy consumed his face, his eyes glittering beneath partially closed eyes as he fought to breathe.

Kimberly let her tongue caress and stroke as her lips moved over him. She drew on him, sucking him as deep as she dared, loving the rasp of his breath, the way his fingers tightened in her hair with his pleasure. It was more than just arousing. It was destructive to her senses, to her emotions.

"Damn, you're pretty like that," he rasped, his teeth snapping together as her tongue wriggled against the ultra-soft flesh just beneath the head.

His thighs tightened at the caress, his abdomen flexing with a convulsive shudder.

"That's good," he bit out. "Suck me deeper, baby. Just a bit harder… Hell…yeah…"

His big body seemed to be racked with fine, fierce tremors. She could feel the hard flexing of his cock in her mouth and beneath her hand, see the effort it took to control his need for release, in the taut contours of his stomach.

"Kimberly," his hips were thrusting his erection deeper into her mouth now, sending the flared, flexing head closer to her throat. "Baby, I'm going to come," he warned her hoarsely, both hands pulling at her hair as he obviously fought to keep from sending his cock too deep into her mouth. "Baby, I can't wait. Let me go if you don't want this."

His hands didn't relinquish their grip though. He held her still for the penetration of her mouth, shuttling faster between her lips as his cock seemed to swell against her tongue.

She moaned, a low, reflexive sound, signaling her own need for his release, the desire to taste the passion she could never fully experience.

"Now." He moved faster, fucking past her lips with a desperation that only spurred hers.

She tightened on him, suckling harder, drawing him deeper until a ragged, almost enraged growl tore from his throat a second before his release began spurting inside her mouth. Deep, hard jets of semen pulsed from the head of his cock. His taste was earthy, primitive, addictive.

She fought to swallow each jetting spurt, her moans rising as her hand pumped his flesh, fighting to give him every second of pleasure that he could wring from the experience while tremors of excitement flashed through her own system.

She was shaking, exhausted, yet her body still ached. A hollow, haunting pain that she feared she would never rid herself of now.

Kimberly licked her lips wearily, tasting the essence of him as he knelt before her. His hands framed her face, his gray eyes staring somberly into hers as his thumbs smoothed along her cheekbones, then her swollen lips.

"You're like a narcotic," he whispered. "So powerful, so damned addictive, you make me fear for my sanity."

Warmth exploded through her system. His touch, his look, both were filled with such gentle amusement, and such heated hunger that she didn't know if she should laugh or cry over the fact that they were only making themselves ache further.

"Jared..." Her hands gripped his wrists, feeling the strength there as he leaned forward, caressing her lips gently with his.

"We better get dressed and get out of here before your spy decides to pick the lock." He grinned as he pulled back and moved away from her. "Son of a bitch, if this room wasn't damned near soundproof then I'd have to kill him yet."

She couldn't say anything. Kimberly felt the words locked in her soul, emotions, frightening in their extremity rising within her. She licked her lips, tasting him yet again, and trembled as her vagina rippled in growing demand.

She followed his example though, dressing quickly, ignoring her shaking hands and the tears that locked in her throat. Just as she ignored the growing certainty that her life, from this point forward, would never be the same again.

Chapter Ten

It didn't take Jared long to find his prey. After escorting Kimberly to her bedroom where she swore she was going to take a nap, Jared went hunting.

Knowing that one of the men Kimberly should be able to trust was no more than a Judas sent by her father was more than he could stomach. The Senator was beginning to piss him off in ways that Jared knew wasn't healthy for either of them.

Kimberly should have never been a pawn in whatever fanatical vision her ancestor had. The Trust was bad enough, holding over her head the preservation of an estate that should have rightfully been hers without such extreme conditions. But to know that her father, the man who should have cared more for her happiness and welfare, cared only about the preservation of her chastity, that should be criminal.

Kimberly hadn't been born to restrain the natural sensuality that burned within her body. It was like a flame, white-hot and intense, threatening to burn the man lucky enough to tap into it. As Jared had. His body tightened at the knowledge that he had released a passion inside her that he knew even she had been unaware existed.

His ears still rang with her screams, her pleas for release. The scent of her arousal had been like the dew, fresh and wild, sweet and clean. Her body had been like a flame, undulating beneath his lips and tongue, spilling the sweet essence of her need to his greedy lips. He'd be damned if he'd let her pay for the pleasure she had found in his arms.

He moved silently through the house, his eyes narrowed as he entered the hall in time to see his office door closing silently. Within seconds, he had opened the door, pushing it forcefully into the bastard on the other side before stepping in and grabbing the bodyguard by the back of the neck and shaking him like a recalcitrant pup.

For a bodyguard, the bastard was a simpleton. Jared had seen more experience in street thugs than he saw in the moron he threw away from him.

"Hey... Dammit, what's your problem?" Tim Adams turned on him, his body moving into an attack position before he saw Jared.

Jared smiled in anticipation. He could see the other man's desire to jump, to attack. It quivered in the muscles of his body, glittered in his hazel eyes and flushed his pale face with an unattractive ruddy color.

"Go for it," he said simply, his body relaxed, ready for any move the other man would make. "I dare you."

Adams tensed, then evidently thought before attacking the man he had been sent to guard.

"This is my office," Jared said simply, warningly as the other man stood down. "You don't have any business here."

Adams' lips firmed as his gaze went around the room before pausing at the couch. There was no mistaking the dampness that still lingered on the center cushion, proof of Kimberly's passion and her need.

Jared watched as fury built within the younger man, his body shaking with it.

"Sorry," he finally snapped with no sign of apology. "Wrong turn."

He moved to pass Jared and escape.

"I don't think so, junior." Jared caught Adams in a neck hold that had him gasping for breath, his body tensing in surprise.

"I think you know just how easy it would be for me to snap your neck right now," Jared kept his tone pleasant despite the fury pouring through him. "Someone as well trained as yourself, Adams, should know better than to ever turn your back on your enemy. And trust me, you just made an enemy," he growled at the other man's ear. "Now you listen here, and you listen good. Kimberly is none of your business. Period. And don't think you can report this to the Senator and get away with it. Won't happen, son, I'll hear about it. And when I do, I'll kill you. You understand me?"

Adams choked with fury, the harsh sounds of his anger and his fight to breathe filled the room for long seconds before Jared loosened his hold enough to allow him to take a breath.

"You understand me, Adams?" he repeated the question, keeping his voice soft, deadly.

"He'll find out," Adams gasped. "She won't get away with it."

Jared smiled tightly. "As long as she remains a virgin, she can get away with whatever the hell she wants to, right?" He tightened his hold as Adams struggled vainly for release. "Answer me, boy, before I break your neck now."

"Yes," Adams hissed.

"Exactly." Jared loosed the grip on his neck further. "But whether she does or not, you're not going to be spreading any tales are you, pissant? You want to know why? Because you know who I am. You know what I can do. And you know I will kill you. Don't you, Adams?"

"Yes." Raw helpless rage echoed in the voice.

"Good boy," Jared commended him mockingly. "Now, you make sure you remember this little lesson, because I would sure hate to have to spill blood in my house. My housekeeper gets real testy when she has to clean up the mess. We wouldn't want that, would we?"

Jared released him slowly, watching with narrowed eyes as Adams tore out away from him. The smaller man turned back, his eyes flashing with anger.

"Do you think the Senator doesn't know what she is?" Adams snarled. "Do you think he won't have her checked first thing after this assignment?"

Jared stilled the need to kill the other man. Hiding the body would be a pure pain anyway.

"Won't matter," he finally said, his voice chillingly cold. "She'll be a virgin. He won't win and neither will you. I'll make certain of it. Now get the hell out of my office before I lose my control and show you just how far you're pushing me right now."

He evidently didn't have to give a second warning. Adams shot out of the room, the curse that fell from his lips echoing in the room behind him.

"Get fucked."

Jared sighed wearily. If only…

Chapter Eleven

Kimberly admitted she had little experience with the male of the species. And she had even less experience with this relationship deal that Jared seemed to want. She felt unprepared for him, inadequate in the face of the experience she was beginning to suspect he had.

She had merely played at The Club. A visit every three months, a quick tumble across whatever table was handy and off she would go. There had been no emotional attachment, no sentiment. And she hadn't wanted any, couldn't afford any.

But she was learning that Jared intended to play the game by a whole other set of rules. The truly frightening part was the fact that rather than feeling intimidated or threatened by the intimacies he had warned her were coming, she was instead, excited, nervous, balanced on a laser point of uncertainty and exhilaration that should have been terrifying.

As she stepped from the shower later that evening and toweled off slowly, Kimberly admitted she was in deep trouble where Jared was concerned. But she had known for months now that he represented a danger to the goals she had kept firmly in mind for the past six years.

She had only five years left to go. Remain a virgin for five more years and she would win. She would do what no other woman in her mother's family had been able to in five generations. She would laugh in the face of the edicts that had governed her life since adulthood and in her father's face in particular.

Five more years.

She sighed deeply as she smoothed lotion over her body, paying particular attention to the waxed folds of her cunt and her firm breasts. Her nipples were peaked and hard, her flesh sensitized as she remembered Jared's touch.

A small smile tipped her lips as she shook her head, drawing her hands firmly away from her body and picking up the blow dryer. The unruly mass of long, red gold curls took forever to dry. But she loved the sensuous feeling of it as it slid over her bare back and curled around her shoulders. She felt feminine, desirable. And when Jared's fingers threaded through it, flexing and tugging at the long strands, sending shards of pleasure and intense sensuality erupting along her nerve endings like wildfire, it increased the wanton sensations.

He was a creature of sexuality, of pleasure. A grin tugged her lips at the thought. Jared would understand why it felt good to lay naked in the sun, or to swim nude in the ocean. He might not do it, man that he was, but he would understand her need to do it.

A frown tipped her brow at that thought. Why should she care if he understood? He wouldn't be a part of her life; she couldn't allow him to be a part of her life. Five years could be an eternity if she let her emotions for Jared get out of hand. Or it could slide by without a ripple if she kept her heart free.

She had a feeling though, her heart was already involved.

She flipped off the dryer and laid it carefully on the sink as she closed her eyes, drawing in deep, controlled breaths. Just the thought of him made her more aware of her own body and the satisfaction she was denying it.

She had accepted years ago that she would be tormented by the same desires that her father claimed were demons inside her mother. An intense sexuality, a need to be touched, a need to feel more than just a tame caress from her lover.

She wanted to be spanked. She loved having her ass opened, feeling a cock boring deep inside that forbidden entrance. Having her nipples roughened, her hands restrained. And the thought of experiencing those acts with Jared sent moisture weeping desperately from her vagina.

"Now there's a look that could bring a grown man to his knees."

Kimberly breathed in roughly as she jerked around, staring back at Jared as her blood began to race through her veins, her heart pounding in double-time to the throb in her clit.

"You don't believe in knocking?" she asked him, wondering at the husky pitch of her own voice.

He leaned against the doorframe, crossing his arms over his chest, and watched her intently as she pulled the blue silk robe from the hook beside the sink and shrugged into it.

"It's my house," he excused himself with an amused smirk as she belted the robe.

"Lord of the manor, huh?" she asked him with a smile, her gaze going over his tall body, and feeling the helpless femininity he never failed to inspire in her.

"If I can get by with it." His eyes gleamed with laughter as the sensual curve of his lips deepened.

She shook her head, feeling something inside her loosen and lighten with his laughter.

"You're too arrogant for your own good," she warned him then. "One of these days, someone is going to knock you down a peg or two, Jared."

He grunted at that, a sound of disbelief and superior male self-assurance all in one.

"You can try if you want, baby," he told her, the smug smile firmly in place as his gaze went over her body. "The struggle could get interesting."

Kimberly licked her lips as she fought the nervousness determined to attack her system. Nerves or uncontrolled arousal, at this point she wasn't certain which it was, the only thing she knew for certain was her inability to fight the attraction building between them.

"Think you'll win, do you?" she asked as she approached him slowly, watching his eyes narrow, darken with lust.

"Definitely." His voice was laced with such arrogance she didn't know if she wanted to grit her teeth in irritation or laugh at the subtle challenge she knew he was deliberately laying in front of her.

"And what is it you're playing for?" She stopped directly in front of him, staring up at him, determined to stay as cool and amused as he appeared.

She could feel the subtle undercurrents though, the tension rising between them as her breasts became more sensitive, her nipples harder. She could feel him, his very presence, sinking into her. It was a strange, oddly comforting feeling, and all the more terrifying for it.

His lips tilted self-mockingly as his eyes gleamed with rueful laughter.

"Whatever the hell I can get," he growled as he reached out for her, his expression changing abruptly from amused arousal to hard, driving lust.

Before she could do more than gasp his name, he was pulling her through the connecting door and into his bedroom. She had a quick impression of heavy, dark wood furniture, reflected in the dim light from the bedside table before he picked her up and tossed her on the thick mattress of the bed.

Kimberly came to her knees quickly, her eyes narrowing as she watched him unbutton the dark blue cotton shirt he wore. His deeply tanned fingers worked at the buttons quickly, freeing the cloth before shrugging it from his muscular shoulders.

She had no intentions of fighting him. No desire to delay the promise she could see glittering in his dark gray eyes. Her lips opened then, her tongue peeking out to dampen the curves as his hands went to the belt of his jeans.

"Am I about to be ravished?" she asked him huskily while her heart raced out of control.

His lips quirked in a sideways smile that had melted her heart for a year. Did he know, she wondered, what that smile did to her?

It warmed her heart, heated her arousal and made her feel like the most beautiful woman ever created. A smile she considered hers alone, simply because she had never seen him smile in such a way with anyone else.

"Ravished, ravaged, eaten alive," he growled. "You have no idea, Kimberly, just how eager I am to possess that sweet little tush of yours."

His words shouldn't have sent heat striking forcefully into her womb, but that was exactly what they did.

Then her breath caught in her throat as he loosened his jeans and began to push them from his lean hips, revealing the full extent of his arousal. His cock was fully erect, engorged with his need for her. She watched, entranced, as the fingers of one hand encircled it, stroked slowly as he kicked the jeans away and advanced on the bed.

"Take the robe off." His voice was deep, dark. A forbidden vein of emotion throbbed beneath it, making her throat tighten in response.

Her fingers fumbled at the belt for a second before the loose knot came free, allowing the edges to fall apart until they draped enticingly over the swollen curves of her breasts.

Her nipples ached, burned for relief. The weight of the gold rings that pierced them was more pronounced, an erotic little pain that reminded her of the rasp of his teeth against the sensitive points.

"Take it off," he ordered again, watching her from beneath lowered lids.

"You take it off." She was breathing so harshly she could barely say the words.

That smile. It flashed again, slightly crooked, a bit boyish.

He was having fun. That knowledge was nearly as strong as the arousal. He was having fun with her. Had anyone ever had fun with her? She was sure they must have, but she had never felt the knowledge that they were like she did now.

"A dare." He appeared to approve. "I think I can handle that, Kimber..." He caught her ankles, pulling her to the edge of the bed with a quick movement. "But can you?"

She expected another of the hard, hungry kisses he destroyed her mind with. Expected him to consume her. Instead, he destroyed her.

He rested his forehead against hers, staring into her eyes, allowing her to see the shifting color, the unchecked emotion, the essence of him as his hands moved to her shoulders and began to slowly, gently ease the silk from her.

"Jared..." Chills of pleasure raced over her body, making her shiver at what she saw, at what she felt.

She blinked back tears, and yet didn't understand why they welled in her eyes, why she felt shaken to the very core of her being.

"Your eyes are darkening, baby," he whispered roughly. "I can see the heat rising within you; see the need growing to a fever pitch. Do you know what that does to me? How hard it makes me to know I can turn those pretty green eyes almost black with hunger?"

The silk slid over her hands as she lifted her arms, pooling about her hips as she raised her hands to his face. Her fingers touched his lips. Trembled. They were warm, not moist or slick but like heated velvet against her fingertips.

She whimpered, her lips parting with a soundless cry as his eyes darkened in turn. Stormy. Like the turbulent center of a storm she feared she would never survive.

She shuddered then as his hands moved as well, cupping the swollen weight of her breasts, his fingers rasping over the hard nipples and sending flares of white-hot heat spearing to the depths of her pussy.

She was burning alive. She could feel the blood racing through her veins, boiling with the intensity of sensation building within her. A touch shouldn't do this, she screamed silently. It shouldn't wrap her, not just in pleasure, but in an emotion that terrified her.

"I could touch you forever." His lips moved against her trembling fingers, his breath a caress she felt clear to her soul. "You're like hot silk and satin, as seductive as sin itself, Kimber."

His head lowered then, turning to brush her fingers against his chin, to nudge them aside as he sought her lips in a kiss so soft it was like the caress of fairy wings against hers.

"Touch me, baby," he whispered the heated plea against her lips. "Touch me, Kimber, like we'll never touch again..."

Like he was touching her.

Chapter Twelve

Each touch was another layer of emotion, of pleasure. It was an unspoken vow, a memory Jared knew he would never be free of.

He watched her eyes; the dark green depths were liquid with her rising passion and the heat and hunger filling her body. Her face flushed, her lips becoming fuller as he nipped at them.

"Are you going to tease me to death?" she asked him huskily as he bent to her, his hands smoothing over her shoulders, her back. Had he ever touched anything or anyone as soft as Kimber?

"It would be my pleasure," he growled, restraining his smile at her soft expulsion of laughter.

"That wasn't what I meant," she informed him, her voice breaking on a moan as his fingers tested the lush fullness of her hips. "I've been teased enough, Jared. I need you."

He could hear the hunger that raged through his own body, heating her voice. Yes, she needed, just as he needed, wanted, craved. She was the air he breathed now, the beat of his heart. Letting her go would eventually destroy him.

"Move up." He gripped her hips, easing her further up on the mattress as he spread her out before him. "This is my fantasy," he told her roughly as he drew the strap he had anchored to the center of the headboard to the middle of the bed. "Give me your hands now."

The long leather strap held two Velcro cuffs at the end. It would allow him to turn her to either her back, or lay her on her stomach without worrying about readjusting the position of the restraints.

He watched her eyes go wild with excitement, her nipples tightening further as a whispering moan left her throat.

"Oh yes, you like this don't you, baby." He smiled tightly as he raised her arms and strapped her wrists into the restraints. "I like this too, Kimber. Having you helpless beneath me, unable to fight your needs, or mine. Seeing you go up in flames has to be the most beautiful sight in the world, baby."

And it was. Jared could think of nothing more exciting, more arousing, than Kimberly's lust. He wanted to fuel it, wanted to see how hot, how high he could make her burn.

He watched her tug at the restraints, saw her realization that unlike those at The Club, there was no escape from the ones he used. She strained against them, her body arching as lust began to overwhelm her.

"There you go," he whispered as his hand smoothed between her breasts to the rounded contours of her abdomen. "Go wild for me, Kimber," he encouraged her as his cock strained for relief between his thighs. "You're nice and safe here. No one can see you, no one will take anything you can't give. This is just for you, baby, all for you..."

Her lust was for him, though. He saw the desperation begin to glitter in her eyes as he reached for the items he had laid out on the bedside table earlier. The tub of lubrication gel, the little vibrating butterfly he would attach around her thighs to rest against the swollen protrusion of her clit, the remote that would activate the different levels of stimulation it was programmed for.

"Now, let's spread those pretty little thighs." He forced her legs apart, smiling tightly as she resisted, bucking against him as her hot little moans fueled his own passions.

Jared moved between her thighs, holding them apart with his own as his hands gripped the upper portion, his thumbs within inches of her glistening pussy. The silken folds were unfurling, a soft blush pink thick with the nectar of her passion.

His mouth watered at the sight of the soft, feminine passion fruit. He moved his hands closer, his thumbs pressing back along the outer lips, watching the little slit widen to reveal the rosy, cream-laden interior.

Kimber was twisting beneath him now, her hips arching as she tried to force the aching flesh firmer into his touch.

"Stay still," he growled, raising one hand and allowing it to fall firmly on the pad of her cunt.

"Oh God. Jared..." She cried out his name as her hips bucked higher, flinching from the pleasure rather than the pain.

Perspiration dotted her face, her breasts, her soft little tummy.

"You like that, don't you, Kimber." He tapped at the delicate flesh again, relishing her lusty growl of feminine demand.

His fingers trailed along the slit as he lowered himself along the bed, tucking his cock carefully beneath him as the thick flesh throbbed painfully.

"Spread your thighs wider, Kimber, or I might have to forget about the little treat I'm dying to taste here. I have to be able to get to it, baby," he warned her, keeping his voice rough, with an edge of danger.

She shivered at the sound, but spread her thighs wide, opening the soft folds further. The tiny entrance to her vagina tempted him, causing him to draw in a hissing, hungry breath. He couldn't fill her there with his cock, but he would make certain he fucked her insane with his flickering tongue.

"Lift up." He placed a hand beneath her buttock, enforcing the demand as he dragged a thick cushion from the bottom of the bed.

It was pillow-sized, but firmer, ensuring that her hips remained elevated for what he had in mind. He pushed it beneath her hips, leaving the lower portion of her buttocks without anything to hamper his desires.

His gaze met hers as he lifted the tube of lubrication then and spread the gel along his fingers. She could barely hold her eyes open, the excitement was rising so high. They lay at half-mast as she fought for breath while the storm of pleasure raged inside her body.

"Are you ready for me, baby?" He smiled down at her, feeling emotions he had never thought he would know with another person. The emotions his father had once described that he felt with his mother.

Tenderness, passion, a wild hunger that no other woman would ever be able to sate. He had been born for Kimberly alone. As trite as it sounded, as much as it went against the hard-edged warrior philosophy he had always lived by, still, he knew it to be the truth. He lived to love her.

"Jared..." She screamed his name, causing his cock to spill a silky stream of cum at the excitement that shot through his own body then.

Her voice was hoarse, ragged, the sexual hunger like a living thing inside her as his tongue slid through the narrow channel of her pussy and his fingers tucked against the puckered opening of her anus.

He felt the taut muscles of her ass flexing, drawing at his fingers as he held them against her while his tongue began to lick at the quivering folds of her pussy, drawing the sweet, seductive nectar deep into his senses.

Her clit throbbed against his tongue, her hips bucked against his caresses as her voice became thicker, pleading, drawing him deeper into the sensual spell she cast over his heart and his loins.

She tasted sweet and spicy on his lips, the flood of her juices only spurred his own lusts higher, made him crave more and yet more of the seductive screams that erupted from her throat.

His tongue circled her clit, his lips sucked at it, drawing it into the heat of his mouth and working it with tender, firm motions. He drew her to the very edge of reason, then slowly drew her back, grimacing at her pleading little moans. His fingers slowly, slowly began to finally sink inside the reflexive clasp of her anus, feeling her open for him, the sensitive tissue stretching for first one finger, then another.

Her hips strained against the impalement, pushing them deeper as her hands gripped the short strands of his hair and fought to hold him to the straining bud of her clit.

He growled against her flesh, feeling her flinch with the impending orgasm a second before he went lower. His tongue rimmed the convulsing entrance to her pussy a second before he began to push it slowly inside her.

One gentle thrust, then another, he filled the entrance, pressed against the tightened muscles and felt her unravel beneath him. Her climax exploded through her, sending her sweet cream rushing to his mouth as the tight tissue surrounding his thrusting fingers began to quiver in response. She shook apart, burning like a flame as she erupted in her pleasure.

Jared didn't give her time to ease down from the storm riding her. Before she could pulse in yet another explosion, he was on his knees, his fingers spreading a thick coating of the lubrication over his cock as he lifted her feet to his shoulders, tucked his cock at the rear entrance and began to press forward.

Kimberly was lost in the orgasm that continued to shudder through her as she felt the thick width of Jared's cock begin to press against her anal entrance. Fire shot through the nerve endings there as pleasure and pain converged, swamping her senses and pushing higher despite the release that still shook her body.

She was only barely aware of him donning the condom before he began entering her, but it in no way affected the sensations ripping through her.

Fiery heat filled her anus as the flared head of his cock opened her ass wide and began to push deeper, deeper inside her. She could feel every vein, every thick inch pushing inside her, caressing sensitized tissue, sending electrical shards of sensation ripping through her body to explode in sizzling bursts of hunger deep inside her pussy.

Her hands gripped his wrists where he held her thighs open, her feet resting on his broad shoulders as he stared down at her intently. She could feel the tension gathering in her body, in his body, as slowly, inch by torturous inch he filled her to overflowing.

"God, I'm worse than a kid with his first woman," he panted above her as his cock throbbed imperatively within the tight clasp of her anus.

"Jared." The excruciating pleasure/pain building within her was more than she could bear. As though the excess juices that flowed from her pussy was desensitizing her yet driving her higher, hotter. She needed more to climax now; she needed the sharp, painful sensations to drive over that furthest edge.

"I know, baby," Jared groaned as he lifted the vibrating butterfly from the bed.

With quick, expert movements, he attached the straps to her thighs before positioning the powerful little device over her clit.

"Get ready, baby." He smiled down at her as she watched him with wide, innocent eyes. She had no idea where she was about to fly.

He flexed his hips, dragging his cock back to the entrance of her tight ass before he flipped the vibrator to its highest setting and plunged inside her again. He knew the sharp, electrical pulses that would attack her sensitive bud would send her screaming toward climax as he raided the hot back channel.

It did just as he anticipated. Her entire body stiffened for a second as her anal muscles locked on his thrusting cock. Then her scream rocked his soul as her release tore through her. Over and over she clenched and jerked against him, the rhythmic milking of her ass on his cock destroying his own control until he plunged inside her one last time and spilled his seed into the latex covering he had barely remembered to don.

His chest heaving for breath, his release shuddering through him, Jared collapsed over Kimberly's shuddering body, groaning in regret as he forced himself to ease from the tight clasp and dispose of the latex protection.

Weakly, he released the straps to the butterfly and removed it from her quivering body. The restraints came next. He pushed the strap back and pulled Kimberly gently into his arms. His hands smoothed down her back, soothing the shuddering tremors, the little whimpers she emitted every so often.

"Okay?" he panted as he whispered a kiss over the top of her head.

"...dead..." she muttered. "Shuttup and let me rest in peace."

He chuckled. A rough, exhausted sound that refused to be held at bay.

"Rest, baby," he grunted, jerking the comforter from the foot of the bed and drawing it over them before collapsing against the pillows.

He would get her up for a shower soon. For now, he wanted just this. Kimberly sleeping against him, holding her tight in his arms, the scent of her filling his senses. His eyes closed, his body relaxed against her and followed her quickly into sleep.

Chapter Thirteen

Keeping up with Jared on the farm would have been an impossible task if he hadn't been willing to let her keep up with him. By afternoon, she was dragging with exhaustion and all she had done was follow from one point to another as he oversaw what she was learning was a vast operation.

Was there anything he didn't do?

First thing that morning he was meeting with some poor farmer who was convinced that the sperm of a prize bull Jared owned was worth more money than Kimberly made in a month. She had sat and listened in amazement as a deal was reached, a check was written out, and some misguided fool left with a test tube of cow soldiers for a price that should have been illegal.

"Highway robbery," she accused Jared under her breath as the happy little man left with a broad smile on his face.

"Do you have any idea how much I paid for that bull?" He arched a brow as he stared down at her in amusement. "Trust me, sweetheart, Mr. Cunningham got a good deal, and he knows it."

Kimberly snorted. "I saw a lot of cows on my way here, Jared," she said, fighting to hold back her laughter. "He could have stopped on the way, jacked one off and gone home without losing a fortune. No wonder farms are failing across the nation; you guys don't let the poor critters breed the natural way."

He swatted at her rear, laughing as she jumped out of his way and tossed him a saucy grin in reply.

"Woman, you're a menace," he had growled, catching her to his chest and dropping a quick kiss to her lips. "Come on, I have to check on the horses before we head back to the house for lunch. I have a ton of paperwork waiting on me."

Kimberly was still waiting for lunch. She propped her foot on the lower rail of the corral and watched at he talked to the foreman. His sun-bronzed face was creased into a thoughtful expression, his sensual, slightly fuller lower lips had tightened, the five o'clock shadow had come early to his chin, giving him a dangerous, sexy look. She wanted to drag him back to bed, run her hands over his body, and lick him from head to toe.

She had nearly accomplished that task earlier that morning. Unfortunately, she made it as far as the thick length of his cock and became sidetracked by the power and promise in that hard flesh.

She propped her hands on the upper rail of the fence, rested her chin on them and wondered what the hell she was going to do now. She was falling in love with him. Hell no, she wasn't. She was already in love with him; had been for nearly a year now and had refused to admit to it.

Was it his smile that first invaded her heart? That quirky, crooked little smile that he seemed to have for her alone? Or was it his eyes, a stormy gray one minute, a soft, gentle slate the next? No, it was all of him—his teasing, his gentleness, the many ways he had found to make their meetings special, to give them an air of fun no matter how crazy he made her. There was something about him; as hard and dangerous as she sensed he could be, she could also see the soft, inner core of him.

The buzzing of the cell phone at her waist jerked her quickly out of her thoughts and back to reality. Jerking the little device from its holder at her side she quickly checked the caller display and grimaced in distaste before flipping the receiver up and connecting to the call.

"I'm on assignment," she said coolly. "What do you want?"

There was a moment of silence across the line.

"Typical response." Her father's voice was as righteous and prim as ever. "Are you ever not on assignment, Kimberly?"

"Not if you're calling," she assured him.

"You should be here at home, where I can see you properly protected," he snapped. "I should have known better than to expect you to take a reasonable course of action. Thankfully, Carolyn's son might be a pervert, but he is trained where you're lacking."

Boy, was that the truth. Kimberly grinned at the sensual knowledge, though she knew her father was talking about an entirely different matter.

"Yes, I'm alive. Jared is alive. The bad guys haven't won yet. Anything else?"

There were days she felt a flare of guilt for the animosity she showed the man who should have been her father. His caustic attitude and sniping tone never failed to dissuade her from the feeling though.

She heard the shuffle of papers through the phone line, felt the tension that suddenly invaded it.

"Stay out of his bed, Kimberly." His voice, when he spoke again was hard and icy cold. "I'll never approve a marriage to him and I doubt seriously that a man of Jared's temperament will be willing to wait the required five years. Don't make the mistake of thinking you can play him as easily as you think you can play everyone else."

Why did it still hurt? For a moment, she was amazed at the ever-present slice of pain that struck her chest whenever he revealed his contempt of her.

"Did you receive the doctor's report last week?" she asked him rather than answering his accusation.

"Of course," he snarled. "They are sent directly to me."

"Then I will assume you are aware I am still a virgin," she said sweetly. "Until the reports say otherwise, anything I do and whoever I do it with is none of your concern. Correct?"

The blatant, falsely sweet tone of her voice would have his face turning red, his hazel eyes nearly bulging. She felt a flare of satisfaction at that thought.

"You think this is about no more than the tests?" he raged. "You are as corrupt…"

"Don't say it." She couldn't bear to hear it. Not now. "I'll hang up the second you do. If you don't have anything pertaining to this assignment to say, then I'll hang up so fast you won't know what's hit you."

"He shares his women, Kimberly, shares them with his friends and God knows who else. No daughter of mine will be part of that."

She wished she wasn't his daughter. It would have made things much easier on her.

"When you're ready to be a father, rather than a moral barometer, be sure to let me know."

She disconnected the call slowly as she stared across the corral at Jared. He was staring back at her with a frown, one that didn't ease when she sent him a quick smile. Her father's accusations flitted through her mind, reminding her of who and what Jared was. A member of The Club. A man whose sexuality was so far advanced, so out of any other male's league, that the sheer scope of it sent her pulse racing.

Yes, if he possessed her, he would share her. He would pick a third, just as the other members of The Club did, and he would share her, stroke her every fantasy and give her a freedom to enjoy it that most women could only dream about.

Did it make her love him less? It made her love him more. It made her hurt more, because no matter how she might dream, or how often she assured herself that five years wasn't that long, she knew better. It could be a lifetime.

"Kimber." He stood on the other side of the fence now, watching her worriedly, his brow furrowed into a concerned frown. "Everything okay?"

"Fine." She swallowed tightly as she stemmed the tears and the knowledge of everything she was being denied. "Are you hungry yet? Lunch was an hour ago, Jared. I think I'm starved, it's been hours since breakfast."

She knew by the narrowing of his eyes that she wasn't hiding anything from him. For the first time in her life she was faced with someone she couldn't fool.

"Kimber." He reached across the fence, his hand cupping her cheek and only then did she feel the slight dampness that had fallen from her eyes to her cheeks.

Her smile fell.

She licked her lips, staring up at him regretfully, aware of the rising emotion that began to fill the air.

"I want too much," she finally whispered. "As always, I just want too much."

She turned away from him then and rushed across the barnyard, heading for the house. She couldn't face him any longer. Couldn't face the past, the future without him, or the demands suddenly whipping through her. She couldn't face Jared, or she would never survive the choice she had sworn she would make.

Chapter Fourteen

Jared watched as Kimberly stalked back to the house. He could see the tension in every line of her body, had seen the hopelessness blooming in her gaze. He propped his hands on his hips and shook his head helplessly.

He had learned patience while in the service. Had learned to sit and wait for what he wanted, what he needed. And though waiting on Kimberly went against every possessive instinct he had, he would do it. But that didn't mean he would watch her suffer.

The sexual tension and anger raging inside her was her own worse enemy. Even with her visits to The Club, she hadn't yet learned how to control that intensity and anger, or how to relieve it.

A smile crossed his lips as he pulled his cell phone from his belt and hit the speed dial for The Club.

"Let me talk to Ian," he said quietly when Thom came on the line.

Ian Sinclair was the owner of The Club. The inheritance had merely stroked the fires of the other man's sexuality. He was the perfect third for what Jared had in mind.

"Jared, you're slacking." Ian's voice was rough, a deep lazy rumble that did nothing to disguise the powerful enemy he could become.

Jared snorted. "Not hardly. But we'll talk about that later. I need a favor."

"A favor?" Amusement crept into Ian's voice. "This sounds interesting."

"You have no idea," he sighed. "I need a third."

Silence filled the line then. It was a well-established rule that Ian did not participate as a third. A first perhaps, the dominance the other man possessed rarely allowed him to take a backseat in anything.

"Why?" he finally asked.

Jared explained the situation briefly, keeping his voice level, his driving need banked. But damn if Ian wouldn't be perfect to join him on this adventure into Kimberly's sexuality. He was restrained, perfectly in control, and despite appearances, a compassionate man.

Once again the other man was quiet. Silence stretched between them for long minutes.

"Son of a bitch," he finally muttered. "Remind me to back whoever's running against the Senator in the next election."

"Let's keep politics out of it," Jared sighed. "Mother's backing him so I don't even want to think about losing here."

Ian snarled. There was no other way to describe the curse that sizzled across the lines.

"Anal or oral sex is a very poor second to the real thing, Jared," he sighed.

Jared knew that well. He was walking around with a hard-on that would eventually kill him. No matter how many times he took her ass or her sweet mouth, he knew he would never know real satisfaction until he managed to fuck her hot little pussy.

"It's her only option right now, Ian," he growled.

"So let me get this straight," he sighed. "No vaginal, period. You know, don't you, that we're both going to have a case of blue balls from leaving that pretty little cunt untouched."

Jared grinned. "Yeah, that pretty much describes it. Come on, Ian, you can get your rocks off anytime. This is Kimber we're talking about. She needs this."

She was a member of The Club, and a woman, and that gave her a certain standing with Ian. It meant he had personally selected, invited and approved her. He likely knew more about the situation than even Jared did.

"Why did I know this call was coming?" he finally asked Jared with a thick vein of amusement. "How will you get rid of the bodyguards? The bedroom is the wrong place for this, Jared. If you're going for intensity, you're going to have to add that extra level of danger for her while keeping her in the security of your home. Otherwise, I would suggest bringing her here to The Club."

"No. We'll use the living room here." Jared shook his head at the alternative. "I have a few of the men from my old team here. We'll arrange the particulars, you just be here."

"Blindfold her, it will roughen the edges of her security." Ian's voice deepened further, indicative of his interest and arousal. "I'll be there at ten."

Jared's cock jerked in the confinement of his jeans. Ian had forgotten more about stroking a woman's arousal and submissive instincts than most men would ever consider.

"I'll have everything ready." He smiled slowly, envisioning the evening ahead. "See you at ten."

He disconnected before turning his head to stare back at the house. There was Adams skulking around the house again. Matthews and Danford were watching him with a frown from their positions. That left the fourth man in the house, most likely watching Kimberly.

Bastards. Lowell and Adams were riding his last nerve and if they weren't careful they would find themselves finishing out this assignment locked in the basement. He paused at the thought. That wasn't a bad idea, actually. Matthews and Danford he could trust. The other two were the problem.

Yes, the basement was beginning to look better every minute.

Kimberly could feel the tension growing in her. It was worse than before. Like a bone-chilling craving she couldn't identify and had no hope of fulfilling. Was this how her ancestors felt? Those women who had been restricted from fulfilling the heightened sexuality that tormented her.

A curse they had called it. She poured a cup of fresh coffee as she breathed out roughly, stilling the trembling in her fingers as she carried the cup to the kitchen table. It was worse than a curse.

She stared through the window, watching Jared as he worked around the barns. Lean hipped, muscular. He moved with a grace she had rarely seen in other men, and he mesmerized her.

Why was he different? Why had he been the one to slip under her guard and steal her heart?

She turned away from him, her hands wrapped around the cup as her head lowered, eyes closing.

She wanted so much more now than she had ever dreamed of. Before learning the terms of the Trust, before the betrayal of the exams, she had decided she would never endure the pain her mother had known. Her virginity had been a matter of pride. Her self-respect and her determination to know a life opposite of her mother's had often been all she'd had to hold on to.

After the shock of the examinations she had fought back in the only way she knew how. Smug, triumphant, she had learned she could have her cake and eat it too. She could assuage the lusts that built within her body and still pass the tri-monthly tests her father demanded.

And that had been enough. Until Jared.

"What now?" she whispered, her gaze returning to the window, to the man. "What do I do now?" Because she knew it was no longer enough, and it never would be again. Now, she wanted it all.

Chapter Fifteen

"Kimber." Jared's voice had her breath catching hours later as she walked out of the bathroom, tightening the belt of her robe.

He stood across from her, leaning against the footboard of the bed, his gaze dark, heavy-lidded, his jeans straining at the crotch.

Kimberly stopped in the middle of the room, watching him somberly.

"I'm sorry about earlier," she whispered. "Sometimes I..." She waved her hand, grimacing at her reluctance to explain the turbulent emotions that filled her.

A gentle smile quirked his lips.

"That's okay," he said softly. "I'm not upset, but I do think I'll punish you for it."

She stared back at him in surprise.

"Excuse me?" Her heart began racing in her chest as she interpreted the dark expression that came over his face.

Now he looked dominant, dangerous. A shocking thrill shook her body, making her tremble in awareness.

"The house is empty and will be for the rest of the night," he began to explain, his voice deep, throbbing with arousal. "You'll keep your virginity, Kimberly, but the rest of you belongs to me. Unconditionally. Agreed?"

She swallowed tightly.

"How?" She licked her lips nervously.

He shook his head firmly. "It doesn't matter how. All I need is your agreement. Unconditional surrender, Kimberly.

Can you sacrifice your control for tonight? No matter what happens, no matter what I ask."

She could feel her body responding to the heat in his eyes, the arousal and demand in his voice. Her clit ached unlike anything she had known in the past. She could feel her vagina moistening, spilling her juices along the folds of flesh beyond.

Her breasts were swelling, her nipples becoming hard and sensitized beneath the silk of her robe.

"All control?" she asked weakly.

She had never dared to attempt such a thing before.

"All control, Kimberly." He would demand nothing less.

She fought to breathe normally, but the rising excitement made it impossible. Her breasts were rising and falling harshly, the blood pumping fiercely through her veins.

Kimberly pushed her hands deep into the pockets of her robe, staring back at Jared intently. What did he have in mind? He wouldn't hurt her, he wouldn't breach her virginity. What was left that she would need to surrender her control?

"No explanations, Kimberly." He forestalled her request for just that. "Either you trust me or you don't. There's no in-between."

"I trust you." There was no question of that.

He smiled again, a crooked, tender smile that caused the muscles of her stomach to clench in response.

"Come here." He held out his hand to her, though there was nothing so weak as a request. It was a demand.

She stepped forward slowly, taking his hand, expecting him to pull her into his arms. She was surprised when he stopped her inches from his chest.

"I'm going to blindfold you," he said firmly. "You will leave it on, no matter what. Agreed?"

She had never been blindfolded. She had never been stripped of even the security of her sight. She shuddered at the demand but nodded in compliance.

Jared touched her cheek with the pads of his fingers before leaning close to touch her lips with his.

"I'll blindfold you here, then carry you to another room. Your safe word is sacrifice; by saying it, you'll sacrifice a pleasure, baby, unlike anything you've known yet."

What could he have planned?

Kimberly nodded jerkily, trembling before him as he picked up the black eye mask from the bed and pulled it over her head. It covered her eyes only, the elastic fitting snugly at the back of her head and blocking all light.

"I've never done this, Jared." She reached for him, her hands gripping his forearm desperately as she became lost in a world of darkness.

"I know, baby," he whispered. "Just let go. I'll take care of you."

She stilled at the small, almost hidden vein of emotion in his voice that she caught then. Despite the arousal, the absolute pleasure, underlying the dominant satisfaction was…sadness?

"I'm going to pick you up," he told her a second before he swung her in his arms. "You don't have to do anything yet, Kimber. Just relax."

Relax? She was blind and becoming paranoid. His voice was making her crazy. What was that emotion, that hint of something in his tone that sent a shaft of pain piercing her heart?

She gripped his shoulders as he cradled her against his chest and began to walk. She tried to picture the path in her mind, but the turns he made didn't make sense, unless he was trying to deliberately disorient her.

"Are you going in circles?" She tried to smile, but felt her lips trembling in the attempt.

"Of course." She heard the smile in his voice. "Where would be the fun in it if you knew where you were?"

He was demanding the complete sacrifice of every shred of control she possessed. And she was giving it to him. That was the part she found truly amazing. She had no qualms in giving it to him, to trusting him to care for her, to protect her.

They stopped moving, and after a pause, she felt him stoop to lay her on the thick comfort of a well-padded mattress. She lay still, listening.

She heard the sounds of him undressing as she shifted against whatever bed she lay on. She wanted him naked, wanted him taking her. She could hear him beside her, but she could feel movement on the other side. A depression to the mattress that made no sense.

"Jared?" She swallowed tightly as she called out to him.

"Yeah, baby." He answered from the position beside her, just as she had heard him.

She whimpered as she felt hands at the robe. Confident, self-assured, they began to loosen the belt. And it wasn't Jared.

"Oh God," she whimpered as the strap loosened and the edges of her robe fell to her side.

Calloused, broad hands lifted her, smoothing the material from her as she shuddered in the grip.

"Easy, Kimber." It was Jared who smoothed back her hair from her neck, uncovering her breast to another's gaze.

She was shuddering, trembling from the inside out with reaction. The hands smoothing along her sides were warm, not rough, but firm, demanding. When they covered her breasts a tremulous cry escaped her lips as her womb convulsed in pleasure.

She knew nothing but sensation. Nothing but touch, sound. Her hands fisted in the sheet beneath her as she arched to the touch, Jared's name bursting from her lips in a plea for what, she wasn't certain.

"Damn, you're pretty, Kimber. The most beautiful sight I've seen in my life." Jared's voice was filled with adoration as he came down beside her, his hand cupping her jaw, turning her head to him. "I want to see you burn, baby. Burn for me…"

Male hands spread her thighs as Jared's lips came over hers. She screamed into his kiss as lips, hungry and intent covered the soaked folds of her pussy.

Kimberly could feel her body shaking, shuddering with pleasure as Jared's hand spread through her hair, gripping the strands and pulling erotically as his tongue danced around hers.

His kiss fed her arousal, fed the wild, untamed fire that burned low in her belly, sending her rocketing into a place of sensation that she had never known existed. Whoever fed from her cunt, licking, sucking, his tongue spearing inside her to fuck her with shallow lazy strokes, was a master at what he did. But there was no pleasure greater than Jared's kiss. Then his lips at her breasts, his tongue stroking her nipples, teeth rasping them, tugging at the little gold rings that pierced them.

Below, between her spread thighs, invading male fingers pressed into the narrow channel of her anus, lubricating the tight little hole, stretching her with sensual, slow strokes.

Blind, her other senses now took over, becoming more sensitized, clearer than ever before. She lifted her hips, bearing down on the fucking fingers as she screamed against the pleasure shaking her soul.

"Yes, baby," Jared urged her pleasure higher. "Burn, sweetheart, let me see you burn."

Her nails bit into his scalp as he sucked at her nipples until his hands gripped her wrists and slammed them to the mattress. She was restrained, helpless beneath them and she burned.

"Let me come," she was screaming the demand, arching to the lips sucking erratically at her swollen clit.

No sooner than she thought her peak would be reached than the lips gentled, lessening the pressure and easing the tightened muscles of her womb.

"Not yet, darlin'." The voice was deep, so deep it rasped over her nerves and sent her shuddering in response. "I like to play, Kimberly. For a long time..."

His tongue swiped through her exposed slit before playing demonically with the little ring that circled her clit. At the same time, Jared pulled at the rings on her nipples. One with his mouth, the other with his tormenting fingers, sending her shrieking with an agony of exquisite pleasure/pain.

She was burning just as he wanted. Burning alive with the need to orgasm, and very well aware of the fact that she would be denied until the men holding her captive deemed the time appropriate.

Despite the evenings she had spent at The Club, she had never been without her control. Her choice. It had never been like this.

"Jared." She strained against his hold on her wrists, terrified as emotions and sensation swamped her.

Her head tossed on the mattress as the fingers tormenting her rear sank deeper, sending flames shooting from her anus to her clit. The two digits scissored inside her, stretching her further.

"I'm here, baby," he soothed her, despite the roughness of his voice as his lips moved to caress her neck, the shell of her ear. "I'm right here."

"Hold onto her," the voice at her cunt warned him then. "I'm going to give her more here. Let's see how hot she can burn."

"Come here, Kimber..." They lifted her, positioning her to her knees though the fingers invading her ass stayed in place.

She knelt on the mattress, following Jared's whispered instructions to lower her shoulders to the bed.

"Anal sex can bring you complete satisfaction, Kimber," he whispered deeply as she felt her buttocks being parted as another finger began to push its way inside her. "If you know how to take it, which you do. If the person giving it knows how, which he does. It can take you places you can never go any other way."

Her back arched as the fingers stretched her further. She was in agony. Pleasure and pain rocked her body as she strained backward, desperate for more.

A second later she screamed in outrage as a hand landed firmly on her buttock. She stilled, thinking it would ease. Believing the swat was for her desperate movements to push his fingers deeper. But it came again, on the other side.

"Bastard," she screeched, intending to jerk away, to push aside the blindfold and face her tormentor.

"Bad Kimber," Jared chuckled when her hand moved to the blindfold. He caught her wrists, holding them before her as he lay beside her now. "Haven't you ever been spanked, baby? Feel it Kimber. Relax with the heat, let it heighten the pleasure. You love the pain, you know you do. It's just another form of it."

The hand landed again, and despite her need to deny it, the pleasure rode a hard edge on the stinging burn. As though in reward, Jared's hand moved beneath her, tucking between her thighs, the palm of his hand exerting a firm, sensual pressure against her clit as he lifted her to lay against his chest.

The hand struck again, and this time the fingers stretching the entrance to her ass moved deeper.

"Oh God…Jared… I can't stand it…" The hand landed again, causing her to tighten on the fingers invading her and making white-hot spears of sensation rip through her pussy.

"More, Kimber…" His voice was rougher now, demanding. "You can take more, baby, you know you can."

Another series of burning slaps were followed by a smooth, even thrust of the fingers into her ass as Jared tugged at the ring piercing the hood of her clit. She was shaking violently, shuddering with the pleasure and intensity as she bucked into each thrust.

"Now, baby..." She was lifted from his chest and propped on hands and knees as he moved before her. "Open wide, Kimber. I want your mouth so damned bad I'm about to come just thinking about it."

She felt Jared's cock press against her lips and opened to him as she moaned in regret for the fingers slowly exiting her rear.

Her mouth was filled with the hot male flesh she loved so dearly. Jared, his cock throbbing against her tongue, his thumbs pressing at the hinge of her jaw as she felt her buttocks being parted again.

She stilled, whimpered.

A second later reality exploded in a kaleidoscope of brilliant bright pleasure/pain as she was invaded. Not by fingers, but a cock that tunneled inside her with one sure, quick thrust that destroyed her.

She lost reason. Madness consumed her. Her lips tightened on Jared's thrusting flesh as her rear burned in ecstasy. She was taken, impaled, possessed in a way she could have never imagined. She could feel every hard inch buried between her buttocks, taste the potent passion in the cock thrusting between her lips. She was possessed, taken, sacrificed to such pleasure that she was certain she would never survive.

She could feel the flames washing over her as the hard body behind her covered her. His hand went between her thighs, his hard fingers moving on her clit a second before he delivered a series of hard, rapid little slaps that pushed her over a precipice she had never known existed.

She exploded, only dimly aware of Jared's semen jetting hot and hard down her throat, and the flex and throb of the cock in her ass releasing as well. All she knew, all she could process was the pleasure burning her, rocking her...destroying her.

She fell to her side, curling into a tight ball as her muscles shuddered and her pussy began to flex in protest. And she knew, despite the agonizing ecstasy that still echoed through her, that never again would the driving pleasure mixed with pain ease the terrible ache in her body. It had only triggered a hunger for more. A hunger she knew only one man would ever ease…

Chapter Sixteen

Jared stood inside the shower, feeling the spray pounding on his back as he leaned his forehead against the tile wall. His eyes were closed, every muscle tight with the effort to control the raging demand that pounded through his body and his mind.

She was his, goddammit. The fierce demand raged through his mind. His heart. His fucking soul and he was wasting away beneath the force of the water rather than laying in satisfied exhaustion in her arms.

The ménage with Ian should have stilled part of the hunger, but it only made it worse. It wasn't enough. Nothing he knew now would ever truly be enough until he took her as he was meant to.

His cock was like living stone, near to bursting with the raging of his emotions. He could taste her on his tongue, feel her on his skin. He could still hear her ragged cry as she convulsed beneath him. Did she even realize what she had cried? Could she know the effect her words had on him?

"…not enough…oh God, Jared, it's not enough…" The words had been a ragged, nearly incoherent cry as she shuddered through her earlier orgasm.

No, it hadn't been enough. It would never be enough.

Would he live another five fucking years before he could claim her? He grit his teeth at the thought of it. It would be a hell he could have never imagined before now. Hell yes, he would wait. But it would fucking kill him.

"Jared?" Her voice was a whisper of hunger, of the needs that raged within him as well.

He opened his eyes, ignoring the water that poured over him as his turned to meet her gaze.

Her green eyes were dark with pain, with goodbye. Fuck. Not yet. He wasn't ready yet.

"The Agency just called." His heart clenched at the sound of her voice, at the misery in it. "The threat has been deemed a prank. I've been called back first thing in the morning."

She had put her robe back on, had belted it tightly around her waist and pushed her hands deep into the little pockets at the side. Her hands were clenched, her fingers bunched together to restrain the pain he saw reflected in her gaze.

"Fuck." What now? Damn them, he wasn't ready to let her go, wasn't prepared to do without her warmth in his bed. Son of a bitch, he had just managed to get her into it.

"Jared..." He watched her swallow convulsively; saw the regret that filled her eyes, and the tears.

"No!" he growled.

Straightening abruptly he jerked her into the shower, ignoring her gasp, pushing aside the knowledge that no matter how hard he wanted, how much he loved, that it was time for her to go.

"I'll always be here." His arms wrapped around her, pulled her against his chest as he maneuvered his body to protect her from the full force of the water. "Always Kimber. I'll be right here, baby, anytime you need me. Anyway you want me. I'll be here."

Her arms tightened around his shoulders, holding fiercely to him as he felt the heat of her tears against his chest. God surely hadn't meant for a man to have to endure this sorrow? He prayed for mercy, because he couldn't cry with her.

* * * * *

Leaving the farm was the hardest thing Kimberly had ever done in her life. She didn't think she would have the strength to do it. Not after the past night. Not after the realizations she had come to herself.

But she did it. She threw her suitcase into the SUV where Matthews sat waiting on her. The others had left hours before, eager to get back to the offices, file their reports and head into more adventurous assignments. Kimberly hadn't been able to tear herself away as easily.

Jared stood behind her silently. He had watched her pack, his expression worn, his gaze turbulent. But he hadn't made any demands, hadn't asked for any promises, he was simply letting her go. Reluctantly, she could tell, but he was letting her go.

She turned back to him as she closed the rear door, staring up at him, realizing that the pain in her chest was more than just regret. It was a hollow, gaping wound she feared would never ease.

"Remember to let Mother know when you're back in town," he told her softly. "She worries, even if she never says anything."

Kimberly nodded, smiling though her heart was breaking. "First thing," she agreed.

"And don't drive too fast," he growled. "Matthews told me you scared the hell out of him on the way up here. The man has a family to feed you know. Stop risking his life."

She would have laughed if it hadn't hurt so damned bad.

"And remember, you always have a place to stay here," he finished. "Anytime, Kimber. All the time."

She wanted to weep at the softness of his voice.

"Jared..." There was so much she wanted to say.

"No." He shook his head regretfully, reaching out to touch her cheek with a caress so light, so tender she felt it rock her soul. "Just remember that, baby. You know where I'm at if you need me. Always."

She had to look away from him or she would never hold back her tears. How was she walking away from him? She could feel everything inside her screaming out in rage that she would do so.

"Go," he said then. "You'll be late getting back if you don't leave soon."

Her lips trembled as she turned back to him. She blinked fiercely to hold back her tears, fighting her head and her heart as she stared up at him.

She loved him. She could feel the emotion exploding within her, violently protesting the decision to leave, to stand firm to the vow she had made so long ago.

"I want..." He cut her words off, laying his fingers against her lips as he flinched slightly.

"Don't, Kimber," he whispered. "Don't make letting you go impossible for me to do. Or for you to do. There's always tomorrow. We aren't saying goodbye, remember?"

She licked her lips, feeling her soul shatter. God help her. He loved her. She could see it in his eyes, in that crooked, pain-filled smile that was hers alone. It was hers alone because he loved her.

She was barely aware of the whimper that left her throat but there was no mistaking the strength, the need in his body as he jerked her against him, holding her tight to his chest, sheltering her with his big body as one hand held her head to him.

"Listen to me," he growled fiercely. "You don't have to say anything, Kimber. You don't have to do anything. Come back when you need to. Know I'll be here. That's all. Damn you, this isn't forever. I won't let it be."

He pulled her head back, his fingers tangling in her hair, destroying the perfection of the intricate braid she had painstakingly worked the strands into. But she didn't care. He was holding her, his lips were on hers, his tongue taking possession of her mouth, wiping away the destructive agony piercing her soul. It wasn't goodbye. Not yet.

One hand gripped her hip, rocking her against his erection as his mouth ate at hers, his groan vibrating against her lips as the hunger that raged between them began to gnaw at her resolve.

"Damn, you're going to send me up in flames right here in my driveway, woman. Is that any example for me to set for my work hands?" He dragged his lips from hers, a weary, entirely false spurt of laughter leaving his lips as he stared down at her. "I'm too old for this, baby. Now get out of here, so I can get some work done."

He stepped back from her, ripping her heart from her chest when he did so.

"Go on," his voice softened as he nodded at the jeep. "I'll see you soon."

She backed away. She couldn't turn away from him.

"Soon?" She heard the desperate plea in her own voice.

"Very soon, baby," he promised. "Anytime you need me."

"What about when you need me?" she wondered aloud.

His expression flinched. A subtle expression of pain that had her stilling the cry in her throat.

"I'll always need you, Kimber," he said softly, roughly. "Always."

* * * * *

She had turned away from him. Walked away. With every step she felt the regret grow, felt the knowledge weighing on her soul. She was making the same choice five generations of women before her had made. She was choosing the past over the future.

The further she drove away from him, the more that knowledge was driven home. In the space of a year, he had steadily weakened her resolve, shown her laughter, patience, and a hunger she hadn't known could exist. He had filled her dreams, waking and asleep, and he had reshaped her views of herself.

"What now?" she asked aloud, unwilling to hold back the pain, unable to bear the separation in silence.

"Only you can answer that one, Kimberly." Matthews reminded her that she wasn't alone, and that the rest of the world wasn't blind. "He's a good man. I hope you know that."

She glanced over at him, seeing the compassion and sympathy in his eyes.

"He's the best," she said slowly, her gaze returning to the road as her fingers clenched on the steering wheel.

"My daddy always said anything worth having was worth waiting on," he finally said philosophically. "Guess you'll have to find that one out for yourself though, huh?"

Jared was worth waiting on, but for what reason? She shook her head as she watched the road, counting the miles as they separated her from the farm and the man awaiting her there. He was worth waiting on. But was she?

Chapter Seventeen

Briar Cliff. A week later, Kimberly turned into the long driveway that led to the stately Pennsylvania estate. Huge oaks lined the paved road, casting a dappled pattern of sunlight and shade over the dark path. She had once found it comforting, the sheltering limbs as they spread over the road, embracing each arrival. Now, she found it oppressive, restraining.

Pulling into the long circular driveway, Kimberly drew in a deep breath as she attempted to control the emotions overwhelming her. She hadn't returned to the home she had been raised in, since her mother's death. The conditions of the Trust would have allowed her to live there; her father would have preferred it because he could not continue residence there without her. Which had been one of the main reasons she had refused to stay.

It hurt, remembering the past. For years she had tried to block the memories, to keep from reliving the pain and fear she had known as a child. To keep from remembering her mother, so frail and fragile, huddled in a corner, her arms wrapped around her body as tears streamed down her face.

She shook her head. She wasn't here to remember, yet somehow she knew that was inescapable.

Opening the door to her beat-up sedan, she stepped outside and stared around the grounds with a sense of déjà vu. She could hear her childish laughter, her mother's voice calling out to her, filled with amusement and…love?

Kimmie, you know your father won't like you climbing that tree. Was it laughter? Her chest tightened with the remembrance of the smug undertones of her mother's voice. It had been like a dare. And Kimberly had accepted it as such.

My sweet Kimmie, don't worry, baby, we won't let mean ole daddy ruin our fun will we, baby…

That hadn't been love in her voice, it had been satisfaction.

She shook her head fiercely. Was this why she had never returned? Why each time she had planned to come back to Briar Cliff something inside her had made her change her mind, there had always been something more important to do.

She pushed her hand into her jeans pocket and pulled out the single key she carried there. It would open the doors to Briar Cliff, and the memories she had fought to hold back for longer than she had realized herself.

The wide, oak, double door opened smoothly. There wasn't a squeak or a hesitation as they swung on their well-oiled hinges.

Kimmie, this is all yours. Yours and your daughter's and your daughter's daughter's. Don't let him ever take it, Kimmie. Not ever…

She had been six, standing in the foyer after yet another of her father's furious exits. Her mother had been in tears, her shoulders heaving with her sobs, her green eyes shadowed with misery.

She stood in the same marble foyer, staring around her, seeing the past rather than the gleaming oak and teak wood trim, or the centuries old antique hall tables and cushioned chairs, or the priceless crystal decorations.

Over two centuries of dedication to the stately home had made Briar Cliff a resource unto itself. It was quite simply, as a whole, priceless. The trust set up six generations before had ensured that there would be no sales, no chance of mortgages, or of loss. It had grown only more valuable over the generations.

But the antiques and delicate wood carved borders were only glanced over. Kimberly had never seen Briar Cliff as a heritage, it had been her home. But now she saw it, felt it as something more. It wasn't a home. It wasn't a heritage. It had been a curse.

She moved slowly through the house, room by room, the voices of a past she hadn't wanted to remember washing over her.

God damn you, you stupid whore. All I asked you to do was play hostess, not the slut…

You fucking bitch, he's gone… Do you hear me? He left. Took the money your father gave him and ran. Are you so fucking lame you can't even remember he didn't want you…

Kimberly wanted to cover her ears, but there was no blocking the memories.

Her mother's tears, her screams for mercy, and her father's voice, rough-edged and filled with fury as he stood over her mother's cowering body.

Whose do you want her to be?

Kimberly shuddered. How could she have forgotten that? She had been seven, hiding outside the drawing room, trembling in fear, terrified her father would actually hurt her mother.

She remembered her mother's voice, slurred drunkenly, smug and amused.

Her mother hadn't been crying. Kimberly stood outside the drawing room now, staring into the shadowed room, and seeing the ghosts of what had been.

Damn you, you lying bitch, I wouldn't believe you either way, he had screamed. She's your daughter. Yours. And likely just as depraved and perverted as you ever were…

What had her mother done?

She moved slowly through the house, room by room. The drawing room, the family room, the dining room. In each area she relived the fights, the screaming matches, her mother's tears, her mother's smug vindictive words laced with her bitter sobs.

He loved me… At least he loved me…

For God's sake, the bastard took your father's money and left. Are you so insane you've forgotten that… He didn't love you, bitch, he used you…

I could have loved you…

I never wanted your love, whore… But her father's voice had been bitter, furious…hurt.

Her bedroom. Her refuge. The one room her father had never stepped foot in. Her bed was still there. The wide, white-canopied confection of lace. It was a room made for a princess.

Remember, Kimmie, you'll be free… Be free for both of us, Kimmie…

Each night her mother had whispered those words to her until her teen years, until her father had put a stop to it. He had sent Kimberly away to school. An exclusive girls' school that had effectively placed a distance between her and the mother who had nurtured her. Who had nurtured a hatred for the father.

Why had she not remembered that?

She moved from her room, down the long hall, and to the room her mother had taken her last breath.

I was wrong… So many things…her mother had wheezed that last day. Don't make my mistakes, Kimmie, swear to me, you won't make my mistakes… I wanted you free, Kimmie… I wanted you free…

Free of what? Free of her father or free of Briar Cliff?

Each room she visited was more of the same. An unending collage of memories flooding her mind, her heart.

In the library, the walls were lined with the portraits of all those who had their time to possess Briar Cliff. From the first, Horace and Catherine St. Montrose. The first Briar Cliff family.

It was said Catherine had been a creature of sexuality, a woman as comfortable with her body and her female desires as she was with the wealth she had inherited from her father, a Lord of the English realm. She and her husband had built Briar Cliff.

Her oldest daughter, Elizabeth St. Montrose Michaels and her husband, Hugh, wore the same happy, contented expressions of the first two. The portraits ranged around the room, a gleam of laughter, of satisfaction in the eyes of those inhabitants until she reached Tabitha Elizabeth Montageau and her husband, Diego Santiago. There was bitterness there, in Tabitha's deep brown eyes, in the pinched contours of her lips. There was a sadness in her face only emphasized by the self-righteous arrogance of her husband.

It had been Tabitha who had established the Trust. Who had broken with willing the entire estate to the first-born daughter and set the restrictive and soul-destroying provisions on the inheritance. It was she, most likely at the direction of her husband, who decided that the desires the women of her line possessed were depraved and perverted and needed to be extinguished.

She had condemned her daughter and all those who came after her to a life of restriction and pain. And Kimberly had been her mother's last hope of breaking the cycle. The Trust terminated in only five more years. But in waiting, in turning her back on what she had seen in Jared's eyes, what would she be gaining? And what would she be losing?

Love endured. If Jared loved her, truly loved her, he would wait. He *would* wait. She had seen it in his eyes, heard it in his voice. He would make that sacrifice for her. But to what end?

She wandered over to the oaken locked shelf that she had been given the key to six years before. She knew what it contained, but she had never had the courage to open it. Five generations of journals and diaries. Accounts of the lives, the loves, and she knew, the pain the women of Briar Cliff had endured.

Slowly, she drew the key from her pocket and opened the door on a past she had sworn she would never visit.

Chapter Eighteen

Father has sworn Matthew Timmons will save me from the demons of lust that are the curse of my birth. I will do as he bids, but my heart breaks, for I know I will never again see my beloved Daniel… Sarah Santiago. She had been Tabitha and Diego's first-born daughter.

Father was right. I am cursed. My female needs torment me both sleeping and awake. James is disgusted by my very presence, of course. I cannot blame him for this. I am a blight upon my family… Samantha Fieldings. Her husband had been James Fieldings, a religious and righteous leader of the community at the time.

God save me. I have wed Davis Eldon as Father ordered. What have I done? I have refused the demand of the one I love for this life. A life of ease, of all I knew should have been mine, for what? For the suffering I now endure. What have I done? My heart breaks for my one true love. My soul aches… Elissa Fieldings Eldon.

They can make me marry as they please, to satisfy the terms of this insane Trust. But they cannot make me suffer. Grayson may be the choice of my father, but it is his brother, Lawrence, to whom my heart and body belongs. I will not suffer the fate of those before me. I will know love, if only in the darkness of the night and the sheltering arms of deception… Karen Eldon Marshal

If only I were as strong as my parents. They loved, they laughed, and they knew at least a small measure of happiness. The man I loved, precious Kimmie, I won't say his name. He was not your father, he was never my lover, and as your father was prone to remind me, he preferred the money. I am too weak, and I know I will not survive this illness. Should I die, then Briar Cliff and its protection falls to you. All that the women of our line have dreamed of falls upon your shoulders, my precious daughter. You can have it all. It can all be yours, just as it was meant to be. But for what? You are inheriting generations of pain, anger, deception and tears. It is truly a curse, and one I pray you deny. Love, Kimmie. Laugh. Let your heart be free and your body be your own. A house, no matter how beautiful, or how priceless, will ever take the place of those things.

I hope you are reading this diary, that you have read those who have gone before, now that I myself have passed on. I hope that the years you have spent away from this house, from me, have given you a chance to grow strong, to break away from the curse this house brings.

So many years I refused your father the truth he often pleaded for. He wanted only to know that you were his true daughter, and I, in my selfishness, refused him that. I realize now, as the end draws near, that I leave you alone, where before I had thought I would be here to see you triumph. I leave you alone. Without the father who perhaps would have treated you with kindness had I not driven the wedge between you.

I suffer now for my selfishness. No, not I, for I will pass on. But I go, knowing I will never rest, because you shall now suffer.

Briar Cliff is the curse, Kimmie, not your desires or your femininity or your gentle heart. It is this estate, and the past that has cursed us all… Claire Marshal Madison. It was dated the week of her death.

When Kimberly looked up from the final diary it was to see that night had overtaken the house. The light beside her glowed eerily, a single point of illumination within to emphasize the darkness that surrounded not just the estate, but her soul as well.

She had been away at school when her mother had become ill, and she hadn't been called home until the last moment. She had believed for so many years that it had been her father's decision to keep her unaware of her mother's health. But now she knew the truth. It had been her mother's.

They had both deceived her, had used her as weapon, one against the other until nothing had been left of the child in their eyes. She had been a sword and she had been the one to suffer.

She wanted to scream, to rage, to destroy the house brick by brick until nothing remained of the agony that resonated through her body. She wanted nothing more than to wipe away the memories of a past that should have never been.

She was crying. She wiped at her cheeks as she closed the diary and laid it beside those she had glanced through before. She stared around the library. Centuries of books graced the shelves and Kimberly knew that many more were in storage. Books that museums would salivate over. In five years, they would have been hers. It would have all been hers.

She shook her head tiredly as she rose from the chair, staring around her as the tears continued to dampen her cheeks. She had been denied her mother as well as her father because of this place. The scars on her soul that her parents had placed there through her younger years would never completely fade. She would never forget that her father's hatred of what her mother had done had extended to her. She would never forget that the mother she had loved, had trusted and believed in, had used her as well.

But was she any better?

She had sacrificed her life, six long years to the battle lines that had been drawn six generations before.

She had walked away from Jared.

A sob racked her body, shuddering through her as pain sliced through her chest. An agonizing burst of never-ending regret shook her, causing her breath to catch as a low, racking moan escaped her. She curled into herself, her arms wrapped around her stomach as she whispered his name.

God, it hurt. It tore through her, echoing through her soul and ripping wide the door she had closed on her heart so long ago. Even before she had learned the terms of the Trust. Before her father had demanded the exams. She had closed herself off from any chance of heartache or pain to ensure that what had happened to her mother could never happen to her.

She had been determined to never love. But Jared has sneaked into her heart with his crooked smile and his stormy eyes. His determination and sheer male presence had stolen past her safeguards and marked her forever.

There had been no jealousy when he had caught her at The Club. There had been only fiery heat and overwhelming hunger. He had catered to her every desire on the ranch, giving her the gift of his touch, his desire…his unspoken love. And he had never demanded more from her than she had thought she could give.

"Kimberly, you're breaking my heart." His voice washed over her senses, a figment of her imagination, a condemnation for walking away from him?

"Baby, you can't cry like this, you'll make yourself sick."

She jerked in shock when she felt his hands grip her shoulders and draw her forward. Her eyes flew open and there he was. His gaze a million shades of gray, lines bracketing his mouth, sorrow in his expression as he drew her to his chest.

"Jared…" She cried out his name, her hands reaching for him, clutching at him as his arms tightened around her, pulling her into his arms as he rose so he could lift her before taking her place in the chair.

She was cradled on his lap, her head buried in his neck as he soothed her. Soft, broken words in a voice ragged with emotion.

"Baby, it's okay," he whispered at her ear before he placed gentle kisses along her brow. "It's okay, Kimber. You're not alone anymore."

He had promised he would always be there, and now, when she needed him the most, he was there. He was holding her, his arms sheltering her, his kisses soothing the gaping wound that had grown in her soul.

"Why are you here?" She tried to stem the tears, but they refused to be held at bay.

Jared sighed roughly. "Mother called when you came for the key last night. She was worried about you."

Kimberly nodded jerkily. Carolyn had watched her too closely and Kimberly had known there was no hiding the proof of the tear-filled nights she had spent since leaving the farm.

She was raw from the inside out. She couldn't sleep for dreams of Jared, couldn't get through the day without his name coming to her lips. Without crying for all she had walked away from.

"I don't want it," she finally whispered. "This place. This legacy, Jared. I can't...I don't want it."

She felt him tense, felt his arms tighten around her.

"Five years isn't so long..." She heard the pain in his voice, heard all the needs that she felt in his soul.

Raising her head, she lifted her hand and placed her fingers against his lips. He stared back at her silently, though his eyes raged with emotion.

"I won't ask for promises," she whispered. "I don't want them. Yet. But I need this, I need you now. Just like this."

His smile, God, she loved his smile, even covered by her fingers as it was.

"I told you," he growled roughly. "I'll be here Kimber, whenever, however you need me. That's not a promise. It's a fact."

He drew her back to his chest, tucking her head beneath his chin as the tears finally eased.

"Just rest, baby," he said then. "Right here, in my arms. Just let me hold you..."

Night moved on, yet Jared never released her. They spoke in hushed whispers, and he listened in silence as she told him of her childhood, of her lonely years in boarding school.

He laughed with her when she told of the pranks she often pulled on the good sisters who ran the school. He hugged her tight when she related the punishments that she considered a fair trade for the fun she had managed to eke out of those years. And he rocked her tenderly when she related the horrifying event of arriving home within hours of her mother's death.

Finally, her eyes closed wearily and sleep claimed her. And Jared still held her, watching her tenderly, his heart breaking for the loneliness she had endured even as his soul swore she would never know it again.

Jared drove her home the next morning after arranging for someone to bring her car in behind them. He held her hand through the hour-long drive, allowing her to sit in silence until they pulled into her driveway.

Kimberly stared at the little brick house, realizing that it had been more of a home to her in the past six years than Briar Cliff ever had been.

"Come in with me," she whispered.

She didn't want to let him go. She didn't want to face the loneliness awaiting her.

Jared sighed wearily as he lifted her hand to his lips, placing a gentle, destructive kiss in the center of her palm.

"I don't have that much control today, baby," he whispered. "I don't think either of us do."

She turned her head, staring at his exhausted face and seeing the same needs swirling in his gaze that burned in her body.

"I'm not asking for your control, Jared," she whispered. "I don't want it..."

He shook his head, stopping her flow of words.

"No, Kimber," he said tenderly. "I won't let you make this decision while your emotions are this ragged. Go inside and rest. I'll see you in a few nights, I promise."

She would have argued with him, she would have pressed him for more, and she knew eventually, he would give in. But if he did, he would never be certain that the decision she had made in the deepest part of the night was made with her heart and not with her pain.

She nodded slowly. "I'll hold you to that."

He smiled that special smile. "You won't be able to keep me away."

He leaned to her, his lips touching hers, the restraint he used evident in the tense lines of his face and the darkening of his eyes.

"Soon," she whispered, pulling back before hurrying from the car.

She had an appointment to make, and she was more than eager to finish it and to begin the life she prayed was waiting for her.

Chapter Nineteen

She faced him, her father, Senator Daniel Madison in the offices of Caruthers, Brickley and Morton, the Estate lawyers who had handled the Briar Cliff Trust from the beginning. Actually, it had been Caruthers senior who had first put together the original Trust. It was his great grandson, Caruthers IV who now faced her from the head of the antique cherry wood conference table.

Across from her sat her father and Attorney Brickley. Morton sat at the other end with a stenographer off to her side.

"Let me get this straight, Ms. Madison, you are rescinding all claim to Briar Cliff, effective immediately?" Brian Caruthers asked her sternly. "This isn't a decision to make lightly, young lady. This is centuries of preservation we're talking about. A heritage anyone can be proud of."

"Proud of?" She flicked the lawyer a glance before returning her gaze to her father's silent face. "I've endured a physical exam every three months to prove my eligibility to hold Briar Cliff. My life, my every move is under scrutiny. I have no pride in Briar Cliff." There, she had said it.

She watched her father's eyes widen marginally before they narrowed in censure.

"She has obviously broken the conditions and doesn't want to admit it," he finally snapped.

Kimberly smiled sadly. Somehow, she had known that would be his first defense. She reached into the briefcase she carried with her and pulled free the doctor's report.

"I saw Dr. Morgan first thing this morning," she said softly. "Here are the results of those tests."

She slid the paper across the table. She knew what it said. The hymen was still intact.

He slid the paper to the lawyer next to him.

"What are you up to?" he growled, his hazel eyes accusing, censorious. "A year ago you sneered in my face and swore I'd never live a night in 'your' home, as you called it."

Kimberly drew in a deep breath as she watched the man who should have been there for her graduation and wasn't. Who should have cared the first time she was wounded during an assignment, but hadn't. The man who should have shared in her joys and her fears, yet he never had.

"I wish I had been given the chance to love you," she whispered then, ignoring the shock on his face. "I wish the Estate hadn't stood between us, and that your own morality and beliefs hadn't eroded what could have been, Father. I wish I could have been the daughter you needed, instead of the tool for revenge that you and Mother turned me into."

He paled. She watched his swarthy expression blanch and shook her head wearily.

"The Trust ends in five years, Ms. Madison," Caruthers reminded her. "Whatever has fueled this decision can surely wait that long."

Make Jared wait? She didn't have the patience.

"I have a life to plan," she said firmly. "Briar Cliff won't be a part of it, because after tonight, I'll never pass another of those asinine exams." She flicked her fingers towards the report. "Five years is too long to wait to tell him I love him."

"No!" Her father's hand smacked imperatively against the pristine polish of the table, the crack resounding around the room as Kimberly flinched at the fury of the sound. "I won't allow you to make such a foolish decision. It's Jared, isn't it?" He sneered the name, his eyes piercing her with his anger. "The little bastard has somehow corrupted you..."

"Enough." Kimberly stood to her feet, pushing her chair back as she faced her father with her own growing anger. "You have it, Father. All of it. Content yourself with that."

"I won't let you whore yourself to him and his friends," he snapped, coming to his feet as well. "Do you think I don't know he belongs to that depraved club?" he spat out. "That I'm unaware of his practices, his lifestyle. Are you insane, girl?"

She lifted her chin, staring back at him with a strength she had never known she possessed. His rages had always terrified her; his harsh words had never failed to rip through her heart. Now, she felt only sorrow, only pity that it had come to this.

"No, I finally found my sanity," she said softly. "You can have the papers mailed to me, Mr. Caruthers," she informed the lawyer. "My time here is finished." She turned back to her father, allowing her regret, a lifetime's worth, to fill her face and her voice. "Goodbye, Father."

She moved away from the table, heading for the door, for freedom. She could feel her heart lifting, her soul becoming lighter with each step.

"Kimberly." Her father's voice stopped her as she opened the door, imperative, demanding.

She turned back to him slowly, seeing so many things she had missed before. Her father had aged in the last six years. He was only fifty, but he looked much older, more bitter than she remembered.

"If you walk out that door you lose it all," he reminded her. "Everything."

She smiled tiredly. "No, Father. I win," she said simply.

He sneered slowly. "You're just like your mother."

Kimberly ignored the pain at the implied insult.

"No, I'm not," she replied slowly. "I'm stronger than she was. I'm stronger than both of you were, because I'm not willing to sell my soul for a piece of land that will neither keep me warm at night, nor love me in return. Unlike you and Mother, I'm not willing to turn my back on love for profit. That was your curse, it won't be mine."

She left before he could reply, before he could hurl the insults she could see gathering on his face. She walked from the offices into a day filled with sunshine and hope and ran toward her future.

Chapter Twenty

He was waiting for her when she arrived. His mother had called and relayed Daniel's fury when he returned from the lawyers' offices. The Senator was coldly disapproving she had said, but Jared had read more than that in her voice.

"Should I come after you, Mom?" he had asked her carefully, concern rising within him.

"No, dear. Daniel isn't a violent man. But neither am I pleased with him at the moment," she had said with a vein of irritation. "You take care of Kimberly. She's renounced Briar Cliff for you. I expect to plan the wedding, of course. And it will take more than a few weeks, young man. I expect six months at the least. I deserve this. You waited long enough to find the woman that makes your lips curve into that smile your father always got with me." Her voice had turned misty with memories, though he had no idea what she meant. "Give her my best, and I'll see both of you soon."

He had hung up the phone, and waited. Night had fallen more than an hour before and still he stood on the front porch, his heart in his chest, his throat tight with the knowledge of what she had given up for him.

She had given up an estate estimated to be worth millions. More than he would ever accomplish in his lifetime, more than he had dreamed his love meant to her. She had only five years to wait, and he would have been there beside her. He would have given her that time.

It both awed and humbled him, and scared the living hell out of him that she had given it up.

Finally, just as he was certain she must have changed her mind, he saw the lights of the jeep topping the rise a quarter of a mile away. And she was there. Everything inside him responded to that sight. His chest tightened with emotion, and his erect cock throbbed in thankfulness. The damned thing hadn't relaxed since she had walked out the door more than a week before.

He held his position on the porch, his arms crossed over his chest as the jeep pulled into the driveway and turned around the circular drive. The engine had no sooner been turned off then the door was opening and there she was.

Her long, red-gold hair flowed around her, unbound, as wild as the passion that burned within her. She was dressed simply in clothing that he figured would take no more than six seconds to tear from her body. A light cream-colored sundress and leather sandals. Four seconds max, he revised.

She moved slowly to him, stepping up on the porch, her eyes dark with emotion.

"I love you," she whispered. "I can't wait, Jared. No matter what. No matter how long you want me, I can't wait."

He drew in a hard, determined breath as he glanced away from her. He couldn't say what he had to say while staring into those beautiful eyes.

"I can ease the desire for you without this sacrifice…"

"No." Tears thickened her voice as pain resonated in it. "We tried that, Jared; it only made it worse. Don't you understand? It's not the need for release. It's not the arousal. It's you. Just you. I need all of you, not just a little bit… I need all of you. You love me, Jared. I know you do. You have to."

He turned back to her, the emotional storm riding within him as unfamiliar as the tears filling her eyes now.

"Love you?" he questioned her roughly. "No, Kimberly. This isn't love. This is a part of my soul that rips out every time I have to let you go. But by God, I won't let you give up everything you've fought for like this. It's only five years."

She shook her head slowly, a single tear falling from her eye, breaking his heart.

"Five years that I can be warm beside you. Five years that I can laugh with you, that I can love you. Five years versus something that was my mother's dream, but never mine. I want you, not the curse that estate has become."

He should have argued further, he thought. He should have made her see exactly what she was giving up, but he couldn't fight past his need to hold her, to kiss her. His need to shelter her and hear the screams he had every intention of fucking out of her.

He reached out, his body clamoring to take and take until he was so sated he collapsed in exhaustion. But nothing could still the need to give until he saw her eyes fill with happiness, with satisfaction.

His fingers touched her cheek gently.

"Be certain," he whispered. "Because I'll never let you go, Kimberly. It would kill a piece of my soul to ever have to let you go again."

Her hand covered his, pressing it to her lips as her lips caressed his palm with a butterfly touch.

"Do I have to tie you down and rape you, Jared?" she asked him with a tearful smile. "Or are you going to tie me down and love me?"

"No restraints," he vowed as his arms went around her and he swept her against his chest. "Just me and you, Kimber. Me and you and the fires that are going to explode around us."

Kimberly gasped at the heat and warmth of Jared's body as he carried her into the house and up the stairs to his room. He didn't exactly walk; his movements were too quick, too filled with purpose for such a sedate pace. But neither did he rush.

Her lips moved to his neck as he stared up the staircase. Her teeth nipped at his flesh, her tongue soothing the ache as a broken growl left his lips. She wanted to give him the pleasure he had always given her. She wanted to consume him, wanted to melt so deep into his body that she never had to worry about being apart from him again.

Finally, he was pushing his way into his bedroom and laying her on the bed as he stared down at her, his gray eyes turbulent with the swirling shades of gray that colored his eyes.

She propped herself up on her elbows, watching as he undressed. He tore his clothes from his body, dropping them carelessly onto the floor until every hard, muscular inch was revealed to her avid gaze.

"Are you attached to that dress?" he growled then.

She glanced down at the dress in surprise. "It's just a dress."

"Good." He reach for her, his hands hooking in the neckline, and before her amazed eyes, he tore the fabric from her body.

Laughter welled inside her and would have escaped her throat if he hadn't covered her lips with his own, coming over her as he pressed her back to the bed, his legs pushing demandingly between her thighs.

"I don't know how long I can wait," he whispered between the kiss. "I'm dying for you, Kimber. So damned starved for you that I feel as clumsy as a callow youth."

"Never clumsy," she panted as his hands framed her breasts a second before his lips moved to her hard, aching nipples.

Pinpoints of rapturous sensation began to tingle over her body as his mouth covered one distended tip. His mouth drew on her with a hunger she couldn't have imagined. She thought she had known him at his most passionate, his most aroused, but she had been wrong. This was Jared, raw, unconcerned with control, but no less intent or powerful for it.

Her head fell back on the bed as her hands moved over his shoulders, his head, her fingers tangling in the short strands of his hair. She wanted, no, she needed to touch him.

She had to feel the bunching muscles of his shoulders, hold his head to her as he sucked at her breast, driving her insane with the pleasure.

When his lips began to move lower, his tongue licking over her flesh, she arched to him, knowing that as the fires inside her began to rage out of control, that Jared would once and for all put out the flames.

"I love your taste," he groaned as his mouth poised over the aching, wet folds of her cunt. "So sweet and hot, Kimber. I could eat your pussy for hours."

"Later," she begged. "God, Jared, I've been in misery for a year now. Make it stop..."

Her eyes closed as a ragged moan escaped her lips. His tongue swiped between the sensitive lips, circled her swollen clit then moved down to tongue the entrance to her greedy vagina.

"Damn you, fuck me," she demanded roughly as her pussy wept with its need. "I've waited long enough, Jared."

She needed him inside her, needed him to fill the empty aching places, not just in her body, but in her soul as well.

"Condom," he panted as he pulled himself to his knees, his eyes wild, his face flushed. "...have to find one..."

"No." Her hands fell to the jutting length of his cock, wrapping around it as they both groaned at the touch. "I'm protected, Jared. I took care of it. I need you like this. All of you."

Her eyes met his. Neither of them had known another's touch without that layer of protection. She needed no protection from Jared. She didn't want any.

As though her words had broken the last threads of his control, he lifted her thighs, opening her further as he came over her, pushing her hands from the rigid length of his erection, and positioned himself carefully.

He was breathing hard and fast, just as she was. Perspiration covered his body, dampened his hair. He stared down at her, his eyes nearly black as he guided the wide, flared head of his cock through the narrow slit of her pussy.

Kimberly whimpered with the pleasure. The mushroomed crest was satin soft and hot as fire as he tucked it against her opening.

"I don't want to hurt you," he groaned, leaning his forehead against hers as he fought for breath.

"I like the pain, remember?" She tried to smile, but her breath was catching in her chest with each new, violent burst of pleasure. "Take me, Jared. All of me..."

He closed his eyes, his hand moving to grip her hip a second before he surged inside her.

Kimberly's eyes flew open wide, not from the pain, but from the filling. He stretched her impossibly, working his cock inside her with stiff, hard strokes that had her gasping for breath, had a scream building in her throat with no air to let it free.

"God, Kimberly," he groaned desperately as she struggled to take the thick width of his erection. "Fuck, you're so damned tight. Too damned tight."

She felt the penetration of the thin membrane she had protected for so long. Her back arched as a cry escaped her, her legs lifting to allow her knees to clasp his hips, to open herself further for him.

Her hands gripped his shoulders, fingers biting unconsciously into his skin as the next hard stroke sent him deeper, stretched her further. Each breath was a gasping cry. Each inch that sank inside her, another slice of ecstasy she feared she would never survive.

Finally, his hands gripped her hips hard as he pulled back a second before he pushed inside her, hard and heavy, a spearing impalement that let loose the scream building inside her.

Electricity sizzled over her flesh as tremors shook her body. She could feel him inside her, every hard, throbbing, heavily veined inch of his cock buried to the last depth of her pussy.

She stared up at him as his eyes opened, gasping for breath, her eyes wide, her hips rocking against him. And she could say only a single word. "More..."

Jared lost his mind. For a second, for one blissful second he thought he could hold on to the control he needed not to ravish her. But that word, that single word, so filled with hunger, with desperation, tore it from him.

He came over her fully, catching his weight on his elbows and began to fuck her with all the driving, greedy desperation he had locked inside his soul for a year now. His hands tangled in her hair, holding her still as his lips came over hers, his tongue pushing past her lips as he surged repeatedly into the fist-tight depths of her cunt.

She was tight. So tight she gripped him like a silken vise, the walls of her cunt dragging over his cock and driving him closer and closer to the edge of release.

Her lips opened to him as eagerly as did the rest of her body, her hands moving over his shoulders. Flames whipped over his body as his chest tightened with a surge of protectiveness and overwhelming emotion.

His arms cradled her close to him as he felt his scrotum tighten almost painfully at the base of his cock. He gritted his teeth against the whiplash of sensation that began to move up the base of his spine. The slick, satin softness of her tight cunt flexed and rippled around his erection. Tiny fingers of bursting sensation speared inside the swollen flesh, striking with destructive results to the depths of his balls.

He couldn't hold back. She was burning in his arms, searing him with her pleasure, her cries urging him to thrust harder, faster, to fuck her with the last measure of strength he possessed. He was helpless against her need, her hunger.

Jared was shocked at the sound of the ragged groan that escaped his chest as he began to hammer inside her. Quick, deep strokes, the sound of her wet pussy sucking at his cock, driving him over the edge of reality.

"Jared...Jared..." She was gasping his name, her body tightening beneath him as he felt the first warning contractions of her cunt around his cock.

She was close, so close.

"I love you, Kimberly," he growled at her ear then, the emotion surging through him like a tidal wave. "Come for me, baby. Come for me now, sweet baby. Right here in my arms."

As though his voice was the trigger needed, she bucked in his arms, her breath strangling past her lips, as he raised his head to watch those incredible eyes as the storm took her.

They were nearly black, wide, unfocused, as a keening cry escaped her lips. Her sweet, sweet pussy clamped down on his cock like the tightest fist as hard, spasmodic shudders began to convulse through her.

Then he felt it. The rush of her release vibrated against his erection as her legs tightened further, her pussy flexing, releasing, gripping and sucking at his hard flesh until his head, his heart, his very soul exploded in a release that had a rough, desperate groan tearing from his chest.

On and on it went. Every pulse of his seed inside the liquid heat of her body was like a whiplash of fiery sensation. His hips pressed deeper, determined to spear into the very heart of her womb as he spilled every drop of his semen into the flexing depths of her cunt.

When it was over, it was like a puppeteer cutting the strings on his creation. Jared collapsed over her, loath to pull free of the velvet depths of her body. He had to be crushing her, but her arms wrapped tight around his neck, her lips whispered, pleaded that he hold her forever.

"I love you, Kimberly," he whispered again, humbled by the emotions that swept through him as exhaustion claimed them both. "I love you..."

Chapter Twenty-One

Three weeks later

"Your mother is insane," Kimberly accused Jared as she hung up the phone and lowered her head into her hands. "Six months? Six months to plan a wedding?" She gazed up at him pleadingly from where she sat at the kitchen table, her coffee cooling in front of her. "I have to wait six months, Jared? That's no fair."

He stood across from her, leaning lazily against the counter, his jeans lying low on his hips, the top snap still undone, his chest bare. God, he was so sexy she just wanted to eat him up.

His dark hair was tousled, his lips still appeared swollen. She barely remembered biting that lower curve as her release rocked her body earlier that morning. Looking at him now, she couldn't imagine how she had managed to keep her hands off him as long as she had.

"Stop looking at me like that," he growled sensually. "After last night and this morning, you're in no shape to follow through on it."

And he was right. She was still amazed that Ian Sinclair had agreed to be the third in their relationship. Ian rarely participated in any of the club members' relationships, and as far as she had known, he had never acted as third. First maybe, but never third.

The experience had been wild, erotic, a giving unlike anything she had ever known as Jared held her in his arms, his gaze locked with hers as Ian began to fill her greedy, soaked cunt.

She shivered now at the memory, staring back at Jared as love exploded in her soul. It still amazed her that he was truly hers.

"Finish your coffee, sweetheart." His voice was a smooth, sexy rumble as the front of his jeans began to fill out demandingly.

She was poised to rise to her feet and attack him when the doorbell chimed, forestalling the sexual intent building like wildfire in her mind.

She rose instead as Jared held his hand out to her in invitation to follow him. Their home. He took every opportunity to prove to her that the house he so cherished was their home. Not just his, but hers as well.

"Expecting someone?" Her ever-present smile deepened as his arm curled around her back.

"Not hardly," he grunted as they reached the wide oak panel. "Let's get rid of them fast though."

Laughter welled in her throat as he gripped the doorknob and opened it wide.

Shock held her immobile.

"Hello, Kimberly." Daniel Madison stood on the threshold, a gaily wrapped box clutched in his white-knuckled hands as he stared back at her coolly.

She stiffened, blinking in disbelief.

"Senator Madison." Jared's icy greeting was less than hospitable. "What do you want?"

He appeared to flinch at the rough tone of Jared's voice, but his gaze never left hers.

"I would like a moment to speak with you," he said austerely. "I promise not to take much of your time."

"You've said enough..." Jared started to growl.

"No." Kimberly pressed her hand to his chest, her gaze never leaving her father's. "I'll talk to him, Jared. This can't hurt me now. I promise you."

She felt his denial of her facing the parent who had attempted to control her for so many years.

"Come into the living room," she invited him warily. "It's a bit messy right now. We haven't gotten around to putting all my stuff away yet."

They had cleaned out her small house the week before, but boxes still littered the living room, packed with a lifetime of memories that she couldn't bear to part with.

Her father nodded, his gaze flickering for a moment, appearing bleak and pain-filled before he glanced away from her.

She led him into the living room, standing uncomfortably as he stepped past several boxes, still clutching the bright pink and yellow box in his arm. Suddenly, he stopped, his gaze caught by the contents of childish mementos that she had kept over the years.

Hesitantly it seemed, he reached into it and pulled free a ragged little book. *Sleeping Beauty.* It had always been her favorite book.

He blinked rapidly as he cleared his throat.

"I used to read this to you," he said faintly. "When you were just a tiny thing. Every night before bedtime, you wanted me to read it to you."

Kimberly watched him curiously. "I don't remember that," she said as she thought back, trying to move past the memories of his rage with her mother to the years before the fights.

He flinched as though she had struck him and carefully laid the book back in its place.

"You were very small," he said. "Too young to remember perhaps. Here..." He handed her the box he carried. "I have a gift for you. Your birthday arrives soon and I saw this..." He shrugged, as though uncomfortable.

Confused, Kimberly took the box. This wasn't the father she remembered.

"I apologize for the wrapping." He cleared his throat again. "I don't know where my secretary was yesterday. I had to wrap it myself."

She could tell. The paper was uneven, clumsily taped, but for a moment Kimberly had to battle back a sob at the knowledge he had wrapped it himself. He hadn't done that since she was five. And she did remember that. The uneven, clumsily wrapped box he brought her and her mother's derision.

You didn't even care enough to have it wrapped properly, her mother had charged, furious. *It's as clumsy as you are, Daniel.*

Her fingers smoothed over the crookedly tied bow as she blinked back tears. Carefully, she untied it, laying the ribbon aside before easing open the paper in the same manner. She would save it. Just as she had saved the ballerina paper he had used so long ago.

Finally, she opened the long box and simply stared down at the contents in amazement.

"It was nothing really," he almost snarled. "I saw it in the shop window. The doll's face reminded me of you."

Reminded him of her? She looked at the little tag on the long white satin wedding gown. It was a Remee, a designer original, and the face resembled her because it was her face. She had long admired the maker's porcelain dolls but had never been able to justify the outrageous price to own one.

Long red-gold curls fell down the doll's shoulders and back beneath a lace and gauze veil. Tiny seed pearls, satin and lace, graced the stunningly white wedding gown, and precious satin slippers covered the porcelain feet.

"Why?" She ran her finger gently over a row of tiny pearls on the long train of the gown that had been folded carefully to the side.

She looked up at him then, seeing someone she didn't know. This wasn't the father she had fought for so many years.

The self-righteous bastard who had, on more than one occasion, all but called her a whore.

He lowered his head slowly, shaking it helplessly as he pushed his hands into the pockets of his slacks.

"I've not been a father to you since you were five," he said, almost too low for her to hear. "I won't excuse myself. There is no excuse, Kimberly. I won't make one. But I wanted you to know…" he swallowed tightly, "I always loved you. Even when I didn't want to. When I tried not to. I loved you."

He shrugged his shoulders uncomfortably as she lifted a slender envelope she glimpsed tucked beside the doll. Curious, she opened it, pulling the papers free. She scanned the legal documents in disbelief before looking at him again.

What the hell was going on here?

"It was always meant to be yours," he snapped then. "If you had married a derelict from the streets, I would not have taken it from you. I married your mother for the money, I admit that. But by God, I didn't get her pregnant for the money, nor was it an accident."

He appeared angry, as he always did. His voice was rough, a little too loud, but this time she saw something she realized had always been there in the past. His pain.

"I can hear you," she said softly. "Don't yell at me, Father."

He grimaced tightly, glancing away again. "I don't mean to yell." He attempted to throttle the sound. "My fellow cabinet members are forever chastising me for it. Sometimes, I don't realize…" He broke off again.

"Why now?" She couldn't figure that part out. "Why come to me now when I needed you years before?" Her voice was roughening with tears, and she hated that. She shouldn't hurt; she shouldn't care.

He cleared his throat again, shifting uncomfortably. "I read her diary. You left it out at Briar Cliff. When you renounced the estate, I was given a letter she wrote me before her death. I went to Briar Cliff to try to make sense of it, and I found the diary." He blinked jerkily.

"When you were five, the evening of your birthday, she led me to believe you may not be mine. It's no excuse," he snapped furiously. "No excuse for what I did. But while I was reading her words, I realized we hurt you. In our selfish attempts to hurt each other, in my own moralistic, self-righteous belief of right and wrong, I had committed an even greater sin. I had denied the child I accepted on her birth. Shouldn't have mattered if she had lied to me, or if she had truly cheated me. I accepted you. And I was wrong."

He stared straight ahead as he spoke, his hazel eyes a bit watery, his hands bunched in his pockets as Kimberly watched him in shock, uncertain, confused. She glanced back down at the doll. It had taken longer than a few weeks for this creation. He would have to have commissioned it more than a year before.

"I don't expect forgiveness," his voice was rising again. "Don't deserve it. But I wanted you know. I know what he does, that man you're marrying. That Club he's a part of. I know what it means. I don't like it. You know I don't like it..." He stopped, obviously attempting to control the volume of his words. "You're my daughter. What you do in your privacy is none of my business... I just want..." He broke off again.

Kimberly stared back at him silently.

"One day..." he continued, "you might have children. Maybe a little boy, too. I want..." He cleared his throat roughly. "I don't want to lose the chance to know your children, as I denied the chance to know you... Dammit, don't cry woman. I won't have those tears," he yelled then.

Before Kimberly could respond he had jerked a handkerchief from his pocket and pressed it to her cheeks. A bit roughly, wiping at the tears before pushing it into her hands.

"Clean it up..." he snapped, gritting his teeth, lowering his voice. "I can't stand to see you cry. Reminds me of too many things, Kimberly. Too much pain I caused in the past. Please don't cry. I didn't mean to make you cry."

"She tried to tell me at the end," she sniffed. "And I misunderstood."

He nodded bleakly. "I know. I heard what she said and I misunderstood as well." He patted her head roughly. "I have to get back. I have work to do, girl. I don't have time to stand around here. Just..." He swallowed tightly. "Be happy, Kimmie. That's all I ever really wanted for you."

He turned and began to stalk to the doorway.

"Father." He paused as she called out to him. "I'm getting married. Carolyn informs me the wedding is in six months."

He grunted roughly. "That woman's a busybody."

Strangely, his voice was filled with a fondness she hadn't expected.

"Yeah, she is," she agreed. "But I'll need someone to give me away," she said hesitantly, wondering if she was only hurting herself with the words.

He turned slowly. It was his turn to be shocked, filled with disbelief.

His lips opened. Closed.

"I don't deserve to," he finally whispered. "I never expected to be able to."

"If you want to," she said, aching for the years lost, the father she realized she never knew. "Love me, love my husband, Father."

He blinked roughly. "He stole my daughter," he growled. "But I was doing a lousy job taking care of you anyway. And I would be proud...damned proud, Kimmie, to give you to him. I sacrificed your love for my own selfish pride. But I'd be damned proud to give you away."

She licked her lips warily. "I never hated you." She couldn't say anything more. Right now, she was stunned, unable to explain to herself how this had happened.

He nodded jerkily. "I'm thankful for that. Now, I have a country to try to help slap back in shape for my grandkids. You keep that man you're marrying in line." He pointed a finger at her demandingly. "He's too damned stubborn and sure of himself. Gives the rest of us a bad name..." He pressed his hands nervously into his pockets again. "Love you, Kimmie."

He turned and left abruptly then, weaving quickly around Jared as he passed him in the hall.

Kimberly met her lover's eyes. He stared back at her in surprise, his lips quirking in sudden amusement.

"Your father has issues," he said with all seriousness.

She shook her head, a smile curving her lips as he came to her, his arms wrapping around her.

"You're worth every sacrifice, Kimberly. He only realized that," he said as he pulled her to his chest a second before her tears flowed again. "Every sacrifice. And trust me, dealing with that pious father of yours is going to be a sacrifice..."

She laughed tearfully at the teasing tone of his voice, because there had been nothing pious about her father. Nothing self-righteous. He had made a sacrifice she had never expected.

She held onto Jared tighter, realizing the gift she had been given in his love. The acceptance, the patience and sheer depth of emotion that now bound them. There had been no sacrifice. Even if she had never seen Briar Cliff again. This, this moment in his arms, was worth losing it all.

Why an electronic book?

We live in the Information Age—an exciting time in the history of human civilization, in which technology rules supreme and continues to progress in leaps and bounds every minute of every day. For a multitude of reasons, more and more avid literary fans are opting to purchase e-books instead of paper books. The question from those not yet initiated into the world of electronic reading is simply: *Why?*

1. ***Price.*** An electronic title at Ellora's Cave Publishing and Cerridwen Press runs anywhere from 40% to 75% less than the cover price of the exact same title in paperback format. Why? Basic mathematics and cost. It is less expensive to publish an e-book (no paper and printing, no warehousing and shipping) than it is to publish a paperback, so the savings are passed along to the consumer.
2. ***Space.*** Running out of room in your house for your books? That is one worry you will never have with electronic books. For a low one-time cost, you can purchase a handheld device specifically designed for e-reading. Many e-readers have large, convenient screens for viewing. Better yet, hundreds of titles can be stored within your new library—on a single microchip. There are a variety of e-readers from different manufacturers. You can also read e-books on your PC or laptop computer. (Please note that Ellora's Cave does not endorse any specific brands.

You can check our websites at www.ellorascave.com or www.cerridwenpress.com for information we make available to new consumers.)

3. ***Mobility.*** Because your new e-library consists of only a microchip within a small, easily transportable e-reader, your entire cache of books can be taken with you wherever you go.
4. ***Personal Viewing Preferences.*** Are the words you are currently reading too small? Too large? Too... ANNOYING? Paperback books cannot be modified according to personal preferences, but e-books can.
5. ***Instant Gratification.*** Is it the middle of the night and all the bookstores near you are closed? Are you tired of waiting days, sometimes weeks, for bookstores to ship the novels you bought? Ellora's Cave Publishing sells instantaneous downloads twenty-four hours a day, seven days a week, every day of the year. Our webstore is never closed. Our e-book delivery system is 100% automated, meaning your order is filled as soon as you pay for it.

Those are a few of the top reasons why electronic books are replacing paperbacks for many avid readers.

As always, Ellora's Cave and Cerridwen Press welcome your questions and comments. We invite you to email us at Comments@ellorascave.com or write to us directly at Ellora's Cave Publishing Inc., 1056 Home Avenue, Akron, OH 44310-3502.

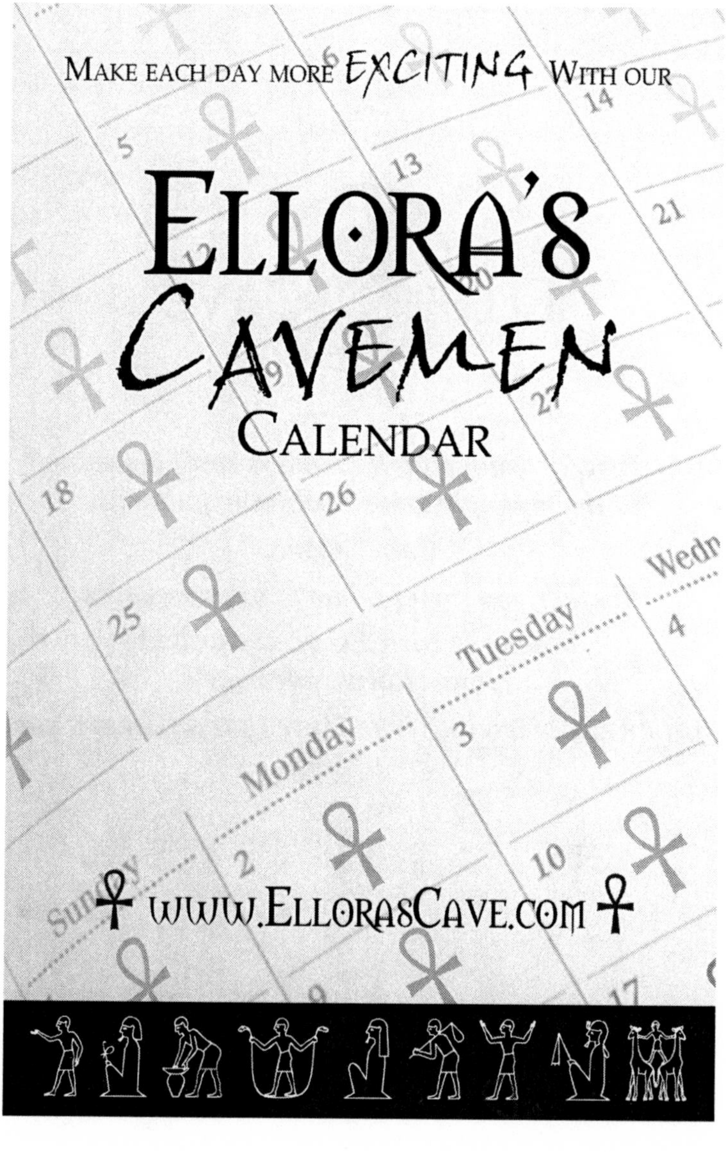
MAKE EACH DAY MORE EXCITING WITH OUR
ELLORA'S
CAVEMEN
CALENDAR
WWW.ELLORASCAVE.COM

LaVergne, TN USA
28 February 2011
218111LV00001B/22/P

9 781419 953965